BRENT VAN STAALDUINEN

DUNDURN
TORONTO

Publisher: Scott Fraser | Acquiring editor: Rachel Spence | Editor: Susan Fitzgerald
Cover desiger: Sophie Paas-Lang
Cover image: utility knife: istock.com/DeadDuck; textures: unsplash.com/BernardHermant and istock.com/sbayram
Printer: Marquis Book Printing Inc.
Lines from "26" © Rachel Eliza Griffiths, 2013. Used with permission.

Library and Archives Canada Cataloguing in Publication

Title: Nothing but life / Brent van Staalduinen.
Names: Van Staalduinen, Brent, 1973- author.
Identifiers: Canadiana (print) 20200155555 | Canadiana (ebook) 20200155563 | ISBN 9781459746183 (softcover) | ISBN 9781459746190 (PDF) | ISBN 9781459746206 (EPUB)
Classification: LCC PS8643.A598 N68 2020 | DDC jC813/.6—dc23

We acknowledge the support of the Canada Council for the Arts and the Ontario Arts Council for our publishing program. We also acknowledge the financial support of the Government of Ontario, through the Ontario Book Publishing Tax Credit and Ontario Creates, and the Government of Canada.

VISIT US AT

 dundurn.com | @dundurnpress | dundurnpress | dundurnpress

Dundurn
1382 Queen Street East
Toronto, Ontario, Canada
M4L 1C9

For Nora and Alida,
who love stories.

How quiet the bells of heaven must be, cold
with stars who cannot rhyme their brilliance
to our weapons. What rouses our lives each moment?
Nothing but life dares dying.

— *Rachel Eliza Griffiths, "26"*

PART 1

HERE

GRADUATION

I plead guilty, of course. It's the only option. No one else used a box cutter on Patrick Scheltz ten days ago. In math class. During the last regular period before our end-of-year exams. Now, I'm not that great at math, but these numbers are easy. Eight stitches. Twenty-seven witnesses. Seven days before summer freedom. One thousand times I've told myself how dumb it was to lose my cool.

The youth-court judge, a stern-looking woman no one in their right mind would mess with, asks me if I understand the consequences of pleading guilty. I nod, but she makes me say it out loud.

"I understand, Your Honour."

Then she clears the courtroom of everyone but me, Mom, the lawyers, the court reporter, my youth worker, and the bailiff, who sits in the chair at the end of my table. Even Gramma Jan and Aunt Viv have to go. The prosecution lawyer starts to object — he thinks Patrick and his parents should be allowed to stay — but the judge silences him with a look over her reading glasses.

"I'll bring them back for sentencing, but there's something I need to talk to Wendell and his mother about first."

First time she's called me Wendell. Until now, I've been "the defendant." I think about what that could mean as I watch everyone file out of the courtroom. Patrick — who everyone calls Pat, which he hates — glares at me as he leaves. A single person remains in the gallery, a woman who's been scribbling madly in her notebook the entire time.

"You too, Ms. Walters," the judge says.

"Judge, I —"

"Especially you."

The woman frowns but gets up without another word and leaves. The judge sighs and nods at the bailiff. "Watch the door, please. I don't want anyone 'accidentally' bursting back in."

I can tell the judge is talking about Walters, a reporter from the local paper — which my mom calls "that right-wing rag" — who lives in my neighbourhood. The bailiff gives a small smile and heads to the door. He shares the judge's opinion.

The judge removes her reading glasses, looks down, and takes a long, deep breath. Her eyes are softer when she looks up and over at the table where I'm sitting. I've seen that kind of look before. It's how people who weren't there look when they talk about it. All helplessness and sadness. She's going to talk about Windsor. My lawyer

2

brought it up in my defence, but I was hoping it would stay locked up in the court records. But no. Now the judge will say my full name again and want me to talk about it.

But I won't. I won't tell anyone. Not in a way they want, anyway. I have memories that live inside my head that are just for me. I was in the Windsor High library when the shooter walked in and opened fire. I didn't see much while it was happening. I was behind a table with my eyes closed. I heard the angry sounds of the bullets destroying everything around me. And the other noises I can't talk about. We all did.

The shooter was my stepdad, Jesse. I found that out later, at home, at the same time my mom did. When the police came to interview her. And me. I also found out that Jesse went to my classroom first. I don't know why. He didn't leave a note or anything. After the shooting, in the strange quiet of our house, I tried to figure it out. Mom hid the TV remote, but there were dozens of reconstructions on the internet. Hashtags and protests and rage and so many people wanting to fight. So much information but so few answers. Computer-generated animations and diagrams and arrows and dotted lines and red X's wherever someone had died. Kids and teachers. The horrible math of it. But I can't say that number. I hope that's all right.

The judge coughs gently.

"A few things have come to light since you were charged," she says, "including the fact that you were at Windsor High School on the day of the shooting. When I call everyone back in, I'm going to pass sentence, but I wanted to tell you in private how sorry I am for what you've gone through. And how much I respect your mother for bringing you home to Hamilton for a fresh start. I've spoken to your math teacher and principal — who both speak very highly of you — and we talked about your situation. They, of course, had no idea."

I sneak a look back at Mom. She's leaning forward on the gallery bench, her arms folded, looking at the judge with narrowed eyes. My lawyer using Windsor is one thing, but Mom won't like that the principal and my teacher know, too. She made me promise not to say anything to anyone, not that I would. Not that I can. I turn back to the front of the courtroom. The judge is still talking.

"You'll be relieved to hear that your expulsion has been reversed and you'll be allowed to graduate from grade ten after all. Quietly, of course. They feel that this one mistake shouldn't keep you from moving forward. I agree. Your school records will be filed away with full confidentiality, which is important to you and your mother. By law these court records will also be sealed. Wendell, I sincerely hope you and your mom can find some peace here. You're a strong young man, and I'm lucky to have met you, despite the circumstances." She leans back and puts her glasses back on. "That said, you broke the law, so what happens next is very, very important."

And with that the judge nods at the bailiff and he opens the door and everyone comes back in. I force my eyes to stay open to keep them dry. I never cry, but I get close a lot. My eyes fill all the time. I can't look back at Mom right now because she'll be a mess. Like me. I can't hear the word *Windsor* without my insides twisting themselves into ropes. But she feels it worse. She feels everything.

BIG BROTHER'S BEST

My probation officer's name is Sean, and he meets me at our house the next morning. He's dressed in khakis and a black golf shirt. He has a thick leather belt with a phone pouch and a gold badge on one side and a handcuff holster on the other. There's a thin cylindrical pouch next to the cuffs. Flashlight, maybe. Pepper spray. Or a collapsible baton. For the ones who don't co-operate.

He opens a map of our neighbourhood on the kitchen table. The boundaries of Churchill Park and Cootes Paradise have been outlined in pink highlighter. We live in an old neighbourhood with the city pressing in on one side and the park and marsh on the other, interrupting Hamilton's urban sprawl. The city, an old steel town tucked alongside the bay at the end of Lake Ontario, keeps growing. Our neighbourhood has seen better days. The houses are small and worn. "War homes," Gramma Jan calls them. Lots of senior citizens.

Lots of families looking to invest as soon as the older folks die off.

Sean repeats the judge's instructions. At-home supervision. Weekly meetings with Sean. Two hundred and forty hours of community service. Picking up garbage from the park and marsh trails from 9:00 a.m. to 3:00 p.m., Monday to Friday, every week until the first day of grade eleven. Then every day after school until the hours run out.

"Alone?" my mother asks.

"For the most part, yes," Sean says. "I'll drop by when I can, but Wendell —"

"Dills," I say. "Call me Dills."

I used to prefer Dilly, but at some point Mom started calling me Dills, and I've come around to liking it. A growing-up thing, I suppose. I'm fine with it. I guess someday I'll even think of myself as a Wendell.

He shakes his head. "Sorry, mate, but no. Let's keep this professional, yeah?"

Sean's about my mom's age but British, so everything he says sounds like it's been stretched out. My name, for instance. Wen-doe, he says. And he drops *yeah?* in behind so many of his sentences.

"Anyhow, I've made an arrangement with Gary, the park manager, for daily check-in. Here." Sean points to a building on the park's eastern side. "He says he'll be there at nine every morning."

"That's the old field house," Mom says. "I always thought it was abandoned."

Sean shrugs, slides the map over to me, and talks about boundaries and limits. Grassy parkland is my priority, but I'll clean the trails, too. The marked, official ones. The little scale marker at the top of the map tells me the area is huge. Bigger than I imagined. I looked it up online, but seeing it spread out on paper is different. I start to feel the weight of the summer ahead of me. Sean puts a plastic shopping bag on the table. Out of it comes a blaze-orange safety vest. Blue construction helmet. Work gloves. A box of industrial garbage bags. Bug spray. A huge blue bottle of sunscreen. SPF 45. My mom's eyebrows rise at that one.

"Uh, I threw that in there," he says. "I've done outdoor work before, and the sun'll burn you quicker than you think."

"That's thoughtful of you," Mom says.

Sean waves away her words, embarrassed. "But stay on this side of the marsh, yeah? South side only."

"Okay," I say.

"Which brings me to the last thing." He digs down to the bottom of the bag and takes out a length of nylon strapping with a black box attached. Unmarked.

"You've got to be kidding," Mom says.

"What is it?" I ask.

"It's a fu—" Mom closes her mouth and stops the word before it comes out. Not a word I hear from her very often. "It's a LoJack."

Sean gives her a look. "Let's call it an ankle monitor, yeah?"

"Big Brother's best."

"No need to be dramatic." He looks at me. "It's a GPS tracker, Wendell, to make sure you stay where the court says you need to stay."

"I can't believe this," Mom says.

"It's standard for house arrest." Sean hands it to me.

It's not heavy. It's not light, either. "I have to wear it all summer?"

He nods. "It also makes my job easier if I need to find you while you're working."

"What about showering? Exercising?" Mom asks.

"Water- and sweatproof. Just keep the strap clean. They can get pretty ripe." He takes the monitor back from me, kneels, and looks up at me. "I have to put it on you now. Which ankle?"

I hear myself telling him to put it on the right side. He talks about tampering and alarms and how violating the court's conditions puts me in a whole different category of youth offender. I've seen ankle monitors in movies, of course, so I get it. But it takes a special, wicked-looking tool to lock it tight and activate it, and the electronic tone as it connects to the satellite sounds sinister. Those scare the crap out of me. The sights and sounds of a screwed-up summer. Stretching out ahead of me a long, long way.

LISTEN

The park manager is a little guy, not much taller than me. He has a mess of twisted scars all up his left arm and bursting up the left side of his neck onto his face. His ear is a ruin. You can see it when he isn't trying to hear anything. When he is, he turns his head to catch the sound with his good ear and the messed-up one disappears. He smells a lot like skunk. The office does, too.

"This is Gary," Sean says.

"Gal," the guy says. "Not Gary."

Sean grunts, takes some folded papers out of his shirt pocket, and squints through all the small lines of text. Frowns. "Thought it was Gary."

No apology, though, even through the long silence that follows. My mom would be pissed about that. *Make it right, right now*, she'd say if she was here. I wonder if Sean's having difficulty with the weed smell. A pot smoker in charge. And if Gal is sensing Sean's issue with his habits. Both of them tense, me dangling in the middle of all that awkwardness. Nothing to do until Gal speaks.

"So you have instructions for me?"

Sean grunts again and goes through his spiel, most of which I've heard before. This time he adds *geofencing* to the vocabulary, which I want to ask about but can't because the two guys are busy moving through the rest of the formalities. They both have accents. Sean's British and flat, Gal's something else: stiff and kind of nasal, with strange vowels, rolled *r*'s, and crumbly consonants, like old cement.

Finally, Sean turns to me. "So that's it, then. Stay busy, yeah?"

"Sure."

Sean walks out of the field house, leaving Gal and me to stand there for a few awkward moments. Gal gives me a quick once-over, head to toe, and waves me out.

"You are on your own, young man."

"Will I see you while I'm —"

"I will not be checking up on you."

Gal turns back to the tiny desk tucked against the wall and picks up his pen. The ratty office chair creaks a protest. Silence again. I feel forgotten already. Just me and my silly safety vest and a million acres of decaying trash.

"Is it gone?"

He turns his head, right ear exposed. "I am sorry?"

"The hearing. In the ear with the scars."

"Yes."

"How does a deaf dude get a job managing a park?"

It's a rude question. That little voice inside is telling me so as I say it, but I'm annoyed enough at the situation to ignore it. Gal scowls, saying something about a million-dollar question. Then he tells me to fuck off and go pick up my garbage. No, really, he says that to me, like I'm somebody his own age and not a teenager he should watch his mouth around. "Feck off and go peck up yoorr rrruhbesh."

BABY

I used to swear. A lot. Sharpening my tongue as soon as I left the house, savouring the taste of the perfect F-bomb, blending in with the other guys. Mom didn't like it. She said it was going to get me in trouble. But after Windsor, those foul words started sounding empty. Puffed up without anything inside. So I stopped. The guys at my new school are just like the guys I left behind. Now that summer's here, they must be blinding themselves with the swearing they can do. I don't miss it. Jesse thinks swearing is a weakness. "It means you've run out of words — a poor substitute for substance," he says. Or, he would say. I wonder if he still thinks about things.

"I feel like swearing now," I say to the trees at the edge of the soccer field.

Specifically, I want to swear at the heat and the bugs and the disgusting stuff that can still come out of long-forgotten garbage when I impale it on my spike.

But I won't. I'll tough it out and head home at lunch. Whenever that is. I've caught myself reaching for my iPod a few times to check the time, but I'm not allowed to have it with me. Part of my sentence.

And I don't own a phone. Mom says I can decide later this year, when I turn sixteen, whether I want one or not but I'll have to get a job to pay for the data. A year ago I'd have said, *Of course I'll want one. I'm a teenager, after all*, but now I'm not sure. Of course, I can do pretty much anything on my iPod I could do on a phone, but between nudie apps and sexting and cyberbullying and the trolls who look to make life miserable for anyone who's experienced tragedy, there's so much wrongness online. You think a lot about safe places after a thing like Windsor.

I've followed a well-worn path into the bush to try to cool down a bit. I didn't know a guy could sweat like this. Ever. I've played sports and felt the little beads running down my face, but this is different. I'm soaked through. Even my undies. I'm getting a rubbed-raw patch between my legs. I should drink more, but the little plastic water bottle has been empty for a couple of hours now. I'll have to get Mom to buy me a bigger one. I've only peed once, running into the bush to go behind a tree — it was dark yellow, and thick, like syrup.

"Hydrate, hydrate, hydrate. Water is the most important thing, troop."

Jesse's words again. Yes, out loud. I do that a lot more these days, ever since the shooting. That's how I got on Patrick's radar. At lunch one day he came around a corner to find me alone, having one of my conversations with Jesse. He told everyone else I was talking to myself, like a baby. But I don't talk to myself — I talk to Jesse. I say his words, too, sometimes. He used to be home all the time, so I could talk to him whenever I needed to, morning, lunchtime, after school.

I feel faint. This is not good. Plus there's a suspicious burning on the back of my neck. Sunburn. Or more chafing from the cheap, rough collar on my safety vest. Both, maybe. *I should head home now*, I think as I spear another faded, collapsed can and put it into my bag. Would Sean know that I left, the stupid box on my ankle broadcasting where I am, my deviation from my work locations? Would he care?

Whatever. I'm going. I stash the stick and the garbage bag and walk out of the woods. Home is right across the field. Sean and the courts would go easy if they knew I was dying out here, right?

Ah, man. Something claws its way up from behind my ribcage and I have to stop midstep and take a few deep breaths to push it down. I can't think about the word *dying* anymore. Even when I'm obviously exaggerating.

"Aww, is Baby crying now?"

Patrick. Sitting on one of the park benches pushed up against the edge of the field. I blink away the blurriness. He's wearing shorts and a sleeveless green and yellow jersey, the scar I gave him on his bicep pink and angry. He flinched when I lashed out at him. Just in time to keep me from cutting his face. We were doing one of those combined lessons that are supposed to teach us how science and math and life are all connected. The teacher gave everyone a box cutter, one of those clicky yellow utility knives. There was a lot of leaf cutting and counting and dividing. Pat and I were assigned as partners. Him whispering taunts. Me lashing out in a moment of pure weakness.

"I heard you got stuck here," he says.

"How'd you hear that?"

"Nice vest."

"What do you want?"

"I want to beat the shit out of you, but who needs the hassle?" He points at my ankle monitor.

"Pat, I said I was sorry —"

He's up and in my face before I finish the thought. "And I told you never to call me that."

Must've been the back of my brain throwing his nickname out there. It's almost funny, but even though he's afraid to hurt me because of my supervision, I know better than to laugh. He can't stand that Pat can be a girl's name. So much that his stupid lizard brain might make the decision for him. Mom says that there are "glands and mysterious forces" that make guys do things. Especially the ones whose parents started them in school late so they could be "more ready." Pat relishes being bigger than everyone. He actually gets five o'clock shadow when he forgets to shave.

I hear myself apologize again.

"Punch me," he says.

"What?"

"Anywhere you want. I won't even hit back."

I'd be lying if I said that the thought of punching him has never crossed my mind. Or that I'm not tempted to bury my fist in his gut to see him fall. But there's a wicked little glint in his eye and a suspicious burn in my throat telling me not to. That's how *I'd* fall. I'd get busted for breaking the conditions of my sentencing. You're not allowed to get in fights, much less with the person you're doing time for hurting.

Jesse would tell me to walk away. I can hear him. *He just wants to bring you down. Don't drop to his level. Clear as mud?*

"Clear as mud," I say.

Patrick is confused. "Huh? What are you talking about, Baby?"

Clear as mud is one of Jesse's favourite sayings. He picked it up in the army, one of a thousand things that sound like gibberish to non-army people. Mud's not clear. It's muddy. You say it when you know what you have to do even when it's not entirely sensible or logical. Jesse always explains the sayings to me. *Get a jag on. On the bus, off the bus. We're all mushrooms, fed shit and kept in the dark.*

Or maybe it's explain*ed*. Past tense. In reality, he can't explain anything to me any more than one of the trees can. He's still in that Windsor Regional Hospital bed. When the police finally swept the school, they found him in a bathroom. Almost dead but not quite. He'd tried to kill himself. At first the cops kept Jesse in restraints and stationed an officer outside the intensive care room. They hoped he'd wake up so they could charge him and lock him away forever. But the doctors say he'll never wake up, that it's not a coma but a "persistent vegetative state." Now everyone is waiting for him to die, which is a little sad. There's been so much death already.

"You shouldn't be here," I say.

"Be a man and hit me."

I shake my head and walk away. I think, *Don't you get it, Pat? I'm not a man. I'm not supposed to be. Not yet.*

Why does everyone expect me to be older than I am? I hear him say dumb things to my back about how sorry I'll be and how he'll be around every day but I'll never know when. Even my own lizard brain knows that you only say those kinds of things when you're out of other options.

Our cool, air-conditioned house is five minutes from the park, my massive, sweltering prison cell. Sean didn't say I can't go home during the day while I'm doing my time, but it still feels like I'm doing something wrong. Even though it makes sense for me to use our own bathroom and eat lunch there. I've been torturing myself.

There's a bright blue Elantra parked at the curb out front, and Mom is talking to someone on the step. It's the reporter from court. Walters. Mom isn't happy to be talking to her. Her arms are folded and she's standing in the middle of the doorway like she's blocking it. You don't stand that way when you're friendly with the other person. You lean against the door frame or turn aside so they can come in.

Walters turns and sees me coming up the walk. She smiles. "Wendell, hello. I'm Cathy, a reporter from —"

"Stop talking to him."

"Vicky, I just have a few questions for your son."

"No, you don't. And you don't get to call me Vicky."

"Hey —"

"I said no. He's still a minor, so it's my call. Dills, come inside and don't say a thing."

She turns slightly to allow me access, but the reporter hasn't moved. I stop. Awkward.

"Get out of the way," Mom says.

"Why did the judge ask everyone to leave the courtroom?"

"Inside, kiddo. Now."

Mom says the last word with extra weight. I know that tone. I call it "Do Not Argue with Me Right Now, Young Man." Walters steps aside and lets me past.

"Don't come here again," Mom says.

She closes the door in her face, cutting off the next question. With a low groan, the door eases open a bit. Mom has to thunk it closed twice more before it catches. Old doors and twisted frames, I suppose. But it steals some of Mom's thunder — Walters is probably out there laughing at the dramatic but missed attempt.

I make for the sink and drain four full glasses of tap water, Mom's eyes on my back the entire time. I put the glass down, my belly as tight and round as a medicine ball.

"Are you all right?"

"I need a bigger water bottle."

"Let me see your neck." Mom moves behind me and grabs my shoulders. Tut-tuts under her breath. "You got some sun, too."

"I'll be fine."

"You're already burned. Didn't Sean give you sun-screen?"

"It was cloudy when I started this morning."

She reaches up and takes down the first-aid kit stashed above the cupboards and hands me a bottle of green aloe vera. It's cool on the back of my neck. Funny how the good feeling makes me more aware of how much I'll feel the burn tomorrow.

"Thanks."

"You're welcome."

I expect her to ask me more questions about how my day is going so far, but she doesn't. She leans against the counter with her arms folded, watching an indistinct point on the fridge across from her. Thinking. Mom's good at keeping things in, like she can lock them up in strongboxes in her heart and mind, but Walters's visit has pulled Windsor back to the surface again.

"She doesn't know anything," I say.

"For now. She's tenacious. Always was. Even in high school."

"You went to school together?"

"She was in the grade below me. Always running around for the school paper and yearbook. Always bugging everyone for stories."

"I'll stay away from her."

"And she's still here. Seems like everyone else left."

"You came back. *We* came back."

"Not by choice."

Her eyes fill, and she's back in Windsor, missing everything about what was good before Jesse walked into my school. Fighting against all the bad that followed.

That we tried to leave behind. Mom is a good fighter. But the tears break free, like they often do. She lets them flow for a bit, then sleeves them away. Stretches tall, breathes in deep.

"I love you, Dills."

"Love you, too, Mom."

Then it's silence in the house. Mom and me and all of this old house's hollow echoes, which I'm coming to know as well as my own breathing. The house has been in the family for a few generations, built by my great-grandpa Gene after the Second World War. He agonized over every joist, every nail, then retreated into the basement workshop and stayed there until he died. Gramma Jan, my grandmother, who was Gene's only child, said the war pushed him down there so he wouldn't have to talk to anyone. "He saw things no one should ever see," she said to me once. I get that.

The workshop is Mom's studio now. My room is down there, too, in the basement guest room, the quietest place in the house. Gene finished the guest room right after the workshop and slept down there every night. The whole basement is soundproofed. Against his nightmares, I guess. And now mine, although for me it's pools of sweat and a racing heart. Dream images fading like the flashes you get when you look at the sun. Not knowing where I am until I can identify the house sounds around me.

My stomach growls. "Okay if I stay for lunch?"

"Of course you can. Why wouldn't you?"

"I almost didn't come home. I don't know if I'm allowed to leave."

She laughs, wiping away a latecomer tear that shines on her cheek. "The judge assigned you to Churchill Park for a reason."

I frown. I don't like being laughed at. "Mom."

"You're supposed to stay close to home."

"Sure, but —"

"I'm sorry, Dills. I sent you out today without talking logistics. Bad mommy moment for me, okay?"

I wish she wouldn't say things like that. Even when I'm pissed at her, I know she's a great mom. I hear myself saying that it's fine, that I'm glad I have the option of a home lunch. I'm glad, too, that I can say that to her. When I'm at my maddest, I don't always give her a break, though she deserves it. Anger is funny that way. Your brain and your heart saying different things, and you know the right thing but your angry heart wins anyhow.

"Actually, I have something you can —"

Mom disappears for an instant without finishing her sentence. Then she's back, holding a faded olive-drab sling pouch. There's a flap over the top, but I know what's in there. Jesse's old army-surplus canteen. He never would have used it when he was in the service — they use hydration bladders now — but he loved to collect old military things. It's a dull olive-green blob with a screw top. Thick, thick plastic. Feels indestructible. I can't believe Mom's holding it. It's not like it was sitting on the hallway shelf, waiting for her to grab it on our way out of the house. It was in Jesse's old footlocker, down in the basement, with his collectibles and other dusty army things. She would've had to go out of her way to get it. Way out.

Mom's speaking as I take the canteen, something about not being able to live with herself if I got heatstroke and passed out in the woods without anyone knowing. Something like that. I notice she's stopped talking and is waiting for me to respond.

"Huh?"

"So you'll use it?"

"I guess. Are you sure? It's Jesse's."

"It's supposed to carry water."

"Well, yeah, but —"

"He'd be fine with you having it. He'd want you to, actually."

"He didn't really share his army stuff with me."

She tilts her head. "Oh, I don't know about that. You should hear all the army-isms that come out of your mouth."

"That's different."

"It is, and it isn't. Just rinse it out before you use it, okay?"

I twist open the cap. A mustiness wafts up, faint but just strong enough for both of us to smell it. Mom makes a face, I make a face, and we speak the same words at the same time. "Sin and corruption," we say. And we laugh because we've both heard it a thousand times and now it's coming out of us almost with one voice. Jesse's voice. "Jesus! Look at the sin and corruption in there!" Something his superiors would yell during inspections when they found anything not completely clean. Dust in corners. Mud in the tread of a combat boot. Smudges on a window. Soot in a rifle's chamber. Sin. Corruption. Both impossible to see or do anything about, yet the saying is so nonsensically, impossibly perfect.

Mom goes serious again and her eyes get all glittery. Mine, too. The canteen didn't do it, but that ridiculous saying did. She wipes her eyes and proceeds to assemble two ham-and-cheese sandwiches, cut them diagonally, and spread them out on two plates. Kettle chips and an apple go in the wedge-shaped gaps. Two meals, made without speaking or thinking.

I don't feel like saying much, either. I never say it out loud, but I miss Jesse so much it's an actual hole in the middle of me. I hate what he did, obviously, but still. Mom misses him, too, though for her the betrayal is so much worse. I can't even imagine. I hope it's all right, but I enjoy our quiet lunch. Sometimes you don't need to say anything.

HEARING JESSE

I'm better prepared when I go out after lunch. White zinc oxide on my nose and ears and the back of my neck. Mom says you can't sweat the zinc oxide away. Sean's sunscreen everywhere else. It smells like coconut, so I smell like the beach.

Before I left, Mom filled the canteen for me and also made me chug another two glasses. Rolled her eyes when I said it would just make me pee more. "You guys love to piss in the woods," she said. Which is true, of course. Although I must've been pretty dehydrated, because even with all the water I drank at lunch, I still don't feel like I have to go. My body needing everything I can give it.

Pat is nowhere to be seen. I half expected him to be waiting for me. Is it likely he'll be out all day, every day, to get me back? No. But knowing doesn't mean I won't worry.

About midafternoon, the temperature drops and the clouds return, this time dark and heavy. I hope it doesn't rain. Sean was clear that I have to work in all conditions. Rain. Wind. Shine. "But not in a thunderstorm, yeah?" he said. "The moment you hear thunder or see lightning, you head for the nearest shelter. Safety first." Mom said she'd go out to buy a bigger water bottle this afternoon, but we didn't talk about rain gear. If I get dumped on this afternoon, all I can do is get wet and keep going. I work my way onto one of the forest paths again, this one linking the park and the marsh, wondering if the forest counts as shelter.

Then, the strangest thing: as the wind picks up, making the leaves rush against each other and the tree trunks creak and groan, I hear Jesse's voice.

I'm here, Dills. Come see me.

I practically jump out of my running shoes. (I have to wear them — "Sturdy trainers, Wen-doe," Sean said. "No sandals, yeah?") What I heard was not the gentle, kind of blurred voice I hear when I talk out loud and imagine Jesse responding. This was as clear as if he was standing on the path next to me. Talking deep and slow, like he always does, like he has all the time in the world. Clear enough to imagine him on his feet and living normally, like before. I feel like I've been punched right above the waistband of my shorts.

I don't want to miss him as much as I do. I want to forget about him and what he did. All those lives. I want to forget that he might've been in the school to get me first. But here's the thing: I can't. He's family. In spite of all his demons, he loved our life together. *Demons.* That's Mom's word for what he carried back from his tours in Afghanistan and Iraq. But we chased them away. On mornings when he'd come into the kitchen with eyes so dark you knew he hadn't slept a wink, or after days away in the woods, he always smiled. For us. "What's up, favourite people?" he'd say.

I wait for him to say something else in his real, right-now voice, but all I hear is the wind and the trees. I wait a long time. I must look like an idiot. Kid in an orange safety vest, standing ridiculously still in the middle of a dirt hiking trail, garbage-sticker in one hand and black plastic bag in the other, staring at the tree canopy. Excitement, anticipation, and disappointment moving across his face like the clouds he can barely see.

Jesse always says I need to work on my poker face. "Two things," he'll say. *Two things* is another Jesse favourite. Keeps a point or an argument simple and easy to break down. "One, people respond better to a little mystery. Two, never give anything away — if they can't know how you feel or what you're thinking, you get the advantage." I always lose the battle for the poker face. Jesse has it down, I can tell you, especially away from home. No road rage or snapping or anger from him, no matter what. Even when he has every reason to rage.

Mom loves that about him. I've seen her watching him as he talks to me, his face calm even when I've screwed up bad. I'll be a mess of knotted ropes inside or as furious as boiling water and he'll remain as still as anything. Mom used to get this little smile when she watched him or talked about him to me. She still does, sometimes. Way less than she used to.

"Jesse?" My voice is low. Even though I'm not talking to myself, saying it out loud is a risk. No one else would understand. Pat, especially. But I still do it — I want to hear more. "Is it really you?"

Nothing.

I wait another minute or so, then put my head down and get back to the garbage. A faded candy wrapper here, a cigarette butt there. There's enough to get into a kind of dirty, distracting rhythm. I wonder if Sean would let me listen to music while I work. I could use Jesse's old MP3 player that Mom uses for yoga, which can't connect to the internet. It only has a few hundred songs on it, all of Jesse's music. She has an iPhone, too, and she listens to streaming music and podcasts on that while she's working in her studio. But the little yellow music player always comes out for her workouts.

The afternoon passes quickly. Just me and the trash and a hundred questions about that voice I heard. Or thought I heard. The rain never materializes.

DEPENDENT

I have this dream where we stay in the classroom and Jesse finds me. There's no talking or shooting. He stands in the doorway and looks at me with his rifle at port arms, an army term he taught me. Held in front, muzzle up. Used in ceremony but nowhere else. Formal. Impractical. He's dressed in his standard jeans and T-shirt, but his face is a mess of camouflage grease-paint. Darker shades on the high points, lighter on the low, which confuses perception and detail. He taught me that, too. The kids in my class are screaming and running to the back. I stay in my desk because I want to hear what he has to say. That's when I wake up. I don't scream like you see in the movies, so no one comes running. I'm always alone when I open my eyes.

I used to get the dream every night. At first, I tried to keep it to myself. Mom would try to make a joke of it and call me "zombie" in the morning, but I could tell she was worried. Eventually, I told her. For her and me.

You can only hold so much for so long. She said I should wake her up, but I never do. No need to have two of us tired in the morning. Two zombies. Since moving to Hamilton, I only get it once in a while, but Mom always knows when I do. Like today.

"Did you see Jesse again last night?"

I nod and reach for the cereal.

"Same dream?"

"Yeah."

"Want to talk about it?"

"No thanks."

She gives me a long look but doesn't press. She sips her tea, the little tag swinging with the movement, and goes back to her iPad. She only drinks green tea flavoured by burnt rice. "Nokcha," she calls it. Orders it online from Korea. Says she got hooked on the stuff in Gwangju when she babysat kindergarten ESL students for a year after university. It just smells like burning to me, though.

I'm annoyed she doesn't want to know more. Usually I'd be fine with it, but today I want her to stop looking at the iPad and tell me it's not healthy to bottle things up. "We're a sharing family," she likes to say. Or used to. We're both a lot quieter these days. Her with her business, the online store where she sells stainless-steel art and jewellery she makes in the basement studio. Me with my nightmares and school troubles.

She asks, "Ready for today?"

"Sure."

"I'm glad you're doing this."

"This?"

"Cleaning the park. Staying close to home. It'll be appreciated."

The word digs at me. Appreciated? How? By who? Churchill Park is huge — I'll never clean it all. A place can look spotless until you're responsible for it. Until you have to pay attention to how little people really care about beauty. Each day takes forever, and I pick up a thousand pounds of garbage, but no one will notice.

"It's not like I have a choice," I say.

"No, but the judge did. There are homes and facilities."

"I wish she'd put me there."

"No, you don't."

"I hate the park."

"It could be wor—"

I stand and slam my hands on the counter. My cereal bowl jumps, the spoon clattering onto the counter, the milk and cereal splashing, forming a soggy constellation. Mom jumps, too. "How, Mom? How could it be worse?"

"Dills …"

"I'm alone all day. There's the heat, the bugs, the garbage — there's so much of it. And I'm on full display. At least at one of those other places, I could be out of sight."

"Doing nothing. Getting —"

"Keeping my dignity."

Mom lets out a slow breath. Her eyes widen a little. I see real hurt there. She folds her arms. "There's no dignity in those places."

"I just —"

"Stop, Dills! Be quiet and listen to me."

The sudden sharpness in her voice makes me sit down again. Mom almost never interrupts like this. "Sometimes all we have is our ability to listen," she likes to say. She takes another deep breath.

"I've never told you this, but I spent some time in one of those facilities."

"Wait, what? You?"

"Yeah, me. I was a little older than you are now. Some friends and I stole a car and drove into a minivan full of kids."

"But —"

"I was driving. No one was killed, but people got hurt."

I kind of hear her tell me the rest, but it doesn't sink in fully. I manage to absorb a few details, like how she and her friends found a car with keys in it, how it was supposed to be a joyride and not a theft. How she bore the weight of the crime because she was driving, so she was sent away for a few months to a juvenile facility. "Juvie," she calls it. Prison for young people. She was incarcerated in a girls' wing with drug pushers, thieves, and murderers. There were fights and injuries and threats and a hundred sleepless nights. But she's sitting in front of me. No criminal, just Mom.

"What happened afterwards?"

"I came home."

"So Gramma Jan and Aunt Viv ..."

"We don't talk about it."

"Why?"

"Because I got to come home, kiddo. Because I had help to get back into my studies, because I lived with people who cheered for and loved me, I was able to get past it."

"Couldn't I do the same?"

"I have no doubt you could. But nothing good happened in there. And boys' juvie is much worse. You can't help but change."

"You changed?"

"Yes."

"How?"

"I used to love loud places, concerts, crowds, protests. I was always the one at the microphone."

I can't imagine her like that. She's all about quiet reflection, listening, thinking twice before speaking. She loves to protest — or she used to, before Windsor — but for her that has always meant writing op-eds and essays for the newspapers, magazines, the little hand-stapled zines she collects. Climate change. Gender parity. Marriage equality. Gun reform. Since moving to Hamilton, though, she's been so subdued. Limiting her anger to the insensitive things the local paper sees fit to print. Small rants over the dinner table.

"Is that why you do what you do? Sitting in your workshop making things?"

"Partially, but —"

"So you're a criminal."

Mom smiles. "No more than you'll be, after the summer. Juvie records are sealed, remember?"

"Right."

"I love making my art. And it sells, too, which allows me to support our family, which is especially important now that —"

"Now that Jesse's out of the picture."

Wow. I can see the physical pain on Mom's face as I say it. Another barb out before I can stop it. I think, *Out of the picture? Come on, Dills, that wasn't fair at all.* "Sorry, Mom, that was —"

She holds up a hand. "It's okay. You're not wrong. The army pension scheme is a nightmare at the best of times, but let's just say they're not sure what to do with him."

"But you can access our accounts from here, right?"

"I can, but I haven't."

"Why not? Aren't we still his dependents?"

"Yes."

"So …"

"I'm still processing things, too. I'm not sure I want his money anymore."

"He was sick, Mom. *Is* sick."

She exhales and nods. Falls silent. She stares into her teacup, where the green leaves and brown grains of rice will be sitting at the bottom, soggy and swollen. I'm quiet, too. I think about families and how we give everything to each other, even when we don't mean to. About the box cutter and Mom's misadventures, how she paid for her crimes. About what she might still be paying for. About how I'm paying for mine. About Jesse and family and influences and the possibility that hurting others might be part of us. In our DNA and bones.

MIA

Every day feels as long as all of human history, yet before I know it, I'm a few weeks into my sentence. Slow days passing fast. A strange, blurry mess of time.

I hear Jesse a lot. Not the imaginary Jesse I used to talk to, but the new voice, all his, that seems right next to me. It happens more frequently now, sometimes four or five times a day. I don't know what to do with it.

I'm here. Come see me.

I've stopped talking out loud to him, though. Two things. First, it feels weird to have the same conversations with him — me talking, him responding in my mind — when his real voice might drop into my day at any time. Second, it keeps Pat away. Without ammunition, he faded quick. I see him from a distance sometimes. He looks bored.

I've tried to tell Mom about Jesse talking to me, but I always bail out. She's so quiet these days. Like every day we're away from Windsor moves us farther away, even though we're still in Hamilton. She's so pissed at him but misses him, too, I can tell. And she worries. Every day, she calls her lawyer in Windsor, who has power of attorney and can receive updates so Mom doesn't have to call the hospital. She'll walk out onto the sidewalk with her phone and pace the width of our property. Voice low. Talking about the man who's legally her spouse, though there's no paperwork to prove it. Apart from army pension cheques he picked up from a post office box somewhere, he never got mail. Everything else was in her name.

I was four months old when Jesse made his vows to Mom. She loves to talk about how Jesse retired from the army and drove from Fort Bragg to Hamilton in a single push as soon as his discharge paperwork was finalized. How he managed to find a tiny tuxedo for me to wear to the church. How cold the church was because it was January and the middle of the week when the building didn't need to be heated. How you couldn't see my tux because of all the blankets. How perfect the service was, though there were only six of us: Mom, me, Jesse, Gramma Jan, Aunt Viv, and the pastor. How they didn't actually get married, because Mom didn't believe in the institution, but the pastor was a family friend who let them trade vows and "forgot" to file the marriage licence. How Gramma Jan and Aunt Viv showed up even though they both thought the relationship was impulsive — a new mom with some nameless other guy's baby in her tummy hooking up with a wounded warrior. Not fitting the mould of what families hope for. I don't know who my bio-dad is. That's Mom's and Jesse's term for the guy who got her pregnant and bailed.

All sorts of gaps, it feels like. The hole of not knowing. The canyon of pain and questions we're going through now. The space between our name and Jesse's, which I'm thankful for. Enough to keep mostly everyone from making the connection. Once the police ID'd him in the hospital, there were warrants for all his records and they found us quickly. Our names appear in detective reports and court documents and more than a few of the little notebooks investigators write in. After it became clear we had nothing to do with what Jesse had done, for the most part they left us alone. They kept our secret. Mom's been so careful about it.

Today, Jesse's voice doesn't arrive until the afternoon. I'm out by the splash pad, which is surrounded by playing fields. On hot days, it seems like every exhausted parent in the neighbourhood brings their kids here. Crowds of squealing, crying, laughing, running, falling kids. But the temperature has dropped before tonight's predicted storm, so there's no one around. A good day to pick up garbage. No one to recognize me. No one to ask what I'm doing.

I'm here. Come see me.

I will, I think. Well, I've decided to try, anyhow — it's a long way to Windsor. Longer still on my own. I haven't worked out the details. There are so many.

I get a good pace going by the splash pad. Out in the open you can walk and stab and keep moving while you work. In the bushes around the park, it feels like you could fill ten bags and not travel more than a few feet.

Trash under every bramble. The poison ivy you want to ignore, but you still have to clear under it.

It's a calm day, too, like the cooler temps convinced the wind to stay away. So I hear Gal singing before I see him. He walks in a strange way, his head turned to the left to take advantage of his good right ear. It always looks like he's about to run into something. He never does, though. And he sings with every step. Low, sad songs in his language. I've never seen him walking without some song keeping him company. Always brutally out of tune, I assume because of the ear thing.

I never know when I'll see him. He goes all over the park, usually carrying a backpack holding whatever tools he'll need for the small repair jobs he does. Rebolting a trail sign to its post. Repainting a playground fixture. That kind of thing. But today he doesn't have the backpack. He's just walking. Sometimes he does that, too. Walks and sings all day, and I'll see him popping in and out of the trailheads at the edge of the grassy areas. He seems to like his job.

I see him stop by the hedges at the far end of the field. The hedges are the remnants of an old living maze. Cedar, I think. Hundred-year-old bushes, with thick, gnarled trunks. Lots of dark hiding spots. There's a faded tourist sign nearby that suggests the park used to be popular with visitors to Hamilton. Grainy black-and-white pictures of people strolling in the park. Women with parasols. Men in top hats.

The woods have mostly reclaimed the area. If you walk through the trees, you can still see the rusted iron framework from the tropical gardens and crumbled stone foundations from mystery buildings. The only remaining feature still in operation is the aviary, a loud, smelly place filled with parakeets, peacocks, all sorts of rainbow birds.

Gal ducks into the hedge and disappears. I haven't worked up the nerve to go in myself, the twisted bushes a bit too mysterious for me. You don't find good things in hidden places like that. There will be lots of garbage. Broken bottles. Beer cans. Used condoms. All sorts of discarded objects from the stoners and love-drunk teenagers who probably hang out there.

So it's weird that Gal would go in. Now I'm curious. I pull out my watch, an ancient silver thing with a cloudy face. I actually have to wind it up every morning. It was Gene's. Gramma Jan said I could use it for the summer since I can't have my iPod with me. It has no band so I keep it in my pocket, a short length of braided paracord acting as a lanyard. Jesse gave me a roll of the skinny green rope and taught me how to braid. Box braid. Running. Trilobite. Herringbone. Cobra. "Once you have paracord around, you'll always find a need for it," he said. "You can use it for anything. Lanyards, laundry lines, belts, you name it." He was right. I'd made a cobra-pattern bracelet for myself the night before the shooting and had it on my wrist when Jesse came into the library. I unravelled it and used it as a tourniquet on my classmate Dakota. On her leg, which one of the bullets almost destroyed. It worked, but her other injuries were too serious and she died anyway.

The watch's blurred hands tell me that it's almost noon, so I walk to a nearby rubbish bin and drop my bag in, stick my picker-upper in the ground, and walk over to the hedges. I can hear Gal's voice as I get close. Then a girl's voice. Both speaking another language. Arabic, I think. Gal says something and the girl laughs. I can smell weed smoke, too. I stop. Shit. There are reasons guys and girls meet in the dark to smoke up. But I hear Gal calling out my name from inside, and I'm busted. Awkward.

"I'm heading home for lunch. I —"

"No, no, please come in," Gal says.

"Uh, that's okay."

"Please. I insist."

"I don't think ... I don't need to ..."

"Do not be shy. Come."

The girl says something too low for me to hear. Gal laughs. She giggles.

Well. If it wasn't awkward before, it sure as heck is now. I start to walk away.

"Wendell, stop," I hear the girl say to my back, laughter still in her voice. "We're not making out or anything."

The curiosity comes back in a rush. She knows my name. Huh. I feel my feet carrying me back to the opening in the hedge, into the darkness. Branches arch up and over the path. My eyes take a moment to adjust, but there's enough light to see them meet overhead, like the bones of a big church. A cathedral, even.

Gal and the girl are sitting together on the ground, their backs against the worn trunks of a pair of trees. Gal's head is turned, ready to hear me though I'm not saying anything. He's not smiling but he looks content. He has a tiny joint in his hand, the smoke swirling lazily around the space. The girl has a blanket over her legs, a book face down on her lap to mark the page. I recognize her right away. From my class. In the dim light, her short hair and her eyes are the same dark colour, almost black. She's wearing a tank top, and I can see her arms. Muscular. Lean. Strong. I don't know much about her. She's a competitive wrestler away from school, so she doesn't hang around. Always sits at the desk closest to the door. Last to arrive, first to leave. No one in my class talks to her. The girls can't relate. The guys are just plain scared.

"You're Mia," I say, a little stupidly.

"Yep. And you're Wendell. Or should I call you Cutter, like everyone else?"

"I'm not —"

Mia laughs. "I know. Kidding. Personally, I think Pat had it coming. The knife was maybe a bit far."

"It was definitely a bit far."

"Most entertaining thing to happen all year."

"Knife?" Gal asks. "Who is Pat?"

Mia laughs again and gives him the ten-second version of my story. Laid out plain and brutal. Hearing it feels like thorns behind my eyes. Am I a terrible person or what?

At the end, Gal simply nods. "So that is why you are here."

"You didn't know?" I ask.

"Not specifically. Your caseworker did not tell me. Confidentiality rules, I imagine." He shrugs. "It is no matter. You are doing a fine job, so I have no need to know."

Between his scowling face and the scars, it doesn't seem like a compliment.

"Want to sit for a bit?" Mia asks. "I have some protein shake, if you'd like."

"I shouldn't. I'm on lunch and then back to work."

But there go my feet again, carrying me in farther. Maybe it was the offer of protein shake, which I have no idea about. It sounds gross. And yet.

I feel some branches snagging on my socks and the ankle monitor. I'm wearing shorts all the time now. It's too hot to wear pants. At first I thought the little black box on my ankle would be like a billboard advertising my delinquency, but no one pays attention to me. I reach down to clear the —

"Wait-a-minute branches." Jesse's voice drifts forward from the past, from the one time he took me hunting. That's what he called the loose branches that snag your clothes. "Two things," he said. "One, never hurry through the brush. Too many bad things can happen when you're not careful and you're carrying a rifle. Two, never break the branches out of the way. No one needs to know you've been there. Clear as mud?" Mom was so pissed at him when we got home. That he'd take me out of school without telling her. That he'd sneak me into the woods to shoot at things. To kill for sport.

Jesse tried to explain that he didn't hunt for fun, but it didn't matter — Mom's mind was made up. Jesse never took me out again. He taught me things at home. I was so mad at her. The memory is as scorching and heavy as the sun, and the dim corridor through the hedges becomes a blurred, conflicted tangle of black and green and blinding white all at once.

"Wendell?" Mia's voice. Concerned.

"I have to go," I say. "I'm sorry."

I can't get home fast enough.

COLD CARROTS

I blunder in through the side door, kick my shoes off, and nearly bowl Aunt Viv over as I rush into the kitchen. I mumble an apology, open the fridge, and stick my head in, savouring the cool air on my hot, red face.

"Hey, kid," she says behind me. "Everything okay?"

"I'm fine."

"You look like someone pantsed you in church."

I shake my head. Then her hand is on my back. Patting, like a new father when he gets his first chance to burp the baby. "Uh, breathe, Dills. Breathe."

It works, though. I calm down enough to close the door and face her. "Thanks."

"So, are you going to greet your auntie properly or what? It's not like I've been gone for a week or anything."

"Oh, shit. Sorry."

I go to give her a hug but she's clearly expecting a high five. There's an awkward clash of hands and arms and shoulders. Some laughter, which is good. I sit down on one of the barstools at the counter. She goes to the fridge and pulls out an old lidded container full of leftovers, sniffs it, shrugs, and leaves it on the counter near me. Not in front of me. She's not like that. I pull it toward myself. Baby carrots and potatoes. I pinch out a carrot and eat it cold.

She leans against the sink and looks long at me. I have to look away. There's an intensity to her gaze I can never meet. She has the darkest, most penetrating eyes ever. Black hair framing her thin face. She's Korean by heritage. Born there. Gramma Jan adopted her when Koreans could get away with sending girl babies away. They wanted boys. Mom's adopted, too. Gramma Jan could never have kids of her own so she took motherhood seriously. All sorts of rituals. She and Grampa Vernon, who died before I was born, had some matching vision for parenthood and resolved to give all their kids V-names. Victoria. Vivian. But they're so different. Mom's rounded corners versus Aunt Viv's hard angles. There was a younger brother, Vincent, who died young. He's in only one of the photographs on the living room wall, his dark brown skin in dramatic contrast to the rest of the family, although it's everyone's smiles you see first. Great big grins. No one talks about him, though.

"So," Aunt Viv says. With purpose.

"So?"

"Saying 'shit' now are we?"

"No, I —"

"Next thing it'll be drugs and F-bombs and tattoos. And pregnant girls. The horror of adolescent malehood. The crisis of —"

"Okay, okay. I got it."

"Good. Definitely don't let Gramma Jan hear you talk like that. She'll have you scrubbing the bathroom floor with your tongue."

"Or Mom."

"Or your mom, exactly."

"You sound like you have some experience."

"I should tell you about the time Gramma Jan washed my mouth out with an actual bar of soap. I was picking bits out of my teeth for days."

"I think you just did."

"Smartass."

"How was your trip?"

With that she lights up, and you could forget that she's as tough as a calloused heel. She explains some obscure internet protocol she's initiated, but I don't understand a word. She's some kind of online-security expert. Travels all over the place to help corporations beef up their online protection. A hacker for hire, although I'd never say that to her face. Mom says that Aunt Viv could bring the world to its knees if she wanted. She's that good.

I sit back and eat the cold leftovers, letting her monologue wash over me. Her enthusiasm is a nice distraction from my embarrassment at having lost it in front of Gal and Mia. Sometimes the memories arrive so quick and huge, I don't know what to do with them. Mom and Gramma Jan and Aunt Viv are used to the moments when I need to stop and get away. But Mia and Gal aren't. Gal? Whatever. But Mia is so strong and never lets anything get to her. The other kids talk, but she walks through the halls at school like she's bullet-proof. Made of Kevlar. I like that strength.

CALL ME DILLS

I'm here. Come see me.

Windsor is about three hundred klicks from Hamilton. Klicks are kilometres in army-speak. Jesse grew up in some hilly place in Pennsylvania before he joined up, hoping for a career. Mom says the war knocked the nobility out of military service for him. He doesn't talk specifics about Afghanistan or Iraq but still has lots of those army-isms, like *klicks*. The army uses them instead of miles. Jesse calls himself "reformed to metric" and now hates that everything is in miles in the U.S. Says it's a stupid way to measure distance. I've never seen him get angry at other drivers, but he sure can rant about the imperial system of measurement.

Mom agreed with him but still ribbed him whenever we were driving and he got into it. "So the Brits aren't civilized?" she'd ask. Then they'd argue in a laughing way about bad teeth and colonialism and the legacy of fish and chips, and they'd look at each other a lot, and she'd run her nails through the stubble on the back of his head and give him goosebumps. When we got home they'd send me to my room. When I was really young they said I needed quiet time. When I was older they said they needed a nap, though they didn't nap and were obviously having sex. Anyhow.

Klicks or kilometres or miles, Windsor is a long way away. No matter how many times Jesse calls to me, getting to him is going to be hard. Not old enough to drive. No job, so Uber or bus or anything requiring money is a bust. Can't ask for the cash. Won't steal it. Can't ask anyone for help or everything will come out, so no. Deal breaker.

The height of the sun and the saturation of my boxers are telling me it's almost lunchtime. I take my helmet off and let the air evaporate some of my sweat. I'm in the woods cleaning the Princess Point Trail so the shade helps, but it's a scorcher today. Thirty-five degrees, feels like. Ninety-five in Fahrenheit, which Jesse never talks about, but I bet he thinks it's another dumb system. Why not measure up and down from zero, rather than from a freezing point of thirty-two? Weird.

I put my helmet back on, tie the garbage bag off, and walk it out. There are large oil-drum trash bins beside every set of benches throughout Churchill Park. The bags go in there when they're full. Well, as full as I can comfortably carry, which is usually about half. Things that decompose on damp ground get heavy.

I heave the bag into the garbage can, stepping back from a cloud of yellow jackets that drones into the air. I haven't been stung yet, but it's only a matter of time. You can't understand how many kinds of bees and wasps and hornets there are until you work outside. They do their thing and don't seem to care much, but you never know when you'll disturb them in the wrong way. Next thing you know, you're being swarmed and stung and they're leaving their stingers in you and dying. I always forget whether it's the bees or the wasps that leave their stingers.

Out here the sun blazes straight down and I have to squint against it. Through the humid haze I can see Mia walking across the grass and waving. I want to wave back, but for an agonizing instant my hand won't work. I just stare. Then my hand creeps up to a low wave and I feel almost human again.

"Hi," I manage when she comes close enough for conversation.

"Hi yourself."

She's wearing another tank top today, a light-blue one this time, and khaki shorts. A few wisps of hair escape from her baseball hat. As she walks up, I can't help but notice how her muscles flex on her legs. Not an ounce of fat on her. She's about my height but wider than other girls our age. But not awkward wide. Powerful wide. Like she's already been given her set of adult dimensions. It feels odd to think of her as a girl. Maybe I should say young woman. A young woman who could bench-press me.

"Leg-press, definitely," she says. "My bench isn't quite there yet."

"Sorry?"

"You were wondering if I could bench-press you."

Oh my god, I think. "I said that?"

A bemused smirk. "You talked to yourself at school, too."

And now I'm blushing and stammering and embarrassed. *Why, Dills?* I ask myself. *This is not news.* And then she looks embarrassed that she embarrassed me. A chorus of awkward noises and apologies. Finally, we both let ourselves off the hook with a good nervous laugh. We meet, kind of.

And for the first time in a long, long time I have a new friend. Just like that. No worries, no doubts, just the pleasant company of another person who can stand you. You lose that feeling early in your life, don't you? Moving to Hamilton in the middle of a school year and not being able to talk about my former life because I might let it slip that it was my stepdad who killed all those kids at another high school like this one is a difficult formula for finding friends. Much less one who makes me itch in a pleasant way. Maybe more than friends. At some point.

"I'm sorry for running away yesterday," I say. "That was awkward."

"Totally."

"And it's Dills."

"Huh?"

"Call me Dills, not Wendell."

"Oh, okay."

"It's weird, but I like it better."

"No, that makes sense. Wendell seems like a birth-certificate name, not a real name."

"Exactly. I like that. I may use it."

"Make sure you footnote me."

I smile and agree to make sure that every time I say it, she'll get the credit. I like that explanation. I *really* like it, in fact, and not because she's a girl and I'm not and there's a kind of magic when a girl notices things like that. I think it explains things. That tension I've always felt about my own name. How Mom avoids my questions about why she named me Wendell, which is a name for old men who wear dark socks and sandals on sweaty days like today. I kind of tune out for a moment thinking about it, and return only to find that Mia is saying something that sounds important.

"Huh? Sorry?"

"I was saying I should apologize for yesterday, too," Mia says. "For how it must've looked over by the aviary."

"Oh, that. Uh …"

"Gal's a friend. A strange friend, but still a friend. That's all."

"I shouldn't have barged in."

"I don't own the hedge."

"No, that's not what I meant. You were having a private talk."

"Yes and no. We were in private, but it was just a conversation. He speaks Arabic, too. I don't get many chances to practise."

"Don't you speak it at home?"

She frowns. "Not anymore. We used to, all the time, but my parents are trying to improve their English. And not get noticed so much."

"Is it okay if I ask where you're from?"

"Hamilton."

Another blush. "No, I mean, uh, where is your family from?"

Nothing.

"Your ethnic background? Your, uh, heritage, culturally speaking? The part of the world, maybe, where you and your parents and their parents and —"

Mia laughs and holds up a hand. "Okay, stop. Watching you squirm was fun at first, but now it's painful."

"Sorry. I've never asked anyone that before. Windsor, where we came from, is pretty white, and —"

I cut my voice off as cleanly as if I've used a box cutter on it, too. Shit. "Windsor" was out before I could stop it. Definitely one of the pieces of information we're trying not to advertise. My mind turns over itself, tumbling damage control around like wet clothes in a dryer. Heavy and ungiving. But Mia looks concerned, like she's gone an inch (2.54 centimetres) too far.

"That's okay," she says. "Hamilton's pretty white, too."

"That's true."

"We're Palestinian, although we hold Jordanian passports."

"Why?"

"Our family was cut off when Israel built another one of its walls. Jordan gives stateless Palestinians passports, and we were able to come here."

"Oh wow."

"Yeah. You couldn't know. Sorry for giving you such a hard time about it."

"I'm sorry, too, for … uh, can you forget I told you where we came from? I'm not supposed to talk about it."

"Windsor's where —"

"Yeah."

A beat. A nod. "I'll keep your secret, Sir Dills. As long as you promise never to tell anyone about my conversations with Gal."

"Of course. I —"

"He's Israeli. That's why it could be a big deal. Plus, smoking up isn't my thing at all, and I don't want that to get attached to my stellar reputation."

"I don't care about that."

"I do. Not about the assholes at school, but what my coaches would think. Weed's terrible for athletes."

"Okay."

"Gal needs the dope. You've seen the scars. He has severe pain almost all the time."

"Oh wow."

"You said that already."

"Right."

As I speak I feel that heat, like it could turn into yet another round of blushing. But it doesn't. A plain old smile rises instead. Mia doesn't seem to notice. She talks some more about her odd friendship with Gal, how he noticed that she likes to spend a lot of time reading in the park. About how her parents would go postal if they ever found out she was speaking with an Israeli, much less developing a fondness for the older, formal, scarred guy in the park who basically represents everything they escaped. She actually said "go postal" like it was no big deal, and I get that itch behind my eyes again. Mass shootings normal enough to create everyday slang. Most people don't think about their language.

"I know all about the hardships Mom and Dad faced," Mia says. "But I can't seem to hate Gal because of where he's from. He agrees that things are messed up over there."

"Why is he here? In Hamilton, I mean."

"He immigrated after he got injured in the army. It was like twenty years ago."

"What's with the scars?"

"His vehicle got hit by a rocket when they attacked Ramallah."

"They?"

"The Israelis."

I shake my head. "Unreal."

"Yeah."

"And now he looks after a park."

Mia smiles. "Can't get much more peaceful than that."

It occurs to me that I'd be fine with staying right here. Now is about the time when you'd ask if the other person would like to sit down on the bench. Maybe carry on the conversation until the sun sets. Or forever. But the ever-present abrasion of my safety vest reminds me that I'm not in the park for fun. How do you tell someone that you can't stay? Such a simple thing. And yet. Mia's gone quiet. A slight breeze feathers the loose hairs, and she tucks them under her hat with an absent, habitual gesture. She looks long across the park. Relaxed. Like she's looking at a good kind of future. Not making it any easier for me to walk away.

"Now that's a woman on a mission," she says.

I follow her look. Mom is striding across the grass toward us. She's in her workshop clothes: stained jeans and tattered UBC sweatshirt and bandana headscarf. The only thing missing is her tool belt, which is full of pliers and solder and other metalworking things. She was born with fair skin, but right now her face looks as white as printer paper, ninety-two bright. I've never seen her walk so fast.

"We need to go," she says when she arrives, slightly out of breath.

"What's wrong?"

"Gramma Jan's at the hospital."

"When? How? For what?"

"Chest pain." Mom exhales quick, exasperated, almost like a growl. "She actually drove herself, then called me. Took Viv's car. Stubborn, stubborn woman!"

"Gramma can drive?"

"She can, but shouldn't. I'll tell you more on the way."

"Okay. But my backpack is by the field house."

"You can get it later."

"I was going to get my water bottle to refill it over lunch, but Mia came, and …"

I don't finish the sentence, distracted by the surprise I see on Mom's face when she looks at Mia. Like she hasn't seen her, though Mia has been standing right here the whole time.

"Mom, this is, uh …"

I can't pluck her name from my brain. I know it. I swear I know it. Really. But she steps forward without a blink of hesitation, her hand extended, and she smiles at Mom. And suddenly I'm aware that no matter what, I'll always be a little in awe of her. Clear as mud for sure.

"I'm Mia, Mrs. Sims. Mia Al-Ansour."

"Oh! I'm Victoria. Vicky, actually. Just Vicky. Not *Mrs.* Sims. I was never a missus. I kept my name."

Mom stops, apparently aware that she might be rambling. Gives me a look. Pleased as sunrise for me, in the middle of everything. Mortifying, all of it. Obviously because it's my mom looking at Mia like she can actually see grandchildren in the shape of her. But also the timing. Poor Gramma Jan. But mostly because, well, Mia. And me. Or not me. The risks and chances I haven't glimpsed yet.

"Mom? Gramma Jan?"

"Right. You're set? Let's go. Nice to meet you, Mia."

"You too."

I give Mia a little wave as we leave, unable to say much more. As we walk across the park, I catch Mom giving me another look, this time with a hint of frustration making lines around her mouth. Well, I know that look. I call it "Boy, Are We Going to Talk About This Later."

METALLIC

Mom usually drives her old Corolla easy, like it'll fall apart at any moment, but today she's treating it like it's a stubborn pack animal that needs to be tamed. Whipping the steering wheel around corners. Mashing the gas pedal to the floor. Crunching the gearshift into place. She's had the car a long time — it's the only car I've ever seen her drive. Its poor little engine screams a few too many times for my liking. I imagine car bits flying off with every bump. Wheel covers. Mirrors. The veteran licence plates Mom insisted on that annoyed Jesse because it made him visible to others. I don't dare ask about Gramma Jan and driving; I won't be the reason Mom wraps us around a telephone pole. We arrive at the hospital and she zooms into the luxury parking lot at the front of the building. Ordinarily she'd circle wider and wider until she found free parking on the street, even if it meant we'd have to walk a few blocks.

"My mother is here somewhere," she says to the nurse at the desk. "Can you tell me —"

"Last name?" the woman says without looking up, her voice a monotone mix of exhaustion and practised boredom.

"Sims."

The nurse manipulates her keyboard and mouse. The computer screen glows blue on her face, dull blue stars glinting in her glasses. There's a waiting room full of sick people behind us. Lots of drawn faces and subdued voices. The nurse doesn't seem to care about any of it. She actually sighs, like she's the one holding the worries of the patients in her tired arms. Mom stares daggers at her, both of her hands on the counter like she might hurdle over it and reduce the nurse to her component elements.

Finally, the nurse looks up. There must be something in Mom's face she recognizes, because her eyes widen for an instant and her expression softens a bit. As she gives us the floor and room number, I'm thinking that she'll never know how much she owes that glimpse of compassion. People have been torn apart for lesser offences than indifference. I can barely keep up with Mom as she bolts down the hallway toward the elevators.

We find the room.

If my mom is a force, Gramma Jan is ten times that. Torn jeans and college T-shirts and baseball hats. No job too demanding. Handy with a hammer and wrench. A garden that's afraid of her. But all of that seems like a memory. Gramma Jan looks like she's weighed down on her bed by wires and pads and sensors. Her face as pale as the hospital gown she's been forced to wear. Her skin is an atlas of veins and spots and wrinkles I've never noticed before. She lies there at the mercy of medicine and all those unanswered questions. I guess I've never thought of her as old. Right now I can't help but think of her as anything else, and it feels wrong.

Her eyes, though. They burn as brightly as ever. She looks like she could spit. "Bastards won't even give me a goddamn glass of water," she says.

That's more like her.

"Mom, language," my mom says, but there's nothing behind it. Her voice drops and she moves to her mother's bedside. The equipment could be barbed wire, it's so scary, and all she can do is place a hand on Gramma Jan's arm. And take deep breaths. Try to, anyhow. It's hard to breathe deep when worry thins the air like it does.

"Shit, Vicky, don't be like that."

"'Shit, Vicky?' That's what I get?"

"I'm fine."

"You're not."

"You shouldn't be here," Gramma Jan says.

Mom snorts. "I called Viv. She'll be here soon. She's grabbing an Uber."

"I told you I didn't want you to come."

"Stop acting like we could possibly stay away. Besides, you stole her car, Mom."

"I borrowed it."

"Good luck explaining that to her."

"She'll be fine."

"And you?" Mom asks. "How —"

"This is all a damn embarrassing mess, is what it is."

Mom goes quiet. Not satisfied with Gramma Jan's response but not wanting to push too hard. Gramma

Jan doesn't say anything more, either. There's not much more they can say, and the silence isn't too awkward. A comfortable tension, if there's such a thing. Like they're reflecting each other in a cracked mirror.

Most of the time you never have reason to see it. Sickness brings it forward. Injury. Death. The last time I saw it was in the ER where they brought us after the shooting. Lots of families momentarily aligned. Divorced parents walking in hand in hand. Working moms and dads, feeling guilty for being so far away, wandering around with their phones in hand, calling names. Everyone shocked at the blood everywhere. Mom, too. The paramedics had bundled me into an ambulance. All that blood and you can't blame them for thinking I'd been hurt. Blood has a smell, did you know that? Kind of metallic. I could smell it on myself, soaked into my clothes from when I slipped and fell beside Ethan, who died with a library book in his hand. And from Dakota, whose leg bled more than I thought possible.

"Hey, Dills, since you're here against orders anyhow, how about a hug and a kiss?" Gramma Jan says.

I try to smile as I move next to the bed. There's a hug of sorts. As awkward and cardboard as it was yesterday with Aunt Viv, but more so because I don't want to hurt Gramma. Who's scared, though she's trying to be brave. Fear has a smell, too. I smelled it while I was waiting for Mom in the Windsor ER hallway where they'd put all the kids who'd been cleared and were waiting to be released by the police back to their parents. Under the blood smell. Fear is sour.

And just like that, I'm back in that hallway, sitting on the floor with everyone else who has been deemed well enough to wait. My friend Maddie and I have given up our chairs because even though none of us have been injured too badly, it seems like everyone else needs them more than we do. There's a sling here, a bandage there, and a lot of bloodstains on all our clothes. Turning dark and kind of brown. We're tagged with our names. There's a cop with a clipboard who checks ID when parents come in for their kids. I think we're all crying. It's cold. The smells of blood and fear fill my nose. Metallic. Sour.

Wait. I can hear voices. Mom's. And Gramma Jan's.

"Dills? Are you okay?" Mom asks.

"I think so?"

Now I'm in a hospital room with my mother and grandmother, who's had some kind of heart thing. It's bad. Must be. Otherwise there wouldn't be so much stuff on her. Wires and pads and clips. The little green and orange and red lights of all the equipment, the fluttering readout screens, the whiteness of the bed and gowns and the open window. I'm all right. But I can still smell that fear. And not only from Gramma Jan. It's everywhere, in the air of the hospital. And it's coming from me again. Why does the room seem all shimmery, like I'm looking at it through water?

I'm here. Come see me.

Jesse's voice. Right next to me, as real in this room as it has been in the park. Is he here? Can he be? Then there's a sudden blackness and I feel myself falling. I don't feel where the fall ends, though.

SCARS

Voices. Familiar ones, I think. But they're all muddy and lost in a swimming darkness made worse by the fact that my eyes won't open. I want them to. Why won't they? Wait. Maybe it's not completely dark. There's a distant redness, like when you shine a flashlight through your hand.

I feel rested. Like I've slept a full night through and am waking up when my mind and body are perfectly ready. What a strange thought to have, given that I don't seem to be in control of either mind or body. And I don't remember dreaming, which is new. No dreams, good or bad. When I was a kid I used to have the wildest, most fantastic dreams. Space adventures and ten-headed creatures and heroics. But they were often gone in the morning, even though I wanted to hold on to them. Now I just have the kind of dreams you're glad to forget in the morning, if you can. I remember too many. Dreams of Jesse's rifle and his camouflaged face. Also ones that feature gunfire or blood or the screams of the other kids.

"Memory dreams," I call them. I think the universe makes you remember those.

"Dills."

That voice is less muddy. Am I waking up? Was I sleeping, or something else?

"Dills, open your eyes."

It's Mom. I can tell because there's the tiniest gravel in the back of her voice. Like she smoked for a while and quit, but not before the hurt took hold. Or maybe the fumes from all the welding and soldering she does in her workshop have seared her vocal cords. I'm glad she's here. It makes it okay to try again to open my eyes.

More light. Flashes. A room that's kind of bright, kind of not. Oh, right. Hospital. Window blinds. Equipment and screens, tiny lights and numbers. Lots of the off-white plastic that everything in hospitals seems to be made of. Mom's face. And Aunt Viv.

"Hi," I say.

"Hi yourself," Mom says.

"What happened?"

"You fainted. How are you feeling?"

I want to say that I feel great, rested, ready to jump out of bed, but I'm not sure how Mom will take that. There's concern in her eyes. And parents have expectations. "Not bad," I say. "Uh, maybe a bit confused."

"Really? You did hit your head on the way down." She looks more concerned now. Parents and expectations and a constant fear of concussions.

Time to downplay. Reassure. Parents can be needy, too. "No, not that kind of confused. I'm wondering what happened."

"Are you sure?"

"My name is Wendell Bartholomew Sims. I'm fifteen years old. I live in Hamilton. I come from a long line of Sims, son of Victoria, grandson of Jan, nephew of Vivian. I'm a criminal mastermind wearing a LoJack —"

"Okay, okay, we get it," Aunt Viv says, rolling her eyes. "Smartass."

"I'm fine."

"Dills, I won't —"

"Mom, chill, okay? I'm good."

"Can you blame me?" Mom asks. "You blacked out, dropped like a stone. Gramma Jan's bed broke your fall, and …"

She stops and points at my forehead. Ah. That explains the strange tightness I feel on my brow, above my left eye. I lift a hand — which feels remarkably heavy, given that it's mine and I've been moving it my whole life — and feel the bandage there. A distant, slight pain behind the dressing. A tightness.

"Stitches?" I ask.

"A few, yeah," Mom says, frowning.

"You'll have a little scar," Aunt Viv chimes in. "And chicks dig scars."

"Cool," I say.

For an instant I believe myself. Maybe every guy dreams about getting just the right scar for just the right story for just the right person. But all my recent history flashes forward. Windsor. Hospital. Pat. Box cutter. I wince. My relationship to scars has changed forever.

"Dills?" Mom asks. "What's wrong?"

"Anyway …" I stretch out the word. I'm so aware of their eyes on me. *Distract, distract, distract.* "How's Gramma Jan?"

Mom and Aunt Viv glance at each other, then practically climb over each other to tell me. The docs think Gramma Jan has an arrhythmia, an irregular heartbeat. She needs to stay in hospital for a few days for further tests. She insisted that Mom and Aunt Viv go with me to make sure I was all right. I can almost hear her peppering her orders with choice language. There's more detail, but I tune out their voices and look around. The bed is in a fishbowl room right across from a nurse's station. Glass on three walls. Curtains on either side of me. In front I can see the top of a woman's head above the station desk. Ducked down, busy, but positioned to look into the room in a nanosecond if need be. A trauma room. For a kid with a cut forehead. It all seems like monstrous overkill.

There are bloodstains on my dingy work shirt and shorts. I'm thinking about the physics of how they ended up there, given that I fell and the blood should've ended up on the floor, when I see the back of someone stopping at the desk and speaking to the nurse. She looks up and nods at the room behind him and he turns, pocketing his wallet. He must keep his probation officer ID there.

Sean.

And he looks annoyed. Not concerned.

He strides into the room and opens his mouth to speak but stops when he sees Mom and Aunt Viv sitting on the stiff chairs. His eyes lock on to Aunt Viv and his mouth closes, this blank expression taking over his face, like he had a speech all ready to go but the sight of her has forced his brain to reboot itself.

"Yes?" she asks, her eyes narrowing.

Her expression is not uncertain in the least. It could cut him into ribbons. Aunt Viv has always had this built-in mistrust of anything institutional. Schools. Courthouses. Churches. She came to my sentencing but steadfastly refused to place a single foot into any of the other buildings associated with my correctional life. "I'm here for *you*, Dills," she said, "not *Them*." The words coming out like they'd been dipped in sewage.

"Well?"

By the way Aunt Viv is disassembling Sean with her eyes — *field-stripping*, Jesse would say — it's clear she views him as the System. Not representing a single portion of it, but embodying the entire thing. There's no response from Sean. Maybe his lower jaw moves a little? I begin to feel bad for him.

Mom steps in. "What are you doing here, Sean?"

Her voice reaches him, and he blinks a few times. You have to do that when you've stared at the sun for too long. "Oh, right. I'm here because, uh, Wendell is in breach."

"In breach?" Mom asks.

"Of his sentencing conditions."

Aunt Viv folds her arms. "What the hell?"

"Um, well, he's geofenced, yeah?"

Aunt Viv's left eyebrow rises a bit. "How?"

"The ankle monitor is GPS-linked, so —"

"Dynamic or static nodes?"

"Dynamic, but only from my workstation."

"Contextually retargeted, undoubtedly."

"In real time, if need be."

"Trigger intervals?"

"Every fifteen minutes."

"Pushed."

"Of course."

Sean holds up his phone and taps open an app. Aunt Viv steps around the bed and stands right beside him, shoulder to shoulder. Their conversation continues as though we aren't there. Which we aren't. Not really. They talk so fast, using terms I don't recognize. It could be their own language. Digitalese, or something. Mom and I give each other a sidelong glance. This conversation has taken a turn toward the surreal. Viv laughs, and Sean lights up like he's glimpsed something golden. Now it's my mother's turn to get grumpy. And my turn to get it. Sean and Aunt Viv are into each other. Flirting. Or some data-stimulated version of it, anyhow.

Mom snaps her fingers in Aunt Viv's direction. "Hey! How about coming back down to reality for a moment?"

"But he —"

"Sean," he supplies, helpfully.

"Right. Sean is e-conduited to the court database. It's —"

"Viv," Mom says.

"— pretty cool, if you think about it."

"Vivian So-Eun Sims."

Hearing her Korean given name, which Gramma Jan insisted she keep on her adoption papers, snaps Aunt Viv back to the present. She shakes her head like she's clearing it of radar jamming and moves back to my bedside. She folds her arms and her face regains its composure, which in her case means the hard stare returns and is directed right back at Sean. He doesn't seem to know what to do with the jarring shift. He fiddles with his phone, suddenly preoccupied by some dirt trapped at the edge of its protective case, before putting it back in his pocket.

"Sean?" my mother asks. "What's going on?"

"Wendell's ankle monitor is linked to a specific geographical location. It alerted me when he left the park area."

"Oh."

"It's sensitive, especially during work hours."

Aunt Viv frowns. "He can't leave our neighbourhood?"

"Of course he can. He's not wearing a shock collar, yeah?" Sean looks at the three of us in turn, his expression brightening a little, but his attempt at humour falls flat. "Right. Well. In off hours, there's some leeway programmed in. If the monitor moves to, say, a grocery store or school or church, we don't worry. But if Wendell suddenly dashes across town in the middle of the day, it'll trigger."

"This is a hospital, Sean," Mom says. "Wouldn't you assume he'd been hurt?"

"I didn't think about it much, to be honest."

"Your concern is heartwarming."

He shrugs. "People go to hospitals for all kinds of reasons."

"You should've told us," Mom says.

"It's common sense. Plus, we went over this at the field house on day one, didn't we, Wendell? You should know better than to desert your post on a workday."

"Desert his what?"

My post, Mom, I want to say. The park. That place where I'm supposed to stay. I can imagine Jesse narrowing his eyes if he was here to hear this. *One, you have a job to do. Two, people are depending on you to stick it out. You don't leave in the middle. Clear as mud?*

Mom leans forward. "So what are you saying, Sean? Spit it out."

"I have to report this to the court. They'll probably look at the circumstances and excuse the breach, but that's up to the judge."

Sean's face has grown harder, too. I hate that. I hate that what I do makes people angry.

"His grandmother is upstairs in the heart ward and you're worried about … about …"

"Breaching, apparently," Aunt Viv offers.

Sean ignores Aunt Viv. "I don't think you appreciate how serious this is, Mrs. Sims. He has to meet the conditions of his sentencing."

"First, don't call me 'missus.' Call me Victoria or nothing at all. Second, I understand that you're processing data and ticking boxes on a thousand bureaucratic forms, but this was a family emergency."

"I have a job to do, Mrs. … Victoria."

"And third, if you think I don't *get* what my kid's been through —"

"He still has to meet the conditions of his sentencing, even if he was at Windsor."

Mom slaps the edge of my bed. "He wasn't just *at* Windsor! Reporters were *at* the school. Parents were *at* the school. Hell, most of the other kids were *at* the fucking school. Dills was —"

Mom stops herself from saying *in the library*. Just a few of our many words to choose from, but they always generate a frenzy of strong opinions and horror and expressions of sympathy. I can't say them. Thinking them is enough. Knowing what they mean is enough.

Mom and Sean and Aunt Viv have all gone quiet. Silence is a strange sort of space, isn't it? You want to fill it. Sean has been knocked into a not-knowing-what-to-say variety of silence. Aunt Viv has retreated into a kind that the loved ones of survivors go into, where there are no words. Mom is looking at me, her silence a mix of the helplessness parents feel and the hope that I'll fill the void. Parents want their kids to say the words, sometimes.

I don't, though. Words can be too easy.

In the days after, during what Mom called "the media storm," news outlets tended to alphabetize the names. Scrolled them like stock tickers. I always knew when Ethan's name and picture would come up. He was my best friend, and his last name began with a *G*, so his was always the fourth. The fourth photo and name listed or slideshowed across all those screens. The same school picture from last year because he was sick on picture day this year. Grade nine and his new braces. Silver hardware and army green for the backings. Mom always looked away when it happened, like when we went shopping or got my hair cut or bought a drink from places where the TVs were always on.

I didn't. In the picture, though he's smiling and clean and polite, which wasn't like the everyday Ethan I knew, he was still so much more him than the Ethan I had to leave on the floor in the library. People can die without faces.

I watch Sean and Mom and Aunt Viv fill the space, but I'm not listening. Mom will tell me the important stuff later.

BELIEVED

The next day, I wake up to a quiet house, which is unusual — I live with three early risers who are always up long before me. But it's a strange morning, all right. Gramma Jan is at the hospital for her tests. Mom's nowhere to be seen. Probably sleeping. Aunt Viv is the only one around, sitting at the kitchen table behind a laptop. Her oatmeal — her breakfast always consists of coffee and a single pack of plain instant oatmeal — congealing and cold beside her as she manipulates the keys.

"Hey, kid," she says when I walk in and begin to assemble my breakfast of Mini-Wheats and OJ. Doesn't look up, though.

"What're you doing?"

She types a long string of code or something, gives a satisfied grunt, and looks up. "Checking out the tech your friend Sean uses to keep tabs on you."

"He's not my friend."

"Just an expression."

"In fact, I'd say he might be more your friend than mine. You two were pretty tight yesterday."

A dismissive wave. "Professional interest."

"Uh huh."

"The tech got me, is all."

"Find anything out?"

"Always."

"What does that mean?"

She points at the computer. "You can find pretty much anything if you have the right keystrokes."

"Please tell me you didn't hack him."

She smiles, a glint in her eye from the laptop screen, sky blue. "Well, *I* wouldn't call it a hack."

"What would you call it? Wait, don't answer that. I don't want to know, do I?"

"No."

"Make sure you don't —"

"Don't worry, Dills. I know how serious this is for you. I'd never jeopardize that."

And I believe her. She has this way of moving through life like it's hers for the taking. Mom told me once that Aunt Viv was top of her class, that she'd been courted by all the tech giants. A bunch of high-six-figure salaries dangled in front of her like golden apples. But she went out on her own. Makes her own hours, chooses her own clients. Mom says she's rich as hell, but you'd never know it by looking at her. Clothes from the same stores everyone shops at. A nicely detailed but small Toyota hybrid in silver, the beige of car paint. Still lives with Gramma Jan in this quiet little neighbourhood. Sleeps in the bedroom she grew up in. Like she doesn't need anything beyond the basics. I like that. You have to respect the lines between need and want.

"Okay, Doc," I say.

She grunts again, reaches over, right into my cereal bowl, and throws a soggy Mini-Wheat at me. She has at least two PhDs, but never talks about them. Hates the prestige factor. It's fun to bug her.

"How's the head?" she asks.

"Fine. No pain."

"Good. Your bandage fell off."

I raise a hand to the tight place. I can feel the roughness of the knots and clipped thread. No pain, though. "How does it look?"

"Like you cut your forehead on the side of a bed."

"Really? I should —"

"It looks fine, Dills. Relax."

I reach for the first-aid box, take it to the bathroom, and check myself out in the mirror. She's right. There's some bruising. But no blood — the wound is clean. I stick a plastic bandage over it and go back to the kitchen.

"You blacked out pretty good yesterday," Aunt Viv says as she spoons coffee beans into the grinder. Her back is to me as she works.

"I guess I did."

The tinny sound of the grinder's blades smashing through the coffee beans fills the kitchen for a few seconds. She pours the freshly ground beans into a basket filter and drops it into the top of the coffee maker. Reaches over to the sink, fills the carafe about halfway, and dumps the water into the coffee maker before hitting the power switch. The machine chugs and hisses.

She watches every drip, not wanting to take the coffee before it's ready. A Jesse thing, something about the proper grind and saturation and timing that he learned in the army. Whenever we'd visit Hamilton, he'd get up first and make coffee for everyone. He'd block the machine if anyone tried to take a mug before it was done. "It'll be worth the wait, troops. Promise," he'd say. Somehow the habit crept its way into our family. Aunt Viv, Mom, and Gramma Jan observing the ritual. They don't realize. I do.

"Do you know what you said before you fell?"

"I said something?"

"You did. 'No, Jesse!' Clear as anything."

The inflection she puts into the words is startling. It sounds like pleading. Like I was pleading. Begging.

"We all heard you, Dills. No one talked about it — I suppose we all figured it was being in the hospital that did it — but I wanted to ask."

"I don't remember saying anything."

"The way you said it —"

And I suddenly know why she's asking. She's imagining what the tone in my voice was saying. Like I was afraid of Jesse. That he could hurt me somehow. In all the ways people fear grown-ups can hurt us.

"Aunt Viv, no, he never —"

"Because you can tell us if anything happened. You know that, right?"

What an odd moment. The hacker aunt I've never lived with asking me if my stepfather abused me. The questions my own mother never asked about my stepfather. The stepfather who, despite a footlocker full of flaws, would never do anything to hurt me. Yet the same stepfather who could march into a school and start shooting. We still don't understand his flaws. And we're afraid of them. Afraid enough to assume. Like Aunt Viv is doing right now, her controlled face a wash of emotions all fighting to take over. *He could never do that*, I want to say. With all of myself I want to defend Jesse, but I've never seen Aunt Viv wrestling so hard with herself, either. What do you do when the could-have-beens are eclipsed by what actually happened?

I guess you begin with what's in front of you. By offering other things. "He talks to me."

"What do you mean? Who talks to you?"

"Jesse."

Aunt Viv tilts her head. "Jesse talks to you."

What seems so clear to me is clearly not so for her. I must sound crazy. "Yes. No. In my head, I think. I mean, I can hear him. When I'm working."

"You've always talked to yourself, Dills."

"No, it's not that."

"Okay."

"He's calling me. I don't know how else to say it."

She exhales, unfolds her arms, and pushes herself away from the counter. Opens the cupboard with a jerky, rushed movement. Grabs a mug. I can tell she's still not able to hold on to what I've told her. And who can blame her? Even I'm starting to hear myself, to hear the crazy in the words.

"Don't worry about it," I say. "I must've hit my head a bit too hard."

"No, keep going."

"Can you not say anything to Mom? She won't like that I —"

"Dills. Keep. Going."

Her eyes have cleared and she's leaning toward me. The body language suggests a change in my favour. But I wait an instant. Not daring to hope too much.

"I believe you," she says, finally.

"Really?"

"Yes."

Okay, then. Her words have settled me. I hear myself telling her everything, the whats, whens, wheres, hows. Telling her that Jesse's voice is a real thing I can almost feel, how it's different from memory or imagination. At the end, I sit back in my chair and watch her as she sips her coffee. She drinks it black. "Full strength," she likes to say. Jesse drinks his the same way. "One, it's easier when you're pressed for time," he once said. "No muss, no fuss. Two, what's the point otherwise? Coffee has to be strong. For the blood. For the brain." Aunt Viv puts down her mug. She's having trouble with the whys.

"So, he wants you to go back."

"Yeah."

"I can't stop thinking about what he did. And now he's talking to you, which is hard to fathom."

"You don't believe me after all."

"I think I do. But I'm worried about what it means for you, in terms of your healing."

"Healing?"

"I'm not going to talk about moving on or any-thing — God knows you've heard enough of that — but accepting what happened."

"I don't hate him, Aunt Viv."

"You don't have to."

"Everyone expects me to. They don't say it, but they do."

"People think hate is the answer for what they don't understand. It's not. But no one can ask him, which makes it worse."

"I can't even hate him when I think that he might've been coming for me."

"Ach, Dills, aside from thinking about all those dead kids, and that you might've —" Her voice breaks and she winces. There is real, physical pain there, pain I've never seen uncovered like this. She swallows, coughs, blinks away a sudden misting of her dark eyes. Tries again. "Thinking about Jesse hurting you is the toughest part for any of us. The wondering. Especially for your mom. You can understand that, right?"

"Do you hate him?"

"I hate what he did. The rest of it, who knows?"

"Does Mom?"

"Would you blame her if she did?"

"He's still Jesse."

"He is and he isn't, if that makes sense."

"I miss him, Aunt Viv. I want to go."

"I know. But can I offer a suggestion?"

"I suppose."

"Keep this to yourself. I'm glad you told me, but your mom might not …" She pauses. "Let's say that she might not get it. Not that I want you to keep secrets from her, but we don't talk about Jesse much these days."

"I get why, I do. But it still feels like a hole in our family."

Aunt Viv puts her mug down and nods. Thanks me for the talk, like we've worked out some everyday thing. There's another awkward hug that she hangs on to for a few extra beats. Then she picks up her laptop and walks out of the kitchen, telling me as she goes to "get out there and pick up some trash." Like she's my coach. Like all that rot and garbage is the goal, rather than the struggle.

DETAILS

Mia finds me before lunch. I've been in the same spot for more than an hour. Near the soccer pitches, there's an access road for the city maintenance fleet to use when they come for their weekly grass mowing and trimming. A dozen iron posts linked by rusted heavy chain line the road from the gate to the soccer field. Hard to know how old the posts and chain are, although they go far enough back to when iron and chain seemed appropriate for kids' play areas.

Only one of the hollow posts still has its original decorative ball screwed to the top. The rest are open to the sky, filled with what seems like a century of garbage. Everything from crushed pop cans to chip bags to cigarette butts to tattered, unidentifiable pieces of clothing. Like a park history in layers of decaying trash. More rotten the farther down you go. The first post cleared out easy, so I thought I'd get the rest. Bad idea. Between the dirt and the rust and the fetid things, each grosser than the last, I'm filthy. And pissed for doing this to myself.

"Serves you right for being so stubborn," I tell myself as I dig into a post with my spike — which I've decided is a far cooler word than *picker-upper* — and lift another dripping, smelly piece of cloth into the sky. This one was black at some point, but is now a faded mess of grey and rust.

A sudden voice behind me. "Stubborn? I'd say you're being thorough, but —"

"Shit!" My heart in my mouth. I fumble the cloth, which falls to the ground and flops open, revealing a cracked silkscreened skull and a single word. *Misfits.* An old band T-shirt. I turn.

It's Mia. Laughing. Hard. "But surely this wasn't part of the deal."

I groan inwardly. I'm blushing to burst. *Please let me not have squeaked out loud. Okay, universe? That's not too much to ask, right?*

"Uh …"

"Hi," she says. Just like that.

"Hi."

"What happened to your head?"

"My head?"

"You have some shiny new stitches."

"Oh, that." I raise my spike-holding hand — it's a tiny bit cleaner than the other one — to my forehead and feel the rough suture knots. I've sweated the bandage away again. I tell her I fainted and banged it against the hospital bed when I went to visit Gramma Jan. I explain it away as an aversion to hospitals and a reaction to how sick Gramma Jan looked. I finish with a dramatic statement about how worried I was and that I wasn't prepared for what came next. Truth mixed with a strategic omission of truth. I'm getting pretty good at leaving things out of my stories.

She nods at the poles and the mess at my feet. Makes a face. "So you're stressed. I suppose it helps explain the reason you gave yourself this particular challenge. Which is totally gross, by the way."

"I didn't think it would take so long. I did the first one, which was easy, and then kind of —"

"Got obsessed."

"Totally."

She smiles. I try to smile. I don't really know whether I'm still embarrassed or not. Caught talking to myself again. Ethan used to make fun of me for it, but in a best-friend way, where you hassle each other for the least important things. He knew about Jesse, how he wasn't my dad but I treated him like he was. How I wanted him to be. When I was a kid, sometimes I'd call Jesse "Dad" to see if it would stick. He didn't like it, though. "Just Jesse, little man," he once said. "One, you know that your dad left your mom when he found out you were on the way. But two, even though you don't like to think of him that way, he's still your dad. I'm not. Clear as mud?" I'd try to argue and say that he was my real dad, but he'd smile and say something like he was lucky to be in my life and he'd take whatever he could get. Though I'm clearly the lucky one. Was, maybe.

"Who's Ethan?" Mia asks.

First, mortal embarrassment. As in *Oh my god, oh my god, oh my god.* Second, I discover another shard of what happened. Right in my middle. And it slices in. Again.

I take a deep breath. "He was my friend. From before."

"From Windsor?"

"Yes."

"Sorry. I was supposed to forget about that, but I can't. I kind of want to know your story, Wendell Sims, a.k.a. Dills Sims."

The nicest feeling in the universe happens when you realize that someone else really wants to know you. I almost miss this one. If her words had arrived at any other time than right now, I'd tell her. Maybe not everything, but enough. Enough to return the interest, at least. My guts, though, are currently focused on stitching themselves up, so I have to let the moment pass.

"Dills Sims ..." She lets her statement trail away, like a question that needs an answer.

"Yes?"

"Sounds awkward, am I right?"

"I suppose so."

"Your mom seems nice, too."

"Huh?"

"She said to call her Vicky, but I think I'd like to call her Victoria. Do you think she'd mind?"

I smile. If there's anything I do know, even amid my confusion, is that my mother hates it when people use her proper name. "That woman named me after a silly Englishwoman," she'll say, sometimes right in front of Gramma Jan. I also know that Gramma Jan reacts as strongly to being called "that woman" as my mom

does to being called Victoria. They argue about it sometimes. Which is funny to watch because it's such a small
thing to get worked up about, I think. Mia, by asking
an innocent question, has landed right in the middle
of it, creating a nanosecond of escape for me. My smile
becomes a grin, which cracks open my face and releases
a laugh so sudden it steals a little of my breath.

"I do think she'd mind, yes," I manage to gasp at the
end of it.

Not what Mia is expecting. Her eyebrows pinch, perplexed. She's unprepared for my bluntness to her earnest
question. Which is even funnier, and I can't stop myself
from laughing more. I have to put down my spike and
my bag. I take my helmet off because it seems too small,
unable to contain the swell of unexpected funniness.

Mia watches me for a few moments. But there
comes a point when even the most well-meant laughter
begins to cut those who aren't sharing it. She frowns and
pulls out her phone and swipes through something or
other. Those familiar movements are like a heavy curtain falling. You worry whether you'll be able to lift it
back up again. My laughter fades, leaving the everyday
sounds of a park in motion and leaving me with that
tight, crinkled feeling you get in your face when you've
laughed too long.

I notice the tiniest shimmer in Mia's dark eyes.
Harsher stabbing and swiping across her touchscreen.
The slight turn of her body away from me. I feel as small
as the point of my trash spike. And as sharp.

"I'm sorry."

"Whatever."

She blinks and continues to manipulate her phone. I wait for her eyes to reclaim their normal mystery. But they stay hard.

"It's just that my mom is so stubborn about some things," I say. "Like her name. It's a perfectly fine name, but she hates it."

"She could change it, if it bugged her enough."

That's a thought I'd never had before. Huh. I hear myself saying "sorry" again, telling Mia that my reaction surprised me, too, that I didn't mean to be so harsh. That the laughter came out so quickly I couldn't hold it back. What I didn't say is that it was the first out-loud laughter I could remember having in a long time. Maybe since before Windsor. Through half a school year at a new school. The cutting incident. Court and sentencing and a daily grind of prying and digging and plucking discarded things from where they'd lain too long. And truthfully, although I was sorry for cutting into her, it felt good, too. Which of course feels horribly wrong. And yet.

Finally, Mia smiles and tells me that it's okay. But I worry that it's not. That I've carved too deep, and maybe the scars won't heal right.

Mia seems to sense my worry. She holds out a hand. "Give me your phone. I'll put my number in there for you."

"I don't have one."

"Oh. Right. The judge doesn't want you to —"

"No, I actually don't own one."

"Really?"

"Sorry."

"Why would you say sorry?"

I don't know. Before Windsor, me having a phone was an "End of Discussion, Young Man" topic. Mom has this thing about cellphones and kids and how rotten their brains are becoming. She can be empowering and progressive about a whole whack-load of other things: religion is misdirection for ignorant people, social justice is everyone's battle, talk to me about anything, there are no stupid questions, you're twelve but here's a box of condoms just in case, et cetera. But on the issue of me having a phone, it's the early 1990s and the web hasn't taken hold yet. She and Jesse are in lockstep about it, too. "No way, kiddo. One, this is your mom's call, but my job is to have her back, so don't triangle me against her. Two, I happen to agree with her. No one knows how to look each other in the eye anymore. Read a book. Get outside. Build something. Get a job." I tried a thousand angles and pitches, but Mom's resolve on this one issue was plate armour. Sixteen for my first phone, and the words "Don't ask again" delivered with a real edge to her voice. I haven't tested it in a while, of course.

"My mom hates cellphones," I say. "She jokes about them being a sign of the end times. I'm not allowed to have one."

"That's —"

"Shitty. I get it."

But I really mean *embarrassing*. Mortifying. Frustrating. Life-alteringly backwards. And yet I don't mean those things, either. I haven't had the urge to use social media since before the shooting, haven't wanted a phone. But here I am, trying to make some offering to the girl in front of me, that obviously it's Mom's issue, right? I know it isn't, yet I can't stop myself.

"No, I was going to say that it's cool," she says. "Sometimes I wish I didn't have to carry one around."

I breathe again. Mia has managed to surprise me and put me out of my misery all at once. "But don't you use all the apps and stuff?"

"Some. Mostly to stay in touch with my wrestling peeps. The rest of it is" — she glances down at her phone — "complicated."

"How?"

"Me being Muslim. Immigrant family. Wrestling body shape. All that. Let's say that social media isn't a safe space."

"I get that."

"Yeah, but boys don't have nearly the —"

"I like how you look."

Her eyes narrow. Ugh. My mouth took over. One silly heart short-circuiting the rest of the system, contacting my lungs, throat muscles, vocal cords, and tongue without first consulting my brain. I'm struck by a sense that it was the wrong thing to say. *Nice one, boss. That was unexpected. Foot in mouth much? Women are more than a sum of their looks, you know.* But right as I'm about to assemble another crack team of apologies — there are some things a guy can never unsay to a girl — Mia smiles. Big and bold and all for me. And beautiful. I hope I can say that.

"Thanks," she says.

And that is how a single word can pull a person back. Give him back his breath. "You're welcome."

"That is literally the first time anyone has ever said that to me."

"No way. That's —"

She holds up a hand. "It's okay, Dills. I've seen the movies and magazines. I know what everyone seems to want."

"I like how you look."

Another smile. "Yeah, you said that already."

"I wanted you to hear it from me for the second time, too."

She rolls her eyes. "Yeah, yeah, that's enough. Now, if you don't have a phone, how —"

"Landline. And email on my iPod. Mom has an iPhone, but I'm not allowed to use it."

"You don't use social media, either?"

I shake my head but don't say anything. The school therapist assigned to me after the shooting advised me to stay away from all things online. "There's too much ugliness there right now," she said. "Too much hate and misinformation. Focus on your real-life relationships and try to lean on them, okay?" It sounded like something she'd gotten used to telling other survivors. I did look at the news reports at first, but I wasn't that big on the online web of social intrigue before, so it wasn't hard to break up with it. I haven't had the desire to go back.

But Mia doesn't question my reasons. She nods and asks for my contact info, tapping it into her phone. Maybe she saw a shadow cross my eyes as I remembered my therapy, another one of a million small but jagged things that feel like they'll be hooked into my insides from now on.

"All right, you, now back to work," she says.

I throw up a salute. "Yes, ma'am. Right away, ma'am."

Parade-worthy, Jesse would call it. Tip of the right middle finger brushing the right eyebrow, hand straight, upper arm parallel to the ground.

Mia giggles and salutes me back. Sloppy and wrong, but that's fine.

"Later, Dills."

"Bye, Mia."

She walks away, and I put on my helmet and adjust my vest on my shoulders. My scratchy, sweaty armour against the rest of the summer. I jab my spike down on a piece of garbage on the ground. No more digging wrong things out of ancient fence posts for me today. I resume my usual rhythm. Look, stick, lift, slide whatever crud I've picked up into the garbage bag. And repeat. This time, though, I let myself include a few extra looks. To anyone observing me, it'll look like I'm scanning for more trash, but I'll actually be watching Mia cross the park as she heads back toward her place. Which I do. Maybe more than a few times.

I'm here. Come see me.

"I know, Jesse. I hear you," I say low, under my breath. "I'm working on it."

But that's not quite the truth, is it? I want to go, but there's a lot of my present life happening around me. Keeping me busy. And keeping me strangely interested in the right now.

SURPLUS

Midmorning snack break is my new thing. When hunger strikes, pretty much wherever I am, I'll drop my bag and stick my spike in the ground and eat. Today I'm close enough to the park chapel to take a couple of steps over and eat in its shadow. Before leaving home, I stuff my pockets. Some days it's cookies or raisins or apples or nuts — whatever I can get, however much — but today it's granola bars. I dig out one of the four I grabbed from the cupboard. Mushy from my body heat, the dark chocolate almost liquid. Gone in two bites. Hunger hits so quick these days, it's almost painful. All the walking and sun and fresh air, I suppose.

The chapel is in the main part of the park, where you'll find the sports fields, the play structures, and the splash pad. The small white cross at the top of the chapel's steeple is visible from almost anywhere in the park. You look there first and next your eyes are drawn down to the white walls and doors. Right now the sun is late-morning high and hitting the place with full force. Blinding against the greens of trees and grass. The chapel sits between four ball diamonds, one at each corner. If you stood at home plate on any of them, the miniature church beyond the home-run fence would be a tempting target. An iceberg to smack a ball at.

I'm not here very often. There's nothing to clean. Everywhere else, the garbage seems to defy physics, wedged tight into impossible places by the smallest breeze. I'll clean another corner of the park until it sparkles, only to find it the next day looking like a rogue garbage truck dumped its load overnight. To spite me. The chapel, though, never seems to get dirty, and trash never collects along its angles.

I wonder how on earth the place stays so white. How anything does. I can't own anything lighter than beige. You can't tell if beige things get dingy because they start that way. Shoes, especially. I gave up on asking for white ones a long time ago. They look great in the store, but on my feet they're scuffed in seconds. By the end of the first day, they look like I've run ten kilometres in them. On a mix of gravel and new asphalt. While kicking old tires. Tagged by rival gangs as I ran.

As I stand and chew, I catch the faintest whiff of burning weed. I wipe the chocolate from my hands and circle the building but see no one. Has to be from inside. I imagine some neighbourhood kid sneaking into the chapel, lighting up, filling the interior with greasy smoke, and dropping the roach on the floor. Grinding the residue into a cross pattern. Giggling at God to do something about it.

And it pisses me off. I have no idea why. We're not a religious family. Maybe I don't like the idea of some kid mocking the chapel's wide-open, welcoming doors by messing the place up. Maybe it's a tiny bit of loyalty because the chapel is cared for by the same local church where Jesse and Mom did their thing and I wore that tiny tuxedo. Maybe it's because it's a clean, cool spot where anyone can escape the sun, sit on polished wood pews, and stare at stained glass.

I step inside and squint against the startling contrast between the light outside and the colourful dimness inside. As my eyes adjust, I see a dim figure sitting in one of the pews. Gal. Leaning forward with his scarred forearms on the pew in front of him. A smouldering joint lightly pinched between forefinger and thumb.

"Mr. Sims," he says.

He brings the joint to his lips and tokes long and hard on it. Exhales. A strange offering. But he looks comfortable here, at peace, like this is routine. I can only see the right side of his face. Almost normal, if you tune out the twisted flesh on his arm.

"You look angry," he says.

"No, I'm not … it's just that …" I fall silent.

"Nice canteen."

He's still looking straight ahead, and I've only just arrived, but he's already taken everything in with his peripheral vision, right down to my accessories. Unsettling.

"Uh, thanks," I say. "Mom's idea."

"Hydration is important."

We're speaking in our normal voices. It's so quiet in here Gal doesn't have to turn his good ear to hear me.

"You sound like her," I say.

"This is a compliment, I am sure."

He tokes again and pinches out the joint with his fingers. No hesitation. No smoke at all. Wow.

"How'd you do that?" I ask.

"Long practice."

"But it was so quick."

He holds up the extinguished end. "If it is small, it is possible. You must do it quickly. Take all the oxygen. No chance to burn."

"That sounds like something Jesse would've —"

That was out before I could stop it. Gal's action like an army thing. *Tactical*, Jesse would call it. Where you act in ways that make you difficult to be seen or heard or found.

"Jesse?"

"Nothing," I say. "He's no one."

Gal looks at me and grunts. Doesn't look convinced. Hard to convince a person if I'm not convinced myself.

"Where did you learn it?" I ask, testing my theory.

"The army."

His voice clipped and final. He doesn't say more. He drops the half-burnt joint into his chest pocket, rises from the pew, stretches, and slides over to the aisle, where he goes down on one knee and crosses himself.

"You're a Chr— uh, a churchgoing type?"

Oh, that was smooth. Nice terminology. Say Christian, *for crying out loud.* Mom fought against the paperwork and rigidity of marriage and she doesn't believe in organized religion anymore, but she still thought it was important to exchange the vows in church. Jesse never had religion and only went along with it because he loved her. Mom grew up attending services twice every Sunday because Grampa Vern was a dyed-in-the-wool church person. Bible studies. Prayer before and after every meal. Church school and catechism every week until he died when she was fifteen. Strict. "Too strict. And no place for women," she told me. "That's why I don't do church." Gramma Jan stopped going after Grampa Vern died. Mom thinks watching him decline wore Gramma Jan's faith away.

Gal tilts his head. "Why would I not be?"

"Mia says you're from Israel, so —"

"You assume I am Jewish."

"Don't you have to be?"

"I was, then. But not now."

"Why not now?"

A long pause. "You might say what happened to me, and what I saw, has complicated my relationship with my heritage."

It almost feels like an opening to ask him about the scars. I want to. But something keeps me from the question. Maybe it's the violence of the past. It complicates everything for me now, too.

Gal doesn't seem to mind my hesitation. He points at the canteen slung across my chest like a satchel. "May I?"

I remove it from its carrier and hand it to him. He smiles a bit when he flips open a miniature cap embedded in the middle of the main lid and points at a small doughnut of faded black rubber resting inside. Tells me it's a hydration port. A straw can be passed through the seal in the canteen and another through an identical seal in a military gas mask. Soldiers can drink in a chemical weapons environment.

"But I could never get the mask to work," Gal says. "Not many could. It is an American design. Useless."

Jesse said the same thing. He said that older NCOs — non-commissioned officers — would talk about them. Practising in gas huts with CS gas, which is like tear gas. Failing because the rubber was too grabby for the straw and they'd give up and breathe and end up on the ground outside, their eyes fused shut, gagging and vomiting from the exposure. Training for NBC warfare, Jesse said. Nuclear. Biological. Chemical. Training for the unthinkable. Bunny suits and booties and gloves and seam tape and decontamination powder. All against poisons and pathogens that you can't see or smell and will probably kill you anyway.

Gal flips the little flap closed. Click. The sound makes him chuckle, his eyes crinkling, lines bursting outward. Like a glimpse of sun between storm clouds. But he grows serious almost right away. His scars don't wrinkle the way the rest of his skin does. They have to feel different. An ever-present reminder keeping him from laughing too long.

He hands the canteen back to me and moves back into the pew. He kneels on the kneeler, crosses himself again, and sits back in his former position. This time he closes his eyes. Folds his hands on the back of the pew in front of him. Serious. Mouthing words of some kind.

EXILED

I can't eat lunch at home today. I walk across the park toward Mia's hedge — that's what I'm calling it now — with a plastic shopping bag dangling by my legs. I don't know if she'll be there, but sitting and eating by myself is better than dealing with the storm brewing at my house.

Mom and Aunt Viv are in a sour mood, arguing about every little thing. Gramma Jan is coming home either today or tomorrow, which you'd think would be good news. But the sisters are jumpy about it. Bickering about who should drive her home. What to prepare for her first meal back. That kind of thing. They tried to bring me into it, but I told them I didn't want to play referee. And could they get over it so Gramma Jan didn't have to deal with their shit when she got home and could concentrate on getting better?

Me dropping the S-word got a half-hearted rebuke from Mom and silenced them for a bit. But by the time I'd assembled a couple of PBJ sandwiches and grabbed an apple and cookies and a few more granola bars, they were at it again. They didn't say goodbye when I left.

Every family argues, right? A good argument is like a pressure valve for all that unconditional love. Mom doesn't talk about it much, but Aunt Viv is happy to share the details of their most extreme shouting matches. A passionate family. Except for Grampa Vern. Mom says he was the calm one in the family. The rain to dampen Gramma Jan's perpetual grass fires. When he died, there was no one to balance Gramma Jan out, so she raised Mom and Viv by her own methods. It was a house where no opinion went unchallenged, no infraction unpunished. Mom says it's why she tries so hard to be gentle with me. Counterpoint to her upbringing. "Building new legacies" was how Jesse put it. "Your mom is changing the game."

But she can still argue. I grew up listening to their flare-ups, which always seemed inevitable. Mom, Jesse, and I would visit Hamilton every now and again. Not very often — Gramma Jan never warmed to Jesse, so the visits were always tense. No one in this family likes to be the first to give in. Gramma Jan and Aunt Viv are different generations of the same person. Mom is calmer but still strong-willed. The three of them feeding off each other is something to watch. Jesse had to take me out of the house a lot when the family would get together.

So the arguments aren't new. There are fewer blow-ups these days, but when they do happen, what comes out is multiplied. Hotter. Like the fury's been stored up. And though no one says his name anymore, Jesse is the cause of all of it. Gramma Jan and Aunt Viv wrestling not only with the horror of the shooting but also with the fact that the shooter is family. Mom fighting against what he did, trying to help me cope, and grieving the loss of their relationship all at once.

This one happened one night a few weeks after we moved to Hamilton, when they thought I was asleep:

"I don't want to talk about it," Gramma Jan said.

"Mom, we need to set some ground rules."

"Victoria Sims, this is my house and I'll decide the rules. You take care of your own."

"I do. He's downstairs and sleeping. That's why I'm bringing this up. He's who we should be worried about."

"Feel free to thank you-know-who for that."

"You're blaming me?"

"*I* didn't bring him into the family!" Gramma Jan said. Like she was spitting. "And I won't say his name one more time. No one will. Not in this space. Ever."

Mom fell silent, hurt and raging all at once. Bearing all of it. Blame. Guilt. Grief. Heartbreak.

You probably can't know what it takes to banish a name from a home. How painful it is, even though it should be easy, given what happened. We were already tiptoeing around it, but anger pushes things. I'd just had one of my first run-ins with Pat at school. He'd pushed my face into the drinking fountain and I'd shoved him back against the opposite row of lockers. Witnessed by a teacher and every student in the hall. A quick phone call and an uncomfortable meeting in the principal's office. Mom took me home. She was calm and reassuring. Gramma Jan was not. Aunt Viv tried to be the referee. They carried the argument into the night. I couldn't sleep and sat on the steps to hear what was being said about me.

"Jesus, Mom. You can't police what we say," Aunt Viv said.

"Watch me. That goes for Dills, too."

"He answers to me," Mom said, although her voice was small against my grandmother's anger.

"He's not answering to anyone right now, is he?"

"Mom —"

"What's Vicky supposed to do with that?" Aunt Viv asked. "The kid's traumatized, for crying out loud."

"He needs structure. Discipline."

"No, he needs time," Mom said. "And love and lots of space. He saw his best friend killed, for —"

Her voice broke, and all three women went quiet. Something reaching all of them at the same time. And of course I was thrown back to that library. Ethan's body. In full HD. I clenched my stomach tight against what could burst out of me.

"That's exactly what I'm talking about," Gramma Jan said, her voice softer but still full of acid. "*He* did that to Wendell. That fucking monster."

"No!" That was me. On my feet and storming into the kitchen. Seeing the emerging horror on three faces, the realization that I'd been listening the whole time. My anger blazing its own supernova. "Stop talking about him that way!"

Gramma Jan stood. "We're just —"

"You think you know why! Everyone thinks they know why! But no one knows anything. Not you, not me. Maybe not even Jesse."

"That doesn't matter. What matters is he took everything away, and he —"

"*Jesse*, Gramma. Say his name."

"No, Wendell. I won't."

And the supernova surged so white I couldn't see anything. I had to burn through. Scream. "You're the fucking monster!"

I turned and rushed out of the kitchen and back down to my room, stomping a thousand pounds on every stair. Thinking about the fact that Mom hadn't spoken at all after I burst into the kitchen. Hadn't defended me. I wanted her to, though there wasn't much she could have said. I screamed into my pillow and made my throat sore. I stared at the little strip of light that cut under my bedroom door. I lay awake for a long time, my anger simmering. Mom never came down, like she always does when we fight. I fell asleep, and of course the dreams came back. I would've preferred to stay awake with the anger.

Today, as I walk toward Mia's hedge, my irritation with Mom and Aunt Viv fades. Like it did after that early argument about Jesse's name. There's something about anger. I find that it can't stay around long, and at some point you're back to normal. It's like the heat of a disagreement seizes up the family engine for a little while but can't hold the tension as the machinery cools. Next thing, you're laughing. Back to the everyday movement of a family. Defending a gramma who sometimes says indefensible things.

A thin layer of cloud has covered the afternoon sky and the air has gone perfectly still. Capturing the humidity, it feels like. The mosquitoes, usually trapped in shadow and waiting for sunset, love this weather. Without the sun to dry them out, they travel far and wide to bite me. Halfway across the park I'm tempted to turn back to grab my insect repellent, a greasy organic concoction cooked up in some herbal kitchen somewhere. Smells like cough syrup and mint and oregano. I don't go back, though. I'm too excited to see if Mia is at the hedge.

She isn't. Pat is. He looks up from the crumpled magazine he's reading.

"Found your spot, Baby," he says with a sneer.

"It's not mine."

"I really like it."

"You shouldn't be here," I say.

"Why not? It's a public park."

He's not wrong. But I don't respond.

He sniffs. "That's what I thought. Too weak to give a shit. Now fuck off and don't come back."

His eyes go back to the magazine. Porn. What a shocker. There's a woman on the front. Jean shorts and a bikini top. Huge breasts. What Pat would call *tits*, I'm sure. *Tats*. *Jugs*. *Funbags*. Words my mom would crucify me for if she ever heard me using them. Still, whatever you might call them, it's hard to pry my eyes away.

Pat sees me looking. "Oh, you like this?"

Turns the magazine around and flops it open to the centre. An extra page flips open. Like my jaw. The dimensions of her. Such a volume of pink, pink flesh. I feel an uncomfortable warmth down below and my shorts are suddenly smaller. A distant part of me feels guilty for responding. Porn's wrong. No one wins. Objectification of women's bodies. All that.

But Pat laughs and closes the magazine, rolling it into a tight tube. Points it at my face. "Nope. Not for you. You're gay as fuck. You and your butch friend."

Now, I don't care if Pat calls me gay. For him, it's an insult of the worst kind, but for me, whatever. I'm not gay, but Jesse and Mom always made it clear that I'm allowed to feel whatever I need to feel. I shouldn't care if he calls Mia butch, because it's the same empty nothingness he threw at me. But I do. It's the casualness of how he does it. As though his messed-up opinions are unbreakable by their certainty. I clench my fists and take a step toward him, like someone else has taken control of my body. He sees it. Drops the magazine and gets up. Those dumb, narrow eyes. I take another step.

I'm here. Come see me.

This time the words aren't spoken, but whispered. Almost hissed. Like a warning. Close enough that my ear seems to itch from Jesse's breath. The discomfort of it, the urgency, knocks me into myself again. I feel this suggestion of imminent shame, like I could disappoint everyone who loves me by stepping wrong. I shake my head and drop my hands and turn away.

Pat doesn't know what to do with the change. As I leave Mia's hedge, I hear him calling me back, huffing and puffing, a comic-book dragon at a loss. Before my next step takes me out of the shadows and onto the park grass once again, my right foot clips against my left and I fall. A classic tripping move. Impossible to recover at speed. I land in the long, uncut grass at the park's fringe, right on my chest, my hands not having time to break my momentum. Lunch bag and watch and granola bars and canteen go everywhere. My breath knocked somewhere into the grey, grey sky.

I get onto my hands and knees, trying to breathe. It's all I can think about as Pat stands next to me, his stupid knees in my peripheral vision. Worst feeling in the world, maybe, to get the wind knocked out of you. Pat is yelling something. I don't hear. I've been sucked into a soundproof tube.

But I feel it when he kicks me in the side, his shoe digging deep into the space between my hip bone and ribcage. There's no breath to drive out, so there's only the pain. The helplessness as I flop over on my back. Half a second in motion but a forever moment on the ground. I close my eyes to concentrate on getting that one elusive breath back. *Focus, Dills*, I think. *Breathe.*

The first sound that reaches me is the scratch of Pat's button and fly. Then he's pissing on me. Still shouting. His urine is warm and yellow and it soaks through my clothes so quickly. Another brief eternity to endure. My lungs finally fill as he finishes. The thick stink of his dehydration is sharp in my nostrils. I open my eyes to see him zip up, almost expecting him to spit on me. The perfect finishing touch to the perfect insult.

Pat sees the canteen. Picks it up, unscrews it, and sniffs the contents. Shakes his head. Holds the canteen over me. A thin stream of water, still cool from the faucet at home, arcs out and lands on me, soaking into my shirt. I hear him mocking me, "Baby playing army" and whatnot, but I'm distracted by his need to sniff the can-teen. What did he expect to find? Tea? Vodka?

"Stop," I gasp.

He's surprised enough at the sound of my voice that he does. "Why?"

"You should have it."

"Have what?"

"The rest of the water."

He snorts. "Like I'd drink —"

"You're obviously dehydrated. Your piss stinks."

"Fuck you, Baby."

Pat raises the canteen and pours the rest out all over me. Mixing with his urine. I don't know where his piss begins and the water ends, or vice versa. I'm simply wet. He looks at the canteen for an instant and slings it over his shoulder, thanking me for it, telling me how awesome it is, telling me I should take better care of my things.

"Hey!"

Pat turns toward the voice. It's Gal, striding across the field in his unique sidelong way, hand up and point-ing. Pat doesn't know what to do with it. His confusion would be satisfying if I couldn't still smell his piss, now cooling. Reminding me of the humiliation that has put me down here.

"Get away from him!"

Pat's sneer returns. He is emboldened, no doubt by the unusual appearance of the reclusive park manager. He sees a non-threat there. A disabled opponent. But then Pat's face changes. Gal's face is dark, his scars pale against his anger, his body tense. I've been distracted by the scars and the weed and his surly manner and have ignored the compact power he still holds. It's fearsome. Pat glances at me on the ground, then back at Gal, and runs away after giving me one final, calculating look. *This isn't finished*, the look says. The canteen bounces against his back as he runs. That's suddenly all I can see.

Gal stands next to me. "Get up now. Go home."

He reaches out a hand to help me up, then draws it back as I reach out my own. Like one of those cruel playground jokes. *Psych!*

"What?"

He frowns. "It is better for me not to touch you."

I exhale through my nostrils, mad at the world for bringing fear into adult-and-kid relationships. Imagining Gal feeling a last-second tug of hesitation about touching the pissed-on kid on the ground. Appropriate boundaries. Bodily fluids. And so on. But then I see him looking all around me. My eyes follow.

"Aw, come on," I groan.

I've landed in a patch of poison ivy. "PI," Jesse called it. "Leaves of three, let 'em be." The memory of Jesse whispering and pointing at foliage as we stalked the bush on our hunting trip. How it all looked the same to me. So much of the forest undergrowth having three-leaf bunches. I didn't take the lesson seriously. Now I do. These low, greasy little plants are defiantly obvious.

"You must wash. With soap. Now."

I stand, my eyes scanning every centimetre of exposed skin. Already feeling the itch, though the reaction is a ways away. Gal's nose wrinkles as the air I disturbed reaches him. Shame drapes me in a blanket soaked in urine. I actually feel like crying. But there's more shame at the idea that I might. I don't cry. Won't. Not anymore. I left my last tears in the triage hallway of a Windsor hospital.

"Don't tell anyone," I say.

Gal doesn't respond. Maybe he doesn't know the proper next steps. His role in all of this, whether he bears any responsibility. Finally, he looks me in the eye. "You have problems with this boy."

"Yeah."

"Is this the one Mia called Pat?"

I nod. "His full name is Patrick, but we call him Pat to bug him. He hates it."

Gal makes a face and a sucking noise behind his teeth. "I would also."

Gal making the connection is worrisome. This can't get back to Sean, who'd obviously have to report it. Or not. Maybe Pat assaulting me isn't his problem. But I wonder about the follow-up. What if it's bigger than him and me? Pat pissed on me, after all. What if the police have to be brought in? I can't imagine the courts ignoring this.

And I think of the box cutter. The one I used to cut Pat. I still have it. I lied to everyone when I said it must have gotten lost afterwards. The principal and the police officer pressed a bit, but not much. Laws and rules about interrogating kids, I guess. But it wouldn't be hard to find. It's in my room, yellow and clicky and stainless and wicked sharp, in a white shopping bag in the bottom drawer of my desk. No blood on it or anything, but still. It could get found and make things worse for me. Any remaining compassion would evaporate faster than the first raindrops on a hot day.

"This is not something he should get away with," Gal says.

"Please don't tell anyone," I say again.

A long pause, thoughtful. A nod. "Go home. And clean yourself."

I pick up my things and walk away, leaving the bag and my lunch on the ground. I'll come back later and use the spike to pick it up and dispose of it all properly. But it bothers me to leave it there. On top of everything, I've made more work for myself. And I'll have to see it again when I come back.

I walk back across the park, taking the shortest possible route home. My worry about poison ivy and the school's knife growing exponentially by the second. I can smell Pat's piss the whole way.

CLEAR

I'm here. Come see me.

The next morning I open my eyes way too early. My single window, which looks south at the world at ground level, is bright. I forgot to close my curtains last night. I wait, feeling as though Jesse might say more. But he doesn't. I close my eyes again to try to grab a little more sleep, but it's clear that my body has had all it needs. Such a good sleep. There were no dreams. Only pure, clear rest. I want more of it. My stomach growls, too, louder than any alarm.

And my right wrist is itching like mad. The rash has arrived. A red, bubbled line up the inside of my forearm, straight as a ruler. Ten centimetres long.

I get up and pad up the stairs to the washroom, a set of clean clothes under my arm. The house is silent. No one else is awake. I strip out of my sleep shorts and T-shirt and stare at myself in the full-length mirror on the back of the door. Bracing for the worst. The wrist undoubtedly a foreshadowing of what's to come. I'm getting a wicked farmer's tan on my face and arms. Body and thighs pale as winter. Pale enough that a rash would be neon lights. But my body is clear. Just sad white skin (and it is a little sad, how pale we can be) and the single rash line on my arm. Itching hot and bright, like it's making up for being the only one. I'll have to cover it. Not to keep it from spreading but to keep my fingernails from wearing a path down to the bone.

As soon as I got home yesterday, I scoured my helmet, shoes, vest, and gloves with a horsehair brush and some ancient soap I found in Gramma Jan's garden shed. I carried the pissy, soapy pile inside to the laundry room, stripped down to what Mom calls "the truth," and dumped everything but the helmet into the washing machine. Poured in a single capful of detergent, then added a bit more for good measure. Set the wash to normal, but on hot, and with an extra rinse. The house was all mine, so I risked a naked dash to the shower and scrubbed myself for what felt like an hour. Did everything right. Urban myth says the blisters spread the rash, but PI only spreads if the oil is still on the skin. The blisters aren't contagious. So I'm good. I know. I googled it.

I called Sean to tell him. About the PI, not Pat. He said I did the right thing by cleaning up and calling him and it was fine to take the rest of the day off. "But assuming you're not lousy with rash, right back at it tomorrow, yeah?" Then he actually thanked me. His thanks were kind of passive, thrown out there before he hung up, but still. I don't think many of his clients do much to keep him in the loop.

The bandage on my forehead has fallen off again in my sleep. The scar is narrow and pink. One of the sutures has come undone, the blue thread sticking out. I pull at one of the loose ends and cringe at a glint of pain as the thread slides through. I use a single square of toilet paper to dab away the tiny bead of blood that has risen from the suture hole. I decide not to replace the bandage — it never stays on for more than an hour or two anyway.

I pull on my clothes and go to the kitchen. My first stop is the first-aid kit, where I cut a length of gauze and then tape it loosely over the rash, an action which is super awkward with only one hand. Then I dig into the cupboard for cornflakes. I'm on my third bowl when I hear Aunt Viv get up. The old house tells me where she is, groaning and popping as she crosses the floor above me. She and Mom each have an upstairs bedroom, the old painted doors facing each other across the small hallway. Aunt Viv comes down, each step creaking, and yawns her way into the kitchen. Ignores me until the coffee maker is hissing and sputtering.

Finally, the last of the water drips through the coffee grounds and filter. The machine groans a final time and falls silent. Aunt Viv clunks the carafe out, sloshes coffee into her mug, and clunks the carafe home again. Morning sounds. She turns and leans back against the counter, taking her first tentative sips with her eyes closed. The mug moves up and down, up and down, flashing a combination of fruits and flowers faded by time and wear and dishwasher heat, the outlines long gone but the shapes themselves still oddly bright. Morning colours. She opens her eyes, sees me, and nods a kind of good morning.

"What's with the bandage?"

"Dressing, actually," I say.

She rolls her sleep-puffy eyes. "Sorry. *Dressing*."

"It's poison ivy."

"From the park."

"Yep."

"God, it's everywhere there. I wish the city would do something about it."

"Ever had it?"

"Once. On my arm, actually, like you. Maybe the other one, though. Itched like a b—" She stops herself and grins into another sip.

"Like a …?"

She shakes her head. "Can't say that stuff anymore."

"Sure you can. Everyone does."

"Getting older means you figure out what needs to get said, what doesn't."

She smiles again, like she's figured out what's good and proper when it comes to bad language. She and I share a few minutes of silent morning. Talking about the PI has made the rash itch a little more. It's probably in my head, but that doesn't make it feel less real.

Aunt Viv doesn't make a move for any food. *The coffee doing the job quite nicely indeed*, Mom would say. I bring my bowl and spoon to the sink.

"So, have you figured it out?" Aunt Viv asks.

"Figured what out?"

"Jesse. How you're going to go see him."

I shake my head. "How could I do that? It's a long way."

"Not too far."

"It is for a guy with no money and no driver's licence."

She shrugs. "You sounded so sure."

I am sure. But it still feels odd that someone knows about it. Like I should keep a little back, maybe to protect my plans, maybe to protect Aunt Viv if I go through with it. Maybe a bit of both. There'd be so much trouble. She doesn't press me about it, though. She retrieves an old, battered travel mug from the cupboard and fills it with the dregs of her first cup. She tops it up from the carafe, steam swirling and disappearing into the air, disturbed by her movement, until she twists the cover on. Sees me looking.

"I've got the morning shift at the hospital."

"Huh?"

"With Mom.

"Mom? Why?"

"My mom. Gramma Jan to you. Your mom stayed last night, so I get today. Like I did yesterday."

"Mom stayed there all night? Why would she?"

"The chair in the room lays flat. They call it a cot, but it's more like a torture device."

"No, I meant why the need to stay? Is Gramma Jan all right?"

A brief shadow moves across Aunt Viv's features, like that single cloud that passes directly overhead on a sunny day. The sudden dimness surprises you. She snorts and makes a joke about how pissed Gramma Jan is that her girls are making all this fuss. When I try for a few more details, Aunt Viv dodges and weaves, chastising me for the shirt and shorts I dropped on the bathroom floor. Uses the old this-isn't-a-hotel standby for whenever adults gripe about the stuff we leave behind. There's grumpy work talk — "I don't get to take a day off," "Can't believe the hospital charges for Wi-Fi," etcetera — as she gathers her car keys, wallet, and laptop and tosses them into her shoulder bag. As though any of it has answered my questions.

DEADLINES

I'm working the near side of the park this morning. I can almost see my house from here. The field is an oval cricket pitch, with a strip of hardpacked crushed stone splitting the middle for the wicket. I work the edge, stabbing garbage along the treeline.

My arm itches like crazy. I was neck deep in PI, so it's a miracle I didn't pick up more. Still, it feels like every itch I've ever had has decided to join forces with every other itch and they're eating themselves into my forearm. All at once. Right now. I find myself having the craziest thoughts as I work. Using knives and forks for the scratching. Pouring boiling water on the rash to distract myself from the burn. Finding the roughest tree in the woods and sandpapering my arm against the bark. That kind of thing.

I let my mind go where it wants because as crazy as they are, those thoughts are also keeping me from thinking too much about the job. Another day in paradise.

Picking up its trash. They work for a while, anyhow. At some point the image of me using that box cutter to cut off my forearm to cure the itch pops into my head, and that's when I decide to stop being so dumb about it. Making light of crudely amputated limbs? I should know better. I've seen what the crazy physics of bullets can do. How fragile we are. But that's all I'm going to say about it. I hope that's all right.

Weird as they might seem, those grim thoughts were also keeping me from thinking about Gramma Jan. And Mom. Now the concern comes back, full force. Of course, there are all sorts of reasons daughters might need to stay at the hospital with their sick moms. But my heart isn't buying the arguments. All it can do is worry.

I'm more worried about Mom. I love Gramma Jan, but she's not the one I grew up with. She's the grand-parent you need to love from a distance. Who you only see a few times a year but who your mother would still drop everything for. You would, too. But to make sure your mom is taken care of. The concern for Gramma Jan more an abstract thing.

I'm here. Come see me.

Jesse's voice arrives at the precise moment I think about heading home to check on Mom. As though he can read my mind and is worried that I might not have enough concern to go around. Like he'd get forgotten if I dared to think about Mom for too long. A flash of pure annoyance washes out the morning.

"Now, Jesse? Really?"

He doesn't respond. Of course. As soon as I close my mouth, the words lost to the grass and trees, I feel stupid about losing my cool. A bit guilty. I haven't been thinking about Mom a whole lot. I should do better. I will.

I walk over to the tree where I've stashed my water bottle and snack bag. The pissing thing with Pat has made me feel weird about stuffing my pockets with food. I don't know why. I take a long drink and walk out to the road. I'll probably find the house either empty or quiet with sleep, and there's no way I'll wake Mom up if she's making up for a sleepless night at the hospital. Still, I have to go and check.

A little blue Elantra pulls up to the curb. Walters. The last thing I want to do right now is talk to a reporter. The last thing I want to do ever. I think about turning around, but I'm still wearing my safety vest and there's no way she hasn't seen me. She doesn't get out. The car is perpendicular to me and I can see the dark outline of her head and shoulders through the tinted side glass. She's turned slightly toward me. Looking at me. Why isn't she getting out? I start to walk again, faster this time, so when I pass the car I can minimize my exposure.

Her car door opening is loud against the morning stillness. The park is quiet, like it always is in the middle of the week. There are a few people walking dogs and out for early hikes, but they're swallowed up by the size of the place. It'll get busier closer to lunch, when parents emerge from their homes, kids tumbling alongside, to head to the play structure and splash pad.

Walters steps around her door and removes a pair of white earbuds from her ears. "Hi," she says.

"You can't be here. My mom —"

She holds up a hand. "I'm not working right now."

Could be the truth. Her hair is tucked under a baseball cap and tied into a ponytail in the back. She's in running tights decorated in a crazy broken-glass pattern and a neon-peach sports bra. And it's clear she runs a lot — she's tanned and fit, and her shoes are scuffed and dirty from the trails. I've seen a lot of trail runners in the park this summer. But the timing of it. And a car? She lives around the corner. Like me.

She watches me checking out the car. "You don't believe me. You think this is an ambush."

I shrug.

"I like to run before work. Usually I'm out here at six in the morning, but I was up late last night on deadline. I'm going in late today."

"Okay."

"And I don't interview in my running gear. Not the most professional."

She looks down at herself and laughs. It's the laugh that finally disarms me. It's genuine. Caught out. She was not anticipating seeing anyone. And the smile around the laugh peels away some of the years between us. Sometimes I have that sense that a lot of the adults in my life aren't that much older than me. Ms. Nieman, one of my teachers at Windsor, was like that. She was our teacher, so obviously she was older, but there were rare moments when she smiled and didn't seem like it. Moments we could sit back and not worry about school or homework or anything. She died behind the library counter, where she'd been helping the librarian check out our books. Research for some project I don't remember. The librarian was definitely an older woman. She held Ms. Nieman's hand as she died. She wouldn't let go when the police cleared the room and escorted us out, or later when they let the paramedics in to help the fallen. I heard she screamed at them to get away a bunch of times. Anyhow.

"There's that look again," she says, her eyebrows rising.

"Huh?"

"When we came back in for sentencing. You and your mom."

Why is it that the worst memories come back right when you're least able to handle them? Why can't you lock them away, bring them out when you need to? The therapist said, "You can't always control how you feel, but you can learn to manage the feelings that do come out." Managing them usually means fighting with them. Fighting back another black, boiling flood.

"And your sentence was so light. What happened?"

"You're not supposed to be talking to me," I say, and walk away.

"You're right. I'm sorry," she says to my back. "But, Wendell?"

I slow and turn back toward her. There's something about adults using kids' first names that's like a tractor beam. "What?"

"Telling your story can help you feel better."

"I don't think that's true."

A pause and a nod. "Okay."

"Okay."

"I'm going for my run."

"You do that."

She smiles at me, puts her earbuds back in, and turns to her phone, swiping into a song or podcast. She runs away, her ponytail swinging. Straight across the cricket pitch and onto the trail into the woods at the far side. A streak of neon disappearing into the gloom. As bright as me in my silly vest.

The morning is silent again. It's cool, too. As I walk home I can feel the dew that has soaked cold through my shoes and socks. Funny I didn't feel it before.

INBOX

The house is quiet. I lock the door behind me, kick off my shoes, and go right to the bathroom to change the dressing on my rash. It's hanging by a single strip of medical tape. How is it that medical people can transplant almost any body part but haven't figured out how to make tape that can stick to sweaty skin? I rinse my arm with cold water, which feels good. The rash is red and angry, as though it resents what I've put it through. I change into dry socks, laying my wet ones over the lip of the laundry hamper to dry. I think better of it, drop them on top of the dirty laundry, and carry the hamper downstairs to the laundry room.

The load from yesterday is a cold, wrinkled heap in the dryer, bunched slightly to the side. That last tumble a half-hearted effort. I lift the pile out and set it on top of the machine. There's no piss smell. Thank God. Nice to know you can normal-cycle away the smell of embarrassment.

I upend the dirty stuff and sort through it. Whites here. Darks there. Synthetics in their own pile. I like doing laundry. The mindless rhythm of it. Lug, dump, sort, wash, fold. Mom taught me the basics when I was six or seven, and now we both watch for the hampers to fill and throw in loads whenever they do. No such thing as laundry day in our house. Any day could be the day.

I see Mom's phone charging on the kitchen counter when I go upstairs. Confirmation that she's sleeping. No devices are allowed in our bedrooms, no phones or laptops or alarm clocks. The fear of blue light and constant connectivity killing proper sleep. My iPod is charging alongside. Both screens are dark. I tap Mom's home button to see if there are any urgent notifications she'd want me to wake her up for. Like phone calls or texts with lots of exclamation points. Her old phone had a code, so I could tap it in and see, but her new phone uses a fingerprint. She likes the security. I still check the screen out of habit. But there's nothing there, only an Etsy photo of one of her metal creations and the phone's clock.

I don't like the new picture. It feels sterile. Her old phone had a photo of Jesse and me doing something in our garage when I was younger. She left it in Windsor and bought a new one when we got here. She says it was a blessing in disguise that she forgot the old phone, because she needed a better camera and more speed. I don't buy it. Nobody forgets their phone when they leave the house to get groceries, much less moving to an entirely new city. It would be like losing a hand or something.

My stomach growls. Lunch hunger hitting me half-way through the morning. I raid the fridge and eat standing beside the sink. Leftover grocery-store chicken in its plastic spaceship. Cold, stiff potato wedges. I munch on some cucumber and celery sticks to "green up the meal," as Mom likes to say. A conscience thing. She is sleeping upstairs.

My iPod's screen blinks on across the kitchen and a low electronic chime announces the arrival of an email. I wipe the grease from my hands on a dishtowel and swipe in. A new message from Mia. Time-stamped now. In my excitement, I almost drop my iPod.

> wendell. (feels weird to write Dills, i dunno why, sorry.)
>
> how r u? u left ur email address with me, so now u cant get away, ha ha. i guess that means were pen pals. or is it touchscreenlap-topkeyboard pals now? anyway.
>
> im at home and bored. not much wres-tling in the summer but lots of weights and running (yawn). but im not writing because im bored. Really. im writing cuz 2day is my 16th bday (insert whistling and fancy bday sounds) and summer bdays are the worst — there are no friends around to spoil u.
>
> UNTIL NOW.
>
> thats right, lucky (only) neighbourhood friend, ur it. u get the job. (insert congrat-ulatory clapping and polite cheering.) now,

this is totally last minute, but u have to come to my bday picnic tonight. (i know, i know, birthday picnic?! lame. but still, its my bday, so u have to come.)

u probably finish ur trash-picking-upping around 5, which gives u about an hr to shower and dress in ur sunday best and come over to the old lawn bowling green for 6. (yes, shower. ull need one after sweating in the park all day. believe me. i know. im bffs with vinyl mats that stink of feet and sweat and unwashed boy, so i know smelly. and yes, sunday best. mia is birthdaying and will be playing dress-up herself (gag). DO NOT MAKE HER DRESS UP ALONE.)

so, ya, thats it. ur invited.
this was long. sorry. (i hope u read it all.)
mia

I read it again. And I nearly drop my iPod again. Me. Invited to her birthday. And she's funny. I laugh in the same places the second time through. Which has to mean something.

I look at the clock. It's not even lunchtime, yet I have this weird need to get ready now. Which is impossible because of garbage and courtrooms and charges and LoJacks and all the time I need to make things right again. I wonder who else'll be there. If I'm the designated summer friend, who does that leave? That thought carries me back to the park to finish my day.

SO GROWN-UP

Here's my afternoon: repeatedly grabbing the paracord lanyard and pulling my watch out to stare at it to see if time is moving any faster, but of course it isn't. I don't know how many times I do that. Takes forever.

When I finally get home, I hear clanging and cursing in the basement. Mom's awake and working. I yell a "Hey, Mom, I'm home!" down the stairs and make straight for the bathroom for a shower. Realize when I'm finished that the towel racks are bare. Mom must've done a load. I dry myself by squeegeeing my body with my hands, but it only goes so far. My clothes are a dirty, damp, not-an-option-dumbass pile on the floor. There's a closet in the hall with clean towels, but it's out there. For a millisecond, I debate a mad run in the buff down to my room, but only a millisecond. Today, the house is not my own.

I crack open the door. Steam wisps around me into the hall. "Mom!"

"What?"

Her response is muffled. Her workshop door is closed. I cringe. A closed door means "I'm Creating. Do Not Bug Me Unless There's Blood or the Apocalypse."

"Can you get me a towel?"

"In the closet! There's a whole pile of them right there! Folded and ready!"

"I'm naked!"

Awkward silence. A door opening, feet stomping up stairs, the closet opening, the soft movement of laundered towels. Annoyed mother muttering about finally getting some work done despite the distractions and teenage boys she'd like to strangle. Footsteps outside the bathroom. I hide behind the door and reach my hand into the hall. But all I grab is air.

There's a pause. A long, long pause full of a mom's unasked questions.

"I'm freezing here!"

"Uh huh. So, why the shower?"

"I always shower."

"Sure, but only after you grab a snack, drink a glass of milk, stare into the fridge for an hour while you scratch your guy parts."

"Mom."

"It's gross. Don't think I don't notice."

"I'm still naked, you know, right here behind this door. A foot away from you."

That's my trump card. My best play. Embarrass the mother who joked about guy parts into action by reminding her of teenage boys and puberty and the changes she never wanted to happen to her baby.

But no. She laughs instead. A dismissive little laugh. "Yeah, I got that. So what's up? Have an accident at work?"

"Mom!"

"I can wait all evening, my friend."

She's enjoying herself enough to make it happen, too. It's nice to hear the lightness that has been eclipsed for the past while. Haven't I been telling myself I need to do more for her? Part of me wants to let her savour it. A small part. The rest of me is butt naked and anxious about a certain girl waiting for me and about wanting to time things so I'm arriving precisely at six so she'll be impressed with my promptness and discipline.

"I'm meeting Mia."

"I figured. The mad shower dash was a classic move."

And the towel is placed into my hand and I can bring it in and close the door. I wait for her footsteps to head back downstairs so she can reimmerse herself in her work and leave me alone. Instead, I hear her head into the kitchen and rattle some things around to make tea. Stall tactic. She doesn't do tea when she's creating.

I dry off, wrap myself in the towel, go down to my own room, and get dressed in a light-blue golf shirt and a new pair of cargo shorts, the nicest clothes I own.

Well, the nicest non-funeral clothes. At the far-left side of my closet there's a suit and a dress shirt and a navy-blue tie with diagonal stripes. All hung on the same hanger in the same clear dry-cleaning bag that lets you see the stripes are red. And the stripes remind you of how you stared down at them all through a bunch of funerals for your school friends and teachers, who probably wouldn't have cared that the stripes look like blood, but you did and felt guilty through every eulogy and tribute. Of how you insisted on going to every service and insisted on wearing that tie even though your mom sensed that it was making things worse and said you didn't have to go. But you kind of did have to. Anyhow.

When I finally go upstairs, Mom is waiting for me. Leaning against the counter and drinking a steaming cup of something, holding the mug with both hands, like it could drop. No burnt-rice smell this time. Instead it's berries and cinnamon and something herbal, like hemp. Jesse called Mom's eclectic collection of rare teas "hippie brews." "Earth mom's getting all unified, man. Far out. Dig it?" he'd joke. It's been a long time since I've seen Mom make a cup of the hippie stuff for herself.

She levers a single finger from the mug and points at my wrist. "What's with the bandage?"

"Dressing," I say without thinking.

"Right. Dressing. PI rash from the park, right?"

"Yep."

"I'm not surprised. You should get your Aunt Viv to tell you some of her rash stories."

"Maybe I will."

She smiles. "You're getting some nice colour, too. From the sun. The white of the dressing really makes it stand out."

"Uh, thanks?"

"You look good. Older. Like your dad."

I don't know what to say to that. My bio-bad (never my *real father* — that title belongs to Jesse) gone but still always casting a shadow on the wall behind us. But Mom is smiling slightly, like she's all right with the reminder of him in me. That's a first.

"He'd like you, I think."

Like. A strange word for dads and sons. Even dads like him and sons like me.

Mom seems to read my face. "I'll have to tell you more about him sometime."

I shake my head. "This is so weird."

"How so?"

"You've always talked about him as the guy who left. Like you didn't want me to know more."

"He did leave me. And you. But he wasn't a bad person."

"Did he know about me?"

"Yes."

"And he still left."

"He was nice enough, but not dad material. He knew it."

We fall silent. A lot to process. Mom suddenly letting on that her relationship with my bio-dad was more than a passing thing. I wonder how long they were together. What they were like. If I might've liked him. That last thought burns. Emotional heartburn for the betrayal against Jesse. I suppose it's natural to wonder about the what-could-have-beens, but I feel like even admitting that I'm curious will stain what Jesse was to me. Is.

"Good thing Jesse stepped up," I say. I can hear an edge to my voice. Almost anger.

Mom looks at me and breathes deep. Nods. "Jesse stepping up was the best gift a mom could ask for, Dills. The two of you were such a good team."

"*Are*, Mom."

"Right. Are."

"How much of him do you see in me?"

"So much I can hardly stand it sometimes. So much goodness, I mean." Her eyes well up as she says it. The twist of heartbreak. Mismatching the man she loved — the man who made so much of me actually me — against the thing he did.

I say, "No, not Jesse. *Him*."

"Oh. I …" She tilts her head, considering. "I'm not sure, really. I'd have to think about it. I haven't thought about him in a long time."

"What was his name?"

"Alan."

"Alan what?"

She wipes her eyes and looks me in the eye. Shakes her head. A quick motion, sharp. "Just the first name, kiddo. Jesse made you who you are. That's where we leave this."

"We should —"

Mom's phone rings, the electronic chimes more like gongs in the quiet of the kitchen. Cutting through the intensity of this new discussion. Drowning it out. We both look over at it, our conversation falling away like a rope cut from a cliff. The screen is lit up and I can see Aunt Viv's face and name in the centre, her expression annoyed, like Mom caught her in the middle of something important when she took the photo for her contact list. The call buttons red and green and huge.

"Weird," Mom says. "She always texts."

Another cycle of chimes begins, as loud and brash as the first. Mom grabs the phone. "Viv, what's —"

Mom falls silent, listening. Some seconds pass. "No, tell me now."

Another few seconds. Five. A thousand, maybe.

"Okay, I'll see you in a few. Bye."

Mom pulls the phone away and stares at it, like she's trying to figure out how to end the call, though it's one of those things we've all done a million times. The red button fades as she watches it. Aunt Viv hit hers first. The screen goes dark to save power.

"Mom?"

"That was Aunt Viv."

"I know. What's up?"

She looks around the kitchen and at the living room beyond the counter, mumbling about corners and dust and doing a load of sheets. Staring at nothing, though. Not really seeing. Her eyes are so wide.

"Mom?"

She grabs a scrap of paper and starts a list of groceries, as though the fridge and cupboards are empty. They aren't. They're as full as we need them to be.

I put my hand on her shoulder. I've seen people do that when they need a person to respond. A person who isn't in the present. I've seen lots of hands on lots of shoulders. Lots of minds struggling to keep pace, struggling to process any of what's happened.

"Mom. Talk. To. Me."

Lots of voices that are firmer than they would be otherwise. So the person will hear them.

Mom turns toward me and her eyes clear. She tries to smile. "Gramma Jan's coming home. They'll discharge her in the morning."

"That's good, right?"

"She was supposed to be in for another few days. I guess the heart thing wasn't as serious as they thought. Your aunt said there was something else, something serious, but she wouldn't tell me on the phone."

"It's after working hours. I can come with you to the hospital."

Mom looks down at me. At my clothes. "Your thing with Mia. You should go."

I look down, too. Creases and laundered cloth. Skin so clean it's almost new. I want to go see Mia but I also want to go with Mom — she looks like she needs the support. I feel the conflict rising, that ancient tension between girl excitement and family obligation. I say that I can see Mia anytime, that this thing with Gramma Jan is more important, but Mom shakes her head.

"I should do this on my own. I don't know what Viv is going to say."

As though to protect me. I get that. "But —"

"Dills. Go get your girl. She's waiting for you."

And Mom turns away from me, ending the conversation. Sending me out. But not making me feel better in the least.

DEFIANT

It feels strange to walk through the park without my safety vest and helmet and trash spike. As though I've forgotten how to be a normal person. I have to resist the urge to stop at every tree and bush to make sure new trash hasn't wedged itself into the places I've already cleaned. Like getting all sweaty and dirty again would be an appropriate penance for abandoning my mother.

I'm here. Come see me.

Jesse's voice seems to walk with me. I can't tell whether it's more or less insistent. My resolve to go see him is finding all sorts of reasons to put itself on hold.

"I should turn around, right?" I ask, hoping he'll walk me through this. Knowing he won't. "Do you think she'll be okay?"

Mom, I mean. Gramma Jan, too. But mostly Mom.

Have you ever found yourself asking questions you already know the answers to? Not knowing why you're asking, yet not able to stop yourself? Jesse would say, *One, your mom is a tough cookie and can handle this. Two, she's not a person you go against. Ever. She told you not to come, so that's it. We honour the requests of people we love, Dills, and we follow orders from those who can order us around. And this was definitely an order. Clear as mud?* Jesse has this way of making everything plainer. Even when it's not.

It's still hot out, the low sun doing nothing against the humidity and heat. My clothes lost their laundry stiffness as soon as I stepped out the door. My rash is itching extra hard. I walk by the splash pad, where families on blankets sit and eat while miniature formations of kids attack the ice-cold spray and mist. Squealing and laughing. I frown at them, but no one notices. Their play like armour.

The bowling greens lie at the southern end of the park. When the community lawn-bowling club went out of business, no one stepped in to maintain the perfectly trimmed greens. Now they're covered in the same grass as the rest of Churchill Park, while the benches and sunshades rust away.

Mia and her family have set up under one of the old sunshades. Smoke from a trio of low silver barbecues rises straight up in the windless air. The smell of grilled meat and veggies makes my mouth water. Sudden, powerful hunger.

Mia sees me. Smiles. That smile like the sun. Melting my cold scowl away. I wave back, noting in a detached way that there are few things more awkward than waving while walking. But not caring.

A few adults stand in a loose circle around the food, men in collared shirts and dress pants offering advice to the guy working the grills, women in dresses and head coverings. There are a couple of toddlers hanging on to skirts. Grade-school kids dashing around like the only reasonable thing to do in such situations is to chase each other. A few older kids, various tweens and teens, sit at the appropriate distance from embarrassing families. When Mia waves, the conversation stops and suddenly every eye is on me, adult and otherwise.

My feet slow down. I don't tell them to, they just do. All that attention. Like I'm walking into the thousand-pound spray of a firehose. Mia turns to all the grown-ups and says something to them. No one moves, their need to stare as heavy as gravity. You can't move gravity. She hisses something at them — a bunch of words I can't hear, then *"Yella, yella!"* That makes them all chuckle and smile and return to their whatevers.

"Hi," she says.

"Hi."

"Thanks for coming. You look nice."

"You, too. You're …" I stop. My goal was to come up with some astute, creative compliment, but my words refuse to try. The sight of her makes them impossible. She's wearing a sundress with a beige and green floral print that would look like camouflage on anyone else. She's tanned and strong, and the dress fits like it's supposed to make my down-belows get all worked up. What she wears isn't about me, I know. But in the moment? All that blood moving south? Sure feels like it is.

"You, too," I say again.

"Thanks."

"Your family?" I ask, nodding at the group, who're trying to respect her wishes not to stare but can't help themselves.

Mia nods and does a run-through of names, all of which I forget as soon as she says them. Except for her parents. The guy on the grill is her dad. The tall woman with the deep purple headscarf and her arms folded is her mom. Neither are smiling. This doesn't surprise me. Boys everywhere never expect anything resembling acceptance from parents. You're trying to steal their biggest accomplishment, after all. And obviously corrupt her beyond redemption.

"What happened to your arm?" She points at the dressing covering my rash.

And just like that, my mind returns to Pat pissing on me, and the buzz I had from seeing her in her dress is gone. Replacing it is a kind of abrasion, sand somehow getting behind my eyes. I didn't get the same feeling when Mom asked. But here, now, I do.

"Nothing much. A little PI."

"PI?"

"Poison ivy."

"I've never had it. Does it itch?"

"I don't want to talk about it."

I can hear my words and tone as they spill out like acid. I should stop them. I want to. Yet I can't. "Foul," Jesse would call it when Mom or I would get grumpy: "Wow. You're acting so, so foul." Saying that would, of course, make it worse. Nothing more annoying than someone else not playing along with your anger.

"Okay," she says, her smile dimming.

"Am I the only one here?"

"The only what?"

"Non-family member."

"Yes."

"Where are your wrestling friends?"

"I don't really have any."

"Why?"

"Well, I'm a girl, and I'm advanced for my age, so I win a lot. No one likes a girl who wins too much."

"That's dumb."

Her eyes narrow. "What's wrong with you? A second ago, you were —"

"I'm fine."

She folds her arms and turns a quarter turn away from me. Closing herself off. Regret in her body language. Inviting this idiot was a bad, bad idea.

What the hell, Dills? I want to ask myself. I've snapped at and interrupted her, which are the rudest things. But my gut is running the show now. My mind is merely a horrified spectator. And guess what gets added next? Replaying my departure, reliving the guilt and worry about leaving Mom to go to the hospital on her own. And I get even angrier at Mia, if you can believe it. Like she's to blame for all of it. My gut opens my mouth, ready to deliver the next perfect, biting remark, and —

"Mia, who is this boy?"

My mouth snaps shut. Her mother has come over to where we're standing. Her accent is strong, but her voice is flat. The tone says, *He looks like trouble and if he speaks to you like that again, I will kill him where he stands.* Up close, she is incredibly tall. Like professional volleyball player tall. Mia's father arrives after a moment, wiping his hands on his apron, which is black and decorated with the words *DON'T LIKE MY COOKING? LOWER YOUR EXPECTATIONS.* He isn't tall. But he looks strong enough to protect a daughter's honour by tearing questionable guys apart with his bare hands. A single hot bead of sweat trickles down my back, between my shoulder blades.

"Mom, Dad, this is Wendell Sims. My friend from school."

"We did not know he was coming," her mother says.

"I invited him." Mia glances at me as she says it. Is there regret in the look?

"Wendell, it is kind of you to come, but this is a family dinner."

Mia's father hasn't said a thing. But his eyes have moved to my shoes. No, wait, not my shoes. The ankle monitor. Shit. I don't think about it at all anymore, apart from when I need to wash around it in the shower. LoJack is the perfect name. Low Jack. Gritty and dishonest, like the kind of person who'd wear it. With shorts. To a birthday party.

"Mom, you're embarrassing me."

"Please ask him to leave. Wendell, it was nice to meet you."

That tone definitely tells me it wouldn't matter if I returned the courtesy. So I don't. I just nod.

"Dills, stay."

There's as much defiance against her parents in her invitation as there is desire for me to be a part of her celebration. I did that. My crappy temper making all this discomfort possible. Without another word, her mother and father turn away and move back to the party. I feel small. And mad. And wrecked. But mostly small.

These days I find myself measuring everything against a piece of metal I keep in the drawer next to the box cutter. I told you about that hospital hallway. The waiting and the blood and the crying and all the things damaged kids can't do for each other. But right after they sat me down, I saw a dark object lying against that smart little curve they put at the base of hospital walls to make sure there are no corners to gather germs. It looked out of place and dirty, so I got myself off the floor and walked over to it. It was small, about the size of a frozen kernel of corn, but heavy for its size, jagged and dense. I put it in my pocket and found it later that day when Mom took me home and let me go up to my room. Rubbing against the cloth in my pocket had shined it up a little. Dark, with flecks of copper. Bullet fragment. I should've given it to the police, but I didn't. I take it out sometimes. Wonder about its travels. Who it might have gone through or fallen out of. It's my new small and huge and every other size.

"You didn't tell your parents about me," I say.

"What would I tell them?"

"Something. Anything."

"Like what? Do *you* know what we are?"

No. Yes. Maybe, is what I think. What I say is "I should go."

"Please stay."

She puts her hand on my shoulder. Her body language opening up to me again, like a door of some kind, even though I'm being such an idiot. The hardness gone from her face, her hand warm through my fancy shirt. The best kind of low heat. She looks over at her family, her eyes moving between the kids, the teens, and the circled adults waiting to eat. Her eyes don't rest on anyone. I realize that she doesn't belong in any of the groups. That we can be strangers in our own families. That she's asking me to be her comfortable. If I'm the threatening outsider, she's the threatening insider, the daughter and niece and cousin no one can talk to. Maybe she's too strong.

"I want to," I say. "But I think you need to work on your parents a bit."

"It'll be fine."

"Maybe I can meet them again sometime when my friend is gone." I lift my foot a bit.

Her eyes go down to the ankle monitor. "Oh my god, I totally forgot!"

"Me, too. But your parents won't."

"We don't need their permission."

"*I* do, Mia."

"Why?"

Because I don't need another question mark in my life, Mia. Another day at odds with another set of parents, or step-parents, or whatever. Though I don't say that. I glance over at her folks, who've been reabsorbed into the adult group. Studiously not looking over at us. Parents are people you want to be loyal to. And you want to have the favour returned.

"Look," I say, "maybe it's too much right now."

"Wait. What's too much? We're hanging out."

"I'm just so … I just have …"

"You sound like you're about to make a lame excuse, Dills."

"No, it is a lot. This stupid LoJack. The sentence. New grade in the fall. Pat. Gramma Jan."

"What's going on with your grandma? Will she get to come home soon?"

I almost tell her. I want to. But, as if on the most awkward sort of cue, my rash lights up again, hotter and itchier than ever. Blots the evening out with the overwhelming urge to scratch and the need not to. And a fresh bloom of anger at the frame my life has been set into lights up, too. The urge to scream at the crappiness of it all. Like really scream at it, raise my sweating face to the sky and yell and shout and scream until my voice obliterates itself.

"No," I say. Mostly to myself. Knowing how little such an outburst would accomplish.

"No what?"

Mia's voice is now as flat and suspicious as her mother's. I read that as the final signal. Affirmation of every speck of not-worthy-and-not-ready in me. "Nothing. I'm going to go."

And I do. I turn away and walk back across the park and into the empty house. To a text on my iPod from Mom, telling me that she'll be staying overnight again. That I should stay put and that Aunt Viv will be home a little later. As though I'd dash across the city right then. She says that Gramma Jan needs to rest so I shouldn't call, that she'll tell me everything in the morning. That I shouldn't worry.

That last one does it.

"Oh, come on!" I yell, pounding my fists against the kitchen counter, hard, listening to the impact moving through the woodwork of the house.

Don't worry.

Right.

Telling someone not to worry is like spraying fuel vapour over a campfire while telling the flames they don't have to grow.

DIGGING

I suppose you could get used to an empty house in the morning. But not by choice. You look for the people you love. When they've always been part of your routines, like Mom, or have become part of them, like Gramma Jan and Aunt Viv, and they're not there, you notice. It feels weird to see every door ajar, every curtain and blind open, every bed unslept in. Everything exactly where you left it the night before. No caring person to reset the house after you go to bed.

I refresh my email on my iPod. Nothing from Mia. The world could've ended as I slept. *The Rapture*, Ethan would've called it. Sheep and goats and all the sinners having to stay on earth. His family was one of those that prays while doing everyday things and uses the word *blessings* a lot, that ends every discussion with "Praise Jesus." Ethan was obsessed with this retro series of books called *Left Behind*, where the Rapture comes and the survivors have to figure out how to survive. I bet he made those the most-read books in the school library. Anyhow.

I eat and get ready for the day in silence. I think about turning on some music loud to keep me company, but that seems crazy. Crazier than trusting myself alone with my worry and guilt about how I left things with Mia.

Before I leave, I wind and set Gene's watch and open the weather app on my iPod. Going to be a scorcher today. Heat alert in effect. Good. Not good for working, obviously, but good for my lunch break and after work. Coming home to a cool house is a rare kind of heaven. Gramma Jan has this thing against air conditioning unless the weather people declare that it is actually hot. The rest of the time, we open windows and use fans to push the hot air around. I turn on the AC. The appearance of the snowflake icons on the thermostat momentarily displaces my worry.

It's so warm there's no morning dew on the grass. The park is dry and still. Bracing itself against the heat. Nothing moves or makes noise, not even the sparrows, who are always moving, always flashing around in fidgety little flocks. A good day to be under cover. There's a path into the woods out past the soccer fields that I haven't gotten to yet. I smear sunscreen everywhere as I walk toward the trailhead.

I'm here. Please come see me.

Please come see me. The *please* is new. Not for Jesse — he's the politest person — but it's the first time he's said it out here. He says that *please* might be the most important word. "So many people don't say it these days," he once said to me. "Like politeness is a weakness or something. But people appreciate when you make the effort. You get more flies with honey than with vinegar." He even uses it when he asks for the time: "May I have the time, please?" It sounds so formal. He'll ask someone at the store or gas station even though he wears his old army watch everywhere and he carries a phone. Creating chances to say *please* to strangers or something. It's weird. But kind of cool.

The trail is wide. Packed hard and well used. Not a lot of garbage, maybe the occasional beer can or snack wrapper. I cover a lot of ground, following the path up and down, toward and away from the marsh, in and out of small ravines and valleys. It's hot and I'm already sweaty, but it's kind of nice to walk for a change.

"Wendell? Can you hear me, mate?"

Sean's voice somewhere behind me, dulled by the heat and the trees but still killing the calm. I slow down but stay quiet. He'll find me on his own — there's only one path, and his GPS will get him here. I don't feel the need to contribute to the noise. I round a bend and find myself at one of the park's scenic lookouts, a wooden platform hanging out over the marsh. Usually these spots are cleaner than the paths, but today I see a jumble of small plastic things, bright against the weathered grey of the platform's pressure-treated lumber. Green. Red. Blue. Yellow. Spent shotgun shells. Scattered all over the lookout, like someone stood right here and shot them all off in one session. For fun. Who does that?

I kneel and pick them up by hand, dropping them into my garbage bag one by one. They landed on the platform, so they're clean. There's the sharp smell of burnt gunpowder. The shooting smell is strong. Like a ton of gunpowder gets packed inside before the shooter blasts them out of his gun and destroys whatever he's pointing at. Not like .22-calibre rounds. They're small. They smell sharp, too, but lighter. Less volume. Jesse has a larger-calibre hunting rifle but also owns a .22 that he uses to shoot beer cans. "Plinking," he calls it. "To keep the hand-eye coordination fresh." One of his army buddies, who moved to Canada and bought a huge plot of land south of Windsor, lets Jesse shoot whenever he wants. I went down with him a few times, long before he took me hunting and got in so much trouble. He'll line up a bunch of cans on a rail and lie down a ways away. Prone is the most stable shooting position. He's so good at shooting, too. He'll tuck the rifle into his shoulder and slow down his breathing and *snap! snap! snap!* he'll knock the cans over one by one with almost no hesitation between them. He can shoot all day. And he does, sometimes.

"There you are."

Sean rounds the final bend, breathing hard. He's holding his phone. As I stand to face him, I can see a pulsing blue dot in the middle of the screen. That's me, I bet.

To my surprise, Aunt Viv appears right behind him. "Hey, kid," she says.

"You're really in deep this time," Sean says.

"But you said I could clean the trails."

"Not *in deep* like that," Aunt Viv says, laughing. "He meant deep in. Far back in the woods."

"What she said," Sean says, smiling at her. "You're fine, Wendell. This is a regular check-in."

"Okay," I say. "But what are you doing here, Aunt Viv?"

"I asked Sean to find you, and he said he was coming out today anyhow. Gramma Jan's being discharged today."

"Yeah, Mom told me."

Her eyebrows rise. "I didn't know that. I was on my way out when she got to the hospital, so —"

"On your way out? But you didn't come home."

"Oh. That. Well …"

And insert awkward pause. So much weirdness happening all at once. Someone using Cootes Paradise as a shooting gallery. Sean in the woods looking like an urban alien. Aunt Viv following him out here. Aunt Viv choosing to follow anyone. Aunt Viv asking for help. If she can hack into his system, surely she can find me out here on her own. Her laughter at Sean's mixed-up words. His smile.

"*I* certainly had a nice time," Sean says.

"Sean," Aunt Viv says, drawing out the word long enough to glare at him. "We talked about this."

"Well, I did enjoy myself, Vivian. And it's pretty clear Wendell's figured it out, yeah?"

Aunt Viv makes a low growling sound and rolls her eyes. Probably because he called her by her proper first name. "Fine," she says.

Sean turns to me again. "But she did ask if you'd be allowed to break early today, so you can be there when your gran comes home. That's what she was going to tell you."

"Both of you had to be here for that?"

"Well, no, but her Prius wouldn't start this morning, so I had to give her a ride home."

"Sean!"

Aunt Viv looks like she could punch him. TMI, clearly. And I get it. It feels sloppy, how goofy he's being around her. What happened to "Let's keep this professional, yeah?"

"Does Gramma Jan know about all of this?" I ask. "She hates it when we make a big deal out of anything."

Aunt Viv nods. "She asked if you could be there."

"Why? What's wrong?"

"She'll tell you herself. She insisted."

"That's more like her, but come on, you can —"

"Be home for eleven."

"Aunt Viv —"

"Stop, Dills. Just be there."

And with that she turns and walks back up the path, disappearing around the bend.

"Sean, what's going on?"

"I don't know, mate. She didn't tell me, either."

He looks at his phone and swipes something away from the screen. Puts the phone in its pouch and looks at me long and hard. "Actually, this wasn't a regular check-in. I have to tell you something. Two things, actually."

"Okay."

"I spoke to the judge about your breach the other day. At the hospital. She's waived any further escalation, so you're off the hook."

"Well, that's good. Mom'll be happy."

"You should be, too."

"Oh. I am."

"You sure? You don't look it."

"I haven't had time … I, uh, haven't thought about it much."

Sean gives me a look, like he can't believe I haven't been obsessing about it.

I ask, "And the other thing?"

"Right. It's about that reporter. From the trial."

"Walters."

"She's been poking around the office and the courts. Bugging me about you."

"I've seen her a couple of times. She knows that something's different about my case."

"So she says."

"Would you ever —"

"Not a chance, Wendell. We don't talk about our cases with reporters. The court, too — they're locked as tight as we are. Still," A pause, thoughtful. "I don't think she's going away. I wanted to warn you to be careful and not say anything."

"I won't."

"When reporters start chewing on something …"

"Yeah."

Sean glances down and sees the shell that's still in my hand. This one is yellow. I drop it in the bag. He looks around the platform at the shells I haven't gotten to yet. Back at me. Sighs. It looks like he wants to say something about them, but he doesn't. Maybe there's a rule somewhere he's trying to interpret on the fly. They're spent, so there's no danger. Or maybe it's about guns and guys like me who live through the unimaginable. I kneel again to grab the next shell, this one signal red. And the next. Blue. Green. Another yellow.

Sean says, "You're all right?"

"All of this is weird, but I'm getting used to it."

"Protect yourself, yeah?"

"I will. Will you tell Aunt Viv?"

He shakes his head. "I have to tell your mum, of course, and I'll have to write it up in my own reports, but no one else. Confidentiality."

"Good."

"Right, then."

And he jogs away back up the path, awkward, looking like he's trying to put a spring in his step. Trying to catch Aunt Viv. He seems so certain about the security of my information, but Aunt Viv can slice through it and barely break a sweat. I trust him, but what about everyone else in the system? My story is different. My life is a scoop. My family is news.

I look at my watch. One hour to go.

COMPLICATED

I'm here. Come see me, Dills. Please.

As I work my way up and down the marsh paths for the remainder of the morning, Jesse calls to me often. As though the woods have provided some extra privacy. Safety to talk to me. Just for today, maybe.

"How, Jesse? How do I get to you?"

His words and voice have become more urgent, and I want to go more than ever. But I'm fifteen. I'm not one of those kids who has worked out how to leave, a plan in his back pocket. I never wanted to run away. Mom and Jesse and I have never been a perfect family, but there's love there. Safety. So many people have assumed that Jesse was always violent, but that's not the case at all. Irritable? Lonely? Impulsive? Sure, sometimes. But he always had time for me, too. Always made sure that his knowledge was my knowledge. Is. I never felt in danger. *We* never felt in danger.

Of course, Jesse doesn't answer. So I walk and spear the occasional trash, my black plastic garbage bag filling slowly, and let my mind wander.

There's the issue of how to get to Windsor. Google tells me there's a bus, but that takes money. Probably ID, too. My student card won't be good enough. Mom keeps my birth certificate and health card. And my passport, a few years old, with a photo of me so young I barely recognize myself. All ears and big new teeth. Hitchhiking is free, but no way. Mom has a car, but I'd bet all the money I don't have that she won't take me. Maybe Aunt Viv can drive.

And that's as far as my plotting gets me. Uncertainty. That three-hour drive might as well be across a demilitarized border, like in Korea. Landmined and razor-wired.

I think about Mia, too. Her parents a different kind of border, just as hard to cross. Me over here, carrying how I feel about her, and her over there with her own feelings. She made it sound so simple. Her parents don't need to know. Parents always find out, though. And I think about Aunt Viv and Sean and Mom and Gramma Jan, and I wonder why life has to be so complicated. *Here, Dills*, the universe is saying, *deal with all of this, will ya? You can handle it, right? It's not like you have any other issues to process.*

I trip over an exposed root. The dressing covering my rash catches on a low branch and tears off. The sudden air against it is a lit match against sawdust. Up it goes. The itch blooming like flame again. The perfect timing of it makes me stop midstep and close my eyes. I feel like swearing.

"Coming through!"

It's a big guy in sweaty running gear. The brightest shades of it. Soaked salmon shirt over his expansive gut, blue shorts covering his spindle thighs. Running hat in construction orange. He has a small dog, maybe a chihuahua, a tiny rat thing that yips and growls at me. I'm so stunned by the sight of them that I can't move, and they're forced to stop a couple of feet from me. Even the dog is decked out for a blinding jaunt though the woods, wearing a ridiculously tiny yellow bandana that matches my safety vest. It's surreal how intense they are against the gloom.

"Out of the way, kid!"

But I don't move. My eyes are locked on the dog as it bristles, teeth bared at me. All the dog shit I've had to clean over the past few weeks. Bagging it for the trash. Flicking it into the underbrush when I can so I don't have to carry it around. Fresh. Petrified. Somewhere in between. The hot, smelly mess of it.

"You should leash your dog," I say, removing my helmet and wiping the sweat from my forehead. "The bylaw's clear. I'm sick of picking up after them."

The guy, shiny with run sweat, folds his arms. "What are you, the cops?"

Instead of replying, I push past him and carry on up the path. The dog growls as I pass, the low burr of a tiny voice box. I can feel all four of their eyes on my back. There was nothing more to say that wouldn't have devolved into swearing and yelling and tearing into him. Not recommended for my situation.

The rest of the morning passes slowly but without further incident. Sweaty and slow. Thinking and waiting and worrying are the worst companions when you want the time to fly.

TERMINAL

I'm late getting home even though I paused my workday in time. At five to eleven I stashed my gear behind a tree and walked to the edge of the park. Something stopped me there, one foot on the end of the sidewalk, the other on the park grass. Awkward. But I remained in that position for five, maybe ten, minutes, staring at the neighbourhood and thinking about everything. Overwhelmed. Forcing myself to breathe. I hope no one saw me.

Mom's Corolla is parked on the street next to the side door. Odd. She's so fastidious about parking in the driveway, which is in the back of the house because we're on a corner lot. More traffic to worry about when you park streetside, more risk of dings and scratches. As I come near, I smell burning. Hot rubber and steel. The car's hood is open. The muffler and the long exhaust pipe rest on the asphalt under the car.

"Mom?" I yell as I close the door behind me.

"You're home," Mom says, appearing in the hallway. "Good."

"What happened to the car?"

"I don't know. It started making all sorts of horrible sounds on the way home from the hospital and died right as I pulled up."

Cars don't die, Mom. They just stop, is what I think. But I can't say that to her. Or to myself, maybe. I kick off my shoes. "It got you home."

"True, but now it won't start."

"That sucks."

"Yeah. Anyhow, come on in. We're in the living room."

We walk in together. Gramma Jan is seated in the easy chair at the far corner of the living room. Aunt Viv is sitting across from her on the good sofa. Mom sits down slowly, carefully, at the other end. A special occasion? Gramma Jan loves to sit and read in that chair, but the rest of the furniture rarely gets used. Aunt Viv and Mom look as stiff as only sitting on an off-white sofa can make a person. You're afraid to breathe. Your breath might stain the fabric. And there are biscuits on a fancy plate in the centre of the coffee table. They're called biscuits, not cookies, because they're in recognizable flower shapes, covered in chocolate, dusted with coconut. Gramma Jan, Mom, and Aunt Viv are each sipping coffee from proper cups and saucers, delicate things with gold edges and hand-painted flowers.

This all clashes. We're more a kitchen-table-and-family-room kind of family. We sometimes sit on the floor. We're mugs and cookies, never fine china, never biscuits. Four-finger mugs. Messy, homemade cookies with smeared chocolate chips. I am instantly on alert.

Gramma Jan smiles at me. She is still so pale, and she looks like she's lost half her body weight since I saw her a couple of days ago. It makes her smile too big. Her head like a grinning skull.

"Wendell!" she says. "Get your ass over here and give your gramma a hug."

I go over to her, but slowly. The language is her, but the instruction is not. I am not a Wendell in this house. You know by now that we are not hugs, either.

"Here, Mom," Aunt Viv says, rising from the sofa, "let me take your cup."

But Gramma Jan has shifted forward and risen from her seat, surprisingly strong.

"Don't worry about it, Viv."

"But the rug —"

"Is just a rug."

Aunt Viv stops, unsure. Glances at Mom, who shrugs. Gramma Jan steps forward and grabs me with a single bony arm. Her other hand somewhere behind me, the cup and saucer clinking an alarming tattoo. She smells of rubbing alcohol and hospital wards and the faintest whiff of urine.

"I missed you, kid," she says. Her voice low and husky. Breaking, kind of.

"Hey, Gramma."

That's all I can get out. Gramma Jan doesn't seem to mind or notice. She holds on for a long time. Tight. The details I've taken in since I walked through the door may have created a general sense of something being off. The hug, though, the length of her need to hold on, tells me with precision that something is wrong. When she finally lets me go and steps back, her eyes are red and shimmering, and the sense of wrongness grows. Gramma Jan is steel and edge, not crying and tears. She eases herself down into the chair again with an audible exhalation.

"Why are you home early?" I ask, finding my voice again.

"They needed the bed," Gramma Jan says.

"Mom," Aunt Viv says, leaving the sentence unfinished. *We talked about this*, the tone says.

Gramma Jan chuckles. "The girls tell me I shouldn't lie to you."

"Lie about what?"

"I said not to burden you, but they're stubborn. Like me."

"Is it your heart?"

"My goddamn heart's fine," Gramma Jan says. "Well, in context, anyhow."

"I don't understand."

"I'm dying, kid."

Mom exhales audibly and brings a hand to her mouth. Aunt Viv makes a face like she could punch the words Gramma Jan just said.

"But you're …"

I stop myself from saying the rest. *You're fine*, I was about to say. But obviously not. That would be stupid. Gramma Jan looks at me. Long. Without speaking. Like she's suddenly aware of how important it is to wait for others to respond to bad news. Mom and Aunt Viv both look like they want to take over. To tell me everything. But they don't. Gramma Jan's news to share.

"Tell me," I say.

So she does. So many details. The heart issue and the tests they ran uncovered certain things. Various elevated levels. Further testing and scans revealed more. Cancer. The Big C. Buried deep, spreading fast. Terminal. Gramma Jan already knew something was seriously wrong but didn't tell anyone. There's an argument about that, about responsibility and sensitivity and pridefulness. But I know that the argument is a symptom of Mom's and Aunt Viv's pain, rather than a need to work through anything. What's done is done.

For my part, I don't say anything. Instead, my mind tries to sort through the infuriating mystery of why bodies fail before their time. I'm still processing why and how the universe can extinguish so many lives by the horrible actions of others. How bodies can be torn apart from the outside. Now I have to process why and how our bodies can turn on us, too. How they can tear themselves apart from the inside. How defenceless we are against any of it.

LIKE NORMAL

"So, do you still hear him?" Aunt Viv asks late the next morning, sitting on the chair beside me.

I take my eyes from my iPod. "Huh?"

We're both in the family room at the back of the house, where the TV and beat-up furniture live. Aunt Viv has her laptop open and is working the keys, her hands a blur. Mom's puttering around in her workshop — she hates the word *puttering*, a Jesse word, and says it diminishes what a person does — more quietly than usual. Earlier, she had the Corolla towed and the tow-truck guy shook his head like it was all over, and now it seems like Mom's grieving the car's absence on top of everything else. Gramma Jan is upstairs, still sleeping. Sean called and said I could take the day off. Aunt Viv must've told him about the diagnosis.

"Jesse," she says.

"Oh. Yeah. Not right now, but every day."

"And Windsor? Still trying to get back?"

"Yes. No. It's complicated."

"Why?"

"Like I said. Mobility challenges."

"So jump on a bus. Get an Uber. Hitchhike, for crying out loud."

"Uh huh. Money? My safety? You haven't offered to drive, either."

"Car's in the shop."

"What about later, after —"

"No."

"Why?"

She scratches a spot behind her ear. "Uh, I don't do highways."

"So we take side roads."

"I can't do those, either."

"I don't understand."

"I have a thing. It has a name, but let's call it fear of road travel."

"A thing."

"A phobia."

"You're messing with me."

"Wish I was, kid. It's real. I've learned to function in the city, but I can't drive farther."

A thought arrives. Lands on me heavy. "That's why you never visited me and Mom."

"Yeah."

"And Gramma Jan doesn't drive."

"She had to give up her licence years ago because of some eye thing she won't talk about. I wonder if it's tied to her recent heart troubles …" She shakes her head and sighs. "Anyhow, before you and your mom came home with an extra set of wheels, I was her taxi."

"Even after Windsor, you couldn't —"

"It sounds weak, but between your gramma and me, it was easy to talk ourselves out of going."

"Mom knows."

"Yep."

"Which is why she never complained about you two staying back here in Hamilton. Huh. I never thought about it. I thought it was about Jesse."

"That, too. I'm sorry."

"I don't know what to say right now."

"But you should still go. I can give you the money."

"It's not just about getting there," I say, holding up my leg. "I'm LoJacked, remember? And why are you encouraging me? You were worried about my healing, didn't want me to tell Mom."

"You seem so preoccupied. And I think you need the chance to …" A pause. "Jesse and you were so … *are* so —" She smacks the table. "Shit, Dills. It's not your fault. Any of it."

"I know that."

"Do you?"

"Of course I do!"

"I don't want to intrude. And yet I do. Feel free to tell me to fuck off."

"No way, Aunt Viv. Never."

"I just want to help."

"I know that, too."

"Okay."

"Okay."

I glance at the screen again. Refresh my email. Again. Willing it to display a little *1* in red. For Mia to reach out, even though it was me who stormed off the other day. The irrational hope I won't have to do anything. That she'll love me for my brand of stubborn crazy. Like one of those scenes in a movie, where the other person appears at just the right time with just the right words in just the right place, even though real life isn't like that and there are so few right times and places. Like this:

> Him: I am so glad you decided to read my mind and appear in the middle of my randomness.
> Her: You are so good to accept my apologies.
> Him: Why, of course it would be okay to call me again.
> Her: I want to kiss you now.
> Him: Yes, we should kiss.
> Her: And look at that sunset!
> Him: It is orange and attractive.

Meh.

"You've been glued to that thing, Dills. It's the girl, right?" Aunt Viv looks excited. Like changing the topic was a kind of rescue.

"How did you —"

"Educated guess. People who stare at screens so much are usually waiting on someone."

"Not you."

"True. I don't wait for them to deliver POL. Proof of love," she explains before I can ask, looking pleased with herself.

"It's not like that."

"Not what your mom says. She says the girl seems nice."

"She told you?"

"She called you 'smitten.'" She makes a face. "I hate that word. It's like roses and chocolates and stupid crushes."

"Me, too."

"But you like her."

I nod. There's no point denying it. She isn't asking.

"Hard to fight, when it hits you like that," she says.

She gets a far-off look in her eyes as she speaks. Well. Who's smitten now?

"Like you and Sean?"

She frowns, coming back to herself. "Maybe. I don't know what to call us. We're having fun. But this isn't about us. What's her name?"

"Mia."

"Italian?"

"Palestinian. Her last name is Al-Ansour."

"Interesting."

"I think so."

"So why isn't she messaging?"

"She prefers email, actually."

Viv rolls her eyes. "How fifteen years ago. Quaint. Maybe you're more roses and chocolate than I realized."

"Aunt Viv …"

"Now I *am* messing with you, Dills."

She looks at her watch and stands. Looks back at her computer. Then moves off into the kitchen where I can hear the fridge door opening and closing. I'd call it aimless, but she's trying to connect. I'm sure her mind is on her computer, assaulting some stubborn code somewhere, racking up her billable hours. Mom's gone quiet in her workshop. It feels weird to have Aunt Viv and Mom not busy. Mom had to take time off from her work after the shooting, of course, but that was not by choice. Aside from Sean giving me the okay to stay home, nothing has been said, but I can tell they've cleared their schedules for the day. Making themselves available for Gramma Jan. And me.

But can we step out of our lives for more than a day? It took me a long time to fall asleep last night. Thinking about what Gramma Jan's diagnosis could mean. For her. Us. It's called "terminal" for a reason. It's not going anywhere. Suspended over us. Today feels like suspension, but tomorrow will push us back into our everyday stuff. Stuff that has to change but still try to stay the same. I have a feeling we'll be looking for a new normal.

Something has changed. Please come.

I know, Jesse. Here, too, I think. I lift my iPod and tap Reload. No change there.

HELD UP

We had a massive thunderstorm overnight. Arrived about three in the morning and rattled the foundations for about thirty minutes. Puddles everywhere and a new coolness in the air this morning when I went out for work. Like the heat and humidity's backs had been broken. I haven't been sweating today even though it's now after lunch, when the heat usually soars.

I'm back at it, working the main park today, dodging parents and kids and the city's grass-mowing crew. Everyone is smiling more. I catch one of the city workers humming as she walks back to her truck, gas trimmer slung over her shoulder. No, not walks. Strolls. She smiles and winks at me as she passes, saying something about being able to breathe again. Her teeth perfect white against her tanned face.

By three in the afternoon, when I usually sit in the shade somewhere and scarf down a couple of granola bars, the section of the park I'm focusing on today is spotless. Not a bit of garbage anywhere. But I'm not moving on. Mia's house backs onto the far side. Her family lives in a row of townhomes, the only ones in the neighbourhood. There are at least five separate occasions where I resolve to walk right into her small backyard and knock on her patio door. Immediately followed by five panicked ones where it doesn't happen.

So now I'm moving up and down the same stretch of treeline, visible from her place, actually pretending to stab things in the brush and put them in my garbage bag. Which remains almost empty, pathetically wrapping itself around my leg with every puff of wind. As limp and formless as my own resolve. I'm embarrassed for myself. Yet can I stop? No.

It's almost a relief to hear Gal's horrible singing. He'll see me and want to check on my progress. Anything to interrupt this ridiculous little play I'm directing and starring in. He emerges at a trailhead a short way down, stops, and heads in my direction. He looks at the ground and at my spike and at my bag, but no change comes across his features. You can't say his face is expressionless — his scars are a riot of expression.

He nods at the bandage on my arm. "The rash is not so severe. I am surprised. You fell into so much poison ivy."

I'd become comfortable with the itch, almost a constant crackling static in the background. But now it flares. I rub it through the bandage. "I was lucky, I guess."

"This is not luck."

This being everything that happened around the PI incident, of course. But there's no need to say anything further about it. I just nod.

"That boy, Pat, the one who pissed on you —"

"What about him?"

"He has been around more. I have had to tell him to leave a few times."

I don't know how I feel about Gal doing that. Fighting this battle for me. "Own your own shit, kid," Jesse says. "One, no one can shoulder it for you. Two, it feels good to be responsible." I remember asking him when to look for help. Jesse told me to try to do things myself but that if I needed to, I could ask him or someone trustworthy. I asked how a person knows if someone can be trusted. "I have no idea," he said. "Some you can, some you can't. Like I said, own your own shit. Remember that. Although if your mom ever asks, I said *stuff*, right?"

"I can take care of him," I say to Gal.

Gal's eyebrow rises. Questioning. Doubting. "I do not think that this boy has much respect for anyone. Be careful."

"I will."

He nods and takes a step away, as though he's heading back into the woods to carry on his walk, but then he stops. Scans the ground, the underbrush at the edge of the woods. Looks at me and across at the fence behind Mia's place and back at me again. The tiniest of smiles breaks on his face, his scars easing.

"This section of the park is very tidy," he says.

"Thanks."

"I would offer to go and tell her you are here, but I think you might like to do this yourself."

As though on cue, Mia appears, stepping out through her sliding glass door and walking across the small yard.

Sees Gal and me. Waves. Unlatches the gate and walks across the grass. Flip-flops, ragged cut-off shorts, and a dark tank top. Everything loose. Functional. Yet showing off her muscles, too. I like that she doesn't hide who she is.

"*Salaam 'alaikum*," she says to Gal when she arrives.

"*Wa'alaikum a'salaam*."

They have a quick exchange in Arabic, rapid fire, back and forth. I'm the awkward spectator with nothing to say. Maybe not even present. I stand and listen, mute, as awkward as a third leg and foot facing the other direction. Mia says something that makes Gal chuckle, and I want to jump in and yell that I'm here, pay attention to me, I'm not pathetic. Gal waves and heads off, singing, his voice fading as he enters the woods at the next trailhead down from the one he emerged from. Leaving me and Mia to stand in silence.

I'm here. Please come.

The word Jesse doesn't say is *now*. He doesn't have to. Now is everything. I have this sense that there are no moments other than now, if you think about it. The past is done and mostly sucks. You can't guarantee a future. You can make plans and save and hoard, but you might never get to use any of it. So what's left? Only the right-nows you try to use as best you can.

"I'm sorry," I say. "About how I acted at your party. I can —"

"No, I'm sorry. I totally put you on the spot."

I'm speechless. Blinded. I was going to tell Mia that I can see her however she wants me to see her. In secret. Out loud. Whatever. Because I think Jesse would be pissed at me if he knew how easily I'd shrugged off this opportunity. His voice telling me without telling me to buck the hell up and to hold what I can. But Mia headed me off with her own apology, and now my words — any words at all — have resettled into the strange places they inhabit in my brain.

"I met your aunt," she says.

"Wait, what?"

"Vivian. She's cool. We had coffee this morning. Well, she had coffee. I had milk. Coffee's gross."

"I don't understand. Why w—"

"She said she wanted to meet me."

"How did she find you?"

"She knocked on our front door. Didn't you tell her where I live?"

I shake my head. "I mentioned your name. She must've googled you."

Now it's Mia's turn to shake her head. "We're not listed, Dills. My parents keep themselves private. Especially after 9/11 and all the crap happening in the States. And that information isn't anywhere on my social media."

And I can't respond to that. I might be used to Aunt Viv's mysterious online ways but only from a distance. Apart. You can trust the space. Not now, though. As I said the word *google*, I knew it was a weak version of what Aunt Viv is capable of. She doesn't need Google. But it's odd that she's taking such an interest in me and in Mia. Aunt Viv and I have never been that close.

Mia watches me thinking. "We made small talk. She said she was an online-security consultant."

"She's much more than that."

"Hacker?"

"She hates the word, but yeah."

"Seriously?"

"Seriously."

Mia looks at the ground, falling into her own thoughts. I think about how exposed she and her family are. She must be realizing the same thing.

Well, I did that. My stupid open mouth. I have to make this right. I have to help. "I'm sorry."

But a change happens. She looks up again, and in the piercing darkness of her brown eyes I can see a new clarity. New strength. No, wait. Not new. More. More of the abundant wonder stuff she is already made of. In a blink, she has weighed all the pluses and minuses and has made her decisions and has made my urge to help, to fix, irrelevant. Not needed.

"It doesn't matter," she says.

"It does, Mia. She shouldn't have hacked you."

"She won't hurt us. I like her. I think I can trust her."

"Still, it —"

Mia lays her hand on my forearm and my voice cuts itself off. There's a strong weight there. Warm. Nice. I'm glad it's a cool day, that my skin is sweat-free and clean so her hand won't slip off. I want to live right here for as long as I can. Soak her in. Her warmth and —

"She told me about Windsor High."

Aw, man, those words. From her, they're bullets. I've been shot through. Two military rounds piercing my body at 3,251 feet per second, 5.56 millimeter caliber, tungsten core, tumbling. All the now and truth and warmth that have filled me up for the past few minutes gush out of me. A trickle at the entrance wound in front, a torrent from the fist-sized exit wound in my back. I've seen those wounds. The blood and bone and bits of flesh that spray out of them, the horrific mess left behind.

Mia's mouth is moving. She's concerned. Asking if I'm all right. But I can't hear. There's a roaring in my ear, a hundred assault rifles on full auto. Drowning out the screams that are immediately behind.

I should have run sooner. Hidden. Behind the librarian's desk. That bookcase. The tables and chairs and catalogue computers. The witness stand. The judge's dais. A tree. Anything.

My legs feel weak. I guess that makes sense. I thought I'd kept it all in, protected, bandaged tight as I heal. But for some reason, Mia's knowing has torn the dressings off and I'm bleeding out. It feels like all that's left is to sink down and wait for it all to end.

Mia raises her hands to my face and kisses me. Not the awkward but tender, swirling, blush-of-romance kind of first kiss, but the who-you-trust-to-save-your-life kind. Firm, dry, strong, and brief. Long enough for my feet and legs and body to understand that they can support me after all. And her arms around me in a long embrace. She could hold me up if she needed to. She is that strong.

"Vivian told me about your stepdad, too. About what he did."

I take a deep breath, exhale into her shoulder. Where to begin? Maybe with the obvious. My obvious, anyhow. "I can't hate him, Mia. Everyone else does, but I can't."

"You don't have to. No one can know him like you do."

"That's so it. Exactly."

"She says he talks to you."

I pull back and look at her. To gauge her expression. Her belief. But her expression is as full of that wonder stuff as before. Wow.

"And you're going to go see him."

"Vivian told you that, too?"

A nod. "I can go with you. We could leave any time."

"I want to, but I can't just go." I explain about buses and unaccompanied minors, the expense of other options, the dangers of hitchhiking. The practical barriers. My ankle monitor. I don't explain about all the other things, the intangibles centred in my head and heart, that might be keeping me here even more.

"We'll figure it out," Mia says.

"I could get in a lot of trouble. You, too."

"I don't care."

"I do."

"You could ask your mom."

"No way. She's dealing with enough as it is. Plus, I think her car died."

"Vivian?"

I shake my head and tell her about Aunt Viv's fear of roads, how she can't leave the city.

"Oh."

We briefly fall silent before Mia's face opens up, bright as that first bit of eastern sun rising over the trees in the morning. "I know who can drive us."

"Who?"

A smile. Teeth as white as trust. "I got this, Mr. Wendell."

"You have it all worked out."

"I am owed a big favour, as they say."

Her tone is formal and serious, though her eyes are bright. I open my mouth to ask the obvious next question, but close it again almost immediately. *As they say.* You never know who *they* are, and yet saying it so often makes it a kind of truth. Especially when it's said by someone like Mia.

"All right, then, Ms. Al-Ansour," I say. "You have my encouragement to pursue this line of inquiry."

"Excellent. I will begin post-haste."

"That is acceptable."

"To me, also."

We laugh, the seriousness and formality feeling somehow right. If I could lift myself like a drone ten thousand feet into the sky, all of Churchill Park laid out below me, I'd see that we're standing precisely, impossibly in the centre of it. Surrounded by grass and trees and swamp. Lots of places to hide. Lots of places to bleed out all alone. But right now, my feet fixed to the earth, it's the place we just happen to be standing, and I have no idea about midpoints and geography and signs. Just that, for the first time in a long time, wholeness doesn't seem so alien. Maybe the dressing hasn't been torn off. Maybe it needed to be loosened. To gauge the healing. To let the air in for a little while.

PART II
THERE

GO

By the time we pull back onto the highway, the sun is
below the horizon. We left Hamilton four hours ago but
one hour out the rear left tire blew. It took five minutes for
Gal to figure out that his spare was flat and almost three
hours for the roadside service guy to find us. He was a
greasy dude, perving Mia out as he filled and mounted
the spare, like she might be ripe enough to squeeze. Gal
got in his face, the service truck's flashing yellow lights
turning his scars into a strobe-lit horror show. The guy
left in a hurry, barely glancing at the cash Gal put in his
hand. The original tire was a lost cause, like a shredded
rubber corpse. We almost left it on the gravel shoulder,
but Gal and I shared a look and put it in the trunk. One
less piece of garbage for someone else to pick up.

"That took way too long," I say from the back seat.

"It is what it is," Gal says, and falls silent.

Gal unintentionally using Jesse's words. *It is what it
is, kid. Lots of things can't be explained. And don't need*

to be. They just are. You wonder how such sayings get passed between different groups of people.

Full dark comes quickly. Our headlights throw a small pool of brightness on the highway ahead. Out here there are no streetlights, so the highway is mostly dark, apart from tail lights on our side of the road and meteor headlights passing the other way.

Please, kid.

I'm coming, Jesse. Finally, I'm coming.

I feel like a coward for waiting this long. Taking a three-hour trip seems like such a simple thing. When you have your own resources, it's simple. When you have the time, it's simple. When you're not chained to the legal system by a sentence and an ankle monitor, it's simple. Yet, when you can have a million excuses but not a single reason that stands up against the reality that you haven't made the effort, it doesn't feel so simple. That you haven't cared enough, maybe. Or that deep down, you have reservations. Complicated reservations.

Gal hums to himself, as off-tune as always, content to drive his Kia hatchback twenty below the highway maximum. On cruise control. The tire guy warned against driving the doughnut spare faster than this, but Gal is in no hurry anyhow. Unlike me. I want to yell at him to speed up. Obviously, I don't. He's driving, after all. Willingly. And he waved away my weak offer to pay for the tire change, clearly sensing that finding the cash would be a challenge.

Mia did this. This trip. This chance to answer some of my questions. The edge of her face lights up and dims with every car passing by in the other direction. I didn't fight too hard back in Hamilton when she called shotgun. The view of her may be the only thing keeping me from screaming that everything is taking too damn long.

"The highway is quiet," Gal says after a while.

"It's Friday night," Mia replies. "And we're in the middle of nowhere."

"Not nowhere," I say. "We're near London. Jesse and I stopped here once."

He called London "a sleepy college town," like the words explained everything. We stopped at a twenty-four-hour supermarket in the northern suburbs to buy some food for our hike into the woodlands nearby, and there were two sleepy students buying snacks in the checkout ahead of us. Not paying attention to the cashier. Jesse snapped at them to wake the hell up. There was an uncharacteristic edge to Jesse's voice. Maybe because he never went to college and wonders if he should have. He's so smart, so he could have, but he likes to talk about the home he made in the military, too. His army family. Mom talks about me going to college like it's a given thing, but Jesse doesn't participate in those discussions. "Education's important," he says, "but it's not school that makes a man who he is. Just keep your choices intact."

"Who is Jesse?" Gal asks.

"Wendell's stepdad."

"Is he the reason we are sneaking from Hamilton on a Friday night?"

I tap Mia on the shoulder. "You didn't tell him?"

"He knows where we're going. The rest of the story is yours."

"He must owe you a heck of a favour."

"Well, that's his story to tell, too. If he wants."

"This little drive will not begin to repay it." Gal says this like he's making a proclamation of some kind.

"Gal, I told you, this'll be enough," Mia says.

Gal makes that sucking sound behind his teeth again and she goes quiet. But in the car's low light, I can see she's smiling. All this history. Inside jokes and stories. I want to tell them to spit it out, that keeping secrets in front of others is rude, but that's not very diplomatic, is it? Or realistic. We keep all sorts of secrets from each other.

We drive in silence for a few more minutes before Gal sighs and glances at me in the rear-view. "You have seen my scars?"

"Of course he has. They're impossible to miss!"

Gal doesn't answer Mia's outburst, but glances at me again and then brings his eyes back to the front. Waits for me to answer. Making space. A kind of permission.

"I didn't want to be rude," I say.

Mia has told me some, of course, but I'm not sure whether Gal knows. Better to keep that to myself. Gal sighs again and expands on the version Mia told me. His national service in Israel. Stationed in a settlement near Hebron but shifted to Ramallah after a couple of Israeli soldiers were murdered there. The complications of control and violent suppression. A rocket attack and an unexploded warhead going off as he placed warning tape around it. Fragments all over his upper body, some of which are still there. Shrapnel. Jesse kept a jar on the dresser in the master bedroom in Windsor with a few shards of metal they took out of him after he got hit on one of his tours. Gal didn't keep his. The surgeries and rehabilitation and a desperate need to leave his country were reminders enough of what happened. Aside from the fragments in his body — the ones he'll carry forever. Or at least to the grave, where they won't decompose with his body. Like Ethan's braces.

"I am healed," he says. "Enough to function. But the pain persists. Especially in my head."

"He smokes pot for the pain," Mia says, excited, still wanting to participate.

"Cannabis has eased my symptoms, yes."

"Okay, but what does this have to do with why you're willing to drive me?"

"Before cannabis was legalized, I was registered to use it medically. But there were times when the amount I was allowed was not enough. Mia helped me a couple of years ago."

"You helped him get weed?"

She glances back at me, rolling her eyes. "Sure, Dills. I'm the neighbourhood dealer. I can hook you up. Did I forget to mention that?"

I give her a look, something along the lines of "Sarcasm Doesn't Help Anyone." But I realize that she can't see me. Right. I feel like an idiot. "So how —"

"She hid my supply when the police raided the field house."

"You did what?"

"It wasn't a big deal," she says.

"Yes, it was," Gal says.

"How much are we talking about?"

Turns out it wasn't a truckload or anything, but definitely enough to have gotten Gal and Mia in serious trouble. Now he can walk into a dispensary and pick out what he wants, but before legalization, his own dealer would sell him enough to keep him supplied for a while. One day Mia walked in on him when he was about to light up, just as the police rolled up, cherries flashing. He told her to leave. Instead, she hid the bag in the waistband of her shorts.

"The cops hardly even looked at me," she laughs. "They had a warrant to search everywhere else but didn't think twice about the bulge on my belly. Just another fat girl."

"Wait," I say. "That's … you're not …"

"Exactly," she says. "But kind of funny, too."

"They didn't wonder why a teenage girl was hanging out with the park manager in his gloomy office?"

"They joked about Gal robbing the cradle, but —"

"They had to leave when they could not find anything," Gal says.

I watch her and Gal laugh about it. But I'm not settled. Too close for comfort, in so many ways that I can't begin to pin them down. I'm glad for their strange friendship — you can't always decide which ones will survive, can you? — but feel lost, not playing much of a part in it. But that's not entirely true, is it? Here I am. Here they are, helping create this piece of my story. And Aunt Viv back home, her car still in the shop, taking Sean out for a long dinner and a movie to keep him from thinking about work.

She hacked the parole system for me. My little blue dot, which turns red when I'm in breach, now moving in short paths around the park and my house. The online equivalent of putting a bank's video feed on a loop while you rob it. The guard snoozing in front of the blinking monitor. No one the wiser. Leaving after work on a Friday was her idea. If anything goes wrong, maybe a reduced weekend staff or Viv supplying Sean with her own distractions will delay anyone noticing too closely. I asked her what would happen if Sean found out, but she laughed and said her digital trail is clean. All he could do is suspect her. They'd have to break up, of course. I said that would seriously suck. "Whatever," she said. "He's not in my league." I'm not sure I believed her.

Mia and Gal's conversation and laughter drop away, leaving the hush of the wind and the tires on the pavement. Mia pulls out her phone. The screen glows against her face, blue in the darkness. Softens her profile more. I want to reach out and rest the back of my hand against her cheek.

"Everything is still a go, team," she says.

"I do not like that your parents do not know," Gal says.

"We've been through this."

"They will be worried."

"Not until the morning."

Mia told them she was heading into the gym for a monster workout to prepare for her upcoming season. It's not unusual for her to be out late when she's at peak training, and they won't wait up. She said her father grumbled in his usual way about the appropriateness of her independence. Her mother simply made an extra-large protein smoothie, like she always does before an intense session. Knowing the importance of sustained energy. Tissue repair.

I agree with Gal and I agree with Mia. I hate the idea of our parents being in the dark. Most of the time we make mistakes in the moment and without a thought to the cost. But this trip to Windsor is on its own level. A more premeditated kind of disappointment for the people who've given everything so we can be safe and loved. Still, a necessity. Mia knows her parents, so the decision rests with her. Just before we left, she said, "It sucks, but there's literally no scenario that sees them being okay with this."

Mom would've locked me in the house rather than let me go. Or worse still, offer to drive, even though the car's dead and she isn't ready to face Jesse. Still, for me she'd stare down every demon and walk me right into the hospital so I wouldn't have to be alone. She'd feel everything yet again.

Up ahead, a police cruiser appears over a rise, moving fast in the other direction, lights on, red and blue. We all tense up, as though the plan has already crumbled and the authorities have been brought in to find us. The lights zip past, and Gal and Mia exhale. I have to close my eyes against the lights still burning behind my eyelids. They flashed all day and night after the shooting, the red of the ambulances and fire trucks, the red and blue of the police. Impossible strobe patterns glinting against the sunlight as we were escorted and carried from the school. Slashing through the night when I finally left the hospital.

"Dills? Are you all right?"

I open my eyes. Mia has turned to the back seat, concerned. I guess she can see me after all. All the light is behind her. I can't see her eyes, though. I nod and attempt a smile and turn my head to look out the side window. But you can't look through glass into darkness, can you? All I see is the darkened outline of my own self and the dimmed reflections from the car's interior.

Somewhere to the north, off to our right, are the woods where Jesse taught me how to walk without making a sound. He was so quiet when he stalked, which is what you call it when you hunt something. He became his surroundings. Watching him move like a spirit through the brush and trees made his former life clearer to me. The things he had to do to succeed and survive. Deadly things that needed absolute silence. "Never hurry," he said. "Speed makes you careless, and careless makes sounds. But you can't go too slow, either, because the deer won't wait for you. Clear as mud?" Hard ground? Heel first, roll to the toe. Leaves and debris? Toe first, testing the surface for the things that can crackle and snap and betray your presence. No talking, just hand signals and eye contact. Every step its own performance. Then the next, with the same considerations. Again and again. It was this exhausting mix of pause and motion, halting but intentional. Getting anywhere took forever.

But now? Twenty below the speed limit feels slow, but it'll get us there. And when we arrive, this will feel like nothing at all, like we arrived as fast as blue and red light. Faster than I thought possible.

INVOLVED

Mia uses her phone's GPS to direct Gal to a tall apartment building on Windsor's east side. We park in one of
three visitor spaces below the building. It's late, about
midnight, but most of the building's windows are lit up.
A lot of nighthawks, doing late-night things. Catching
the late shows. Writing the next great novel. Binge-
watching Netflix. Feeding babies. Staring at phones.

Mia taps a contact on her phone, watches it dial.
"Moment of truth."

"She doesn't know we're coming?" I ask.

Mia shakes her head and listens to the phone ringing on the other end of the line. On the way down from
Hamilton, she told us about Noor, her wrestling friend
who lives here. I assumed it had been all arranged.
Another complication. More people involved. This whole
trip becoming way, way more complicated than I antic-
ipated. I closed my eyes when I saw the first city-limits
sign from the highway, thinking I could avoid seeing the

name *Windsor*. But it's everywhere. Gas stations. Corner stores. Faceless industrial buildings. Schools.

No one's answering. Mia frowns and ends the call. "I didn't want to take the chance that she'd tell someone we're coming. We're friends, but not good friends."

"Risky."

"Life is risk, Mr. Sims," she says, smiling.

"You both are behaving very strangely," Gal says.

His tone is deadpan. Hard to know whether he's trying to participate in the humour or genuinely perplexed. And no way to confirm either way, as he's not saying anything more to help.

Mia tries the call again. Another wait. No luck. "Now what?"

"Hotel?" I ask.

"Perhaps it would be best if a solitary middle-aged man did not attempt to check in to a hotel with two minors."

"Right," Mia laughs. "Good thinking."

"The hospital?" I ask. "I'm sure we could find a waiting area."

"Mmm ... hospital chairs," Mia says, drawing out the words like they're the world's best chocolate.

"Hey, come on," I say, feeling chastised. "I'm just trying to —"

Mia's phone lights up and buzzes, cutting me off, bright and loud in the confines of the car. A photo of a dark-haired, dark-skinned woman comes up on the screen. *NOOR* in big block letters. Mia smiles and taps the green emerald to accept the call. There is a quick exchange in Arabic and some laughter.

I glance at Gal. "Mia's friend must have asked if she should put on some clothing," he says, looking embarrassed. "Mia has told her that you and I are here, so yes, she should."

Now I'm embarrassed too. "Oh. Okay."

Mia ends the call and slaps Gal lightly on the shoulder. "She's putting on a housecoat over her pyjamas. She wasn't naked or anything. Let's go."

Gal winces and mutters something I don't understand under his breath as he gets out. She steps out, too. Their doors close with a metallic clunk, leaving me alone. They walk to the front of the car, talking. The parking-lot lights are bright enough to outline them in an amber glow. Like halos. I think about my earlier thought, about how the complications are becoming harder and harder to control, and I want to take it back. I'm glad they're here, these two odd people who have determined I'm worthy of their time and efforts. Unexpected angels, for sure. Even in their impatience, as they bend to look at me in the car and make hurry-up gestures, wondering why I haven't come out.

COOLING GLASS

"Done," Mia says, sliding the balcony door closed and joining me at the railing. "But wow, does it feel weird leaving my phone out there, hidden or not."

She went down to stash her phone in a park across the street from the apartment complex. Aunt Viv's idea. Just in case Mia's parents contacted the police, who'd track her phone before doing anything else. I offered to accompany Mia down, but she said no. Insisted, in fact. Telling me I needed plausible deniability, like we were sneaking state secrets out of the White House itself.

"Did you see anyone?" I ask.

"No. Still felt like there were a thousand eyes on me, though. Gal's out?"

"On the couch. Snoring about five seconds after he turned off the light."

Mia laughs. "Must be the weed cookies. Too tired to smoke, maybe."

"He did drive the whole way."

"He's good people."

"Quite the little crew we make. Noor, too."

"Our very own miniature UN."

"I'm not sure she got the memo that you two aren't close friends."

Mia smiles. "Sometimes my skin is thicker than it needs to be. There aren't too many Muslim girls in our sport."

Noor and Mia could be sisters, they're so similar. They look like they were cut from the same tree, raised from the same seed. The hardest wood. Grown for putting strong people down.

"Who's better, you or her?"

"She is, big time. Same weight class, but older. Smarter. Kicks my ass all over the mat every single time."

"Nice of her to let us stay."

"I actually laughed at her when she offered: 'If you're ever in Windsor …' I feel bad about that now."

"Does she have family?"

"In Toronto. She left them to come out here. College wrestling, full scholarship. She's that good."

You're that good, I almost say. But don't. Saving myself from a further layer of something embarrassing.

We lean on the railing and fall into a comfortable silence. Suburban Windsor lies before us, a spread of low buildings, yellowish street lamps, stoplights, and business signs. We're only eight floors up, but from here we can look out across the uniform roofs of a dozen master-planned communities and feel like we're in a skyscraper. Jesse and I climbed higher hills together, but this is the first time I've been in a building with more than a few floors. It's dizzying, being so high.

My house is out there. Our house. The home Mom and Jesse and I made. I can't see it in the street-lit darkness, but it's just south-southwest from where I stand, about five minutes away. And the school is another five minutes beyond that. I could find my way to both places with my eyes closed, but I won't go back. Ever. From the porch of our Windsor home, you can see the front doors of the houses where three dead kids used to laugh and yell at their parents. None of the wounded were from our street. Just the dead. I'm glad we arrived at night.

"Did you power off?" I ask.

"Huh?"

"Your phone. Down there."

Aunt Viv told us that powering off would make it even harder for the police to triangulate. "And make sure you stash it somewhere other than where you're staying," she said.

"Oh. Right. That's an affirmative, Agent Sims."

"Mia …"

"Right. No real names. You can be Agent Smith. Like in —"

"*The Matrix*."

"You know it? It's kind of old school."

"Yep."

"I like that you know it."

I blush. And blush more when I realize it. And even more when I realize there's just enough light reflected onto our faces from the city below that Mia can see me. She giggles and kisses me on the cheek. Which of course, makes my face bloom even more.

She goes into a two-sided recitation of some of the lines from the movie, asking herself if she can dodge bullets and then telling herself when the time comes she won't have to. She laughs. I don't. I feel my blush cooling, fading to pale. Bullets in movies don't do the things real bullets do. And there's no supernatural dance around them. What they find, they destroy. It's that simple.

So instead of talking, I pull out the small phone Aunt Viv bought for me and power it on. I watch the screen brighten and the wireless bars dance as they search out the nearest tower. "It's a burner," she said. "We're safe for texting or calling, and you can use the GPS. No email or social media, though. Those are beyond my immediate, uh, powers." She has an identical device. Untraceable. "Can't very well have you using my real number, can I?"

The phone chimes as it connects. Text from Aunt Viv.

— Let me know when you arrive

I tap out a quick response.

— windsor

She responds in precisely fifteen milliseconds.

— Good. All clear here too
— sean?
— Clueless. The perfect crime

A smile at her choice of words sneaks onto my face.

— i bet

— ;) You ok?

— i think so

— …

— well maybe a bit nervous

— Ok. (I would be, too.) G'nite

There's no reason to text more. Aunt Viv does not do extended goodbyes. Hates them, in fact. She railed about it just the other day after running an errand. Acted it out.

"They stand there right in the store, gushing over each other's farewells like they mean something. Like they're not going to see each other two minutes later in the car. 'No, you say goodbye.' 'No, *you*.' (Insert awkward, pregnant pause by both parties.) 'I was waiting for you!' 'And I was waiting for *you*!' (Insert giggles.) 'Okay, now really, you say goodbye.' 'No, *you*!' And so on. People are pathetic."

I slip the phone into my pocket.

Mia is watching. "You got so quiet before Viv's text arrived. Did I say something wrong?"

"No."

"Are you sure? I feel like I messed up somehow."

"It was just your words. Normal words. I'm just unprepared for them sometimes."

Her eyes get wide. "It was *The Matrix* scene, wasn't it?"

"Yeah."

"I'm so sorry."

I shrug. "You couldn't know."

"Does it happen often? Where you get sad, I mean?"

"It's not sadness!"

I say it too quickly. Too sharply. And I can see it on her face. When you speak like that, it stretches out before it's ready and becomes brittle. Like molten glass cooling into shape too quickly. It'll break if you don't ease some warmth back into it.

"No, wait," I say. "I am sad, of course, for everything we lost, but what hits me is more of a darkness. A shutting down, if that makes sense. And yeah, it happens often enough. You saw it the other day."

"Have you talked to anyone about it?"

"Not since leaving here. The school board had counsellors everywhere. For a little while, anyway."

"How was that?"

I pause, considering. You get this sense that there are all these people who want to help, but in the end, they weren't there. They haven't lived what you've lived. They haven't seen death like you've seen it. Counsellors all over the place for a few days. Daily sessions in offices far removed from the school. Then dwindling to once a week. Too big to imagine, much less fix. No one gets that. Every survivor will stay broken forever.

I wonder if Mia only wants to hear the good stuff. The TV news stuff. That I'm grateful for the help. One day at a time. Community heals. #windsorstrong #istandwithwindsor #neverforgotten. The stuff that makes politicians feel better about taking money from gunmakers. That kind of thing. Or maybe she doesn't — maybe she wants the truth.

"Useless," I say.

"For real?"

I nod. "It's not their fault. People think you can fix anything if you talk about it enough."

"You can tell me anything."

"I know."

Next comes the urge to call Mom. Surprising and not surprising all at once, out of nowhere but right inside me the whole time. I can feel the burner phone's warmth against my leg. It would be so easy to tell her I'm all right. I left a note saying I was meeting Mia in the park, but she'll have noticed I'm not home by now. She'll be carrying the worry as fully as she does everything else.

"What about your mom? Do you talk to her?" Mia asks, like she can reach into my mind with one of her strong, calloused hands and grab what I'm thinking. Turn it over. Inspect it for a while.

"I can, but we don't. Not much, anyhow. It's hard for her. She gets torn between loving Jesse and what everyone thinks about him."

"Like you do, too."

"For her it's multiplied by, like, a thousand. Because they're married. And Jesse is just —"

I pause, cutting off my own voice, feeling horrible about what was about to come out.

"Just what?"

"I was going to say *just* my stepdad, but —"

"Jesse was more than that."

"*Is* more than that. He's always been there, right from day one."

"I thought he and your mom got married after you were born."

"They did. They met while she was pregnant with me, though."

"By someone else."

I nod. "Jesse was on leave and met Mom, love at first sight, all of that. She told him about the baby. He said he was 'so rocked by her' he didn't care. He didn't drink for the rest of his leave so she wouldn't feel uncomfortable."

"To respect the pregnancy. Wow."

"Right? That's the Jesse I know. I know what happened at Windsor. I know he did it. But it wasn't him. Mom has tried to tell that story. I've tried, too, but —"

"No one wants to hear it."

"No one wants anything to do with it."

"Thank you for telling me."

"Thank you? You're thanking me? For —"

Well. That shatters me into a million and four pieces, and my voice hitches. I am that thin strand of cooling glass after all. Being thanked for sharing a bit of myself is enough to break me. It shouldn't be. My glass core should be vaulted in tempered steel rather than this delicate, fragile thing we call a body. Not defeated by a simple *thank you*, much less being thanked for being honest about a guy who made everything so dark and wrong but who built me up with such strength and light. Like I could be anything else. Because of him.

I open up for the first time since I was a kid. The flood we all hold back, every day, set loose on that balcony. Big and messy and raw. With the girl I'm crushing on resting at the railing beside me and watching the same city and not saying another word. Or doing anything you'd expect if you've watched anything on TV or online or in a theatre or anywhere at all. No hugs or kisses or attempting to say the right thing. You'd think it was an effed-up scene in the most effed-up, unsatisfying movie. Unless you were me, ugly-weeping for the mass murderer no one understands like you do. You'd be thankful for the space. And maybe a calloused hand on a shoulder. Warm and strong. Again.

JUST FINE

The next morning I sit at the kitchen table, staring at the massive breakfast Noor has loaded onto our plates. Eggs, beans, toast, fruit. Bowls of muesli and containers of yogurt, too. Noor and Mia eat like they're bulking up, chatting between mouthfuls. In English now, maybe for my benefit. Memories of holds, pin-downs, wins, almost-wins. Gal eats slowly but steadily, in silence. Everyone is up early. Visiting hours still a couple of hours away. My stomach has shrunk itself to the size of a marble. Two sips of orange juice and I feel like I've feasted.

Mia and I talked until well past midnight, then fell into a comfortable kind of quiet, watching the city and listening to a line of distant thunderstorms that never reached us. Then a quiet goodnight. Mia in the guest room and me on an air mattress on the living room floor, kept company by Gal's snoring. No attempt to sneak into the guest room to try anything more than what happened on the balcony. Content to rest, knowing about the big day ahead and that we'd be facing it together. Neither of us with the desire to talk all night or make out or get into trouble. Smashing teenage clichés by the dozen.

I can't look at this food any longer. I stand and excuse myself to the bathroom, leaving my heaping plate untouched. I lock the door and lean against it, drawing a long, deep breath. To still myself against the nerves and energy that are building.

Please come. I need you.

"I know!"

Jesse's voice is a surprise. My response too loud, too sudden. I hear Mia calling to me down the hall and asking if I'm all right. Me yelling back that I'm fine.

Come, Dills.

"As soon as I can, Jesse," I whisper. "Promise."

Noor has stacked clean towels on the vanity and triangled a couple of washcloths on top. A bowl next to the sink holds a motley assembly of wrapped hotel soaps and tiny shampoo bottles. There are a few new toothbrushes and travel tubes of toothpaste, all still in their packaging. Flourishes of unexpected hospitality. I run the shower full blast, steam quickly filling the small space, and step into the spray. It's too hot for comfort, but it feels right, too, the scalding water scouring my pores. I changed after work yesterday but putting clean clothes on a dirty body is like painting an old wall without stripping it first. All grit and flaking paint.

My clean skin feels like a kind of armour against the day ahead, too. I'm going back. Back to the hospital, where I was bathed in the sights and smells and sounds of an unimaginable aftermath. Where I really noticed the stains for the first time, the blood and the other things I can't mention even to myself. The stains I know are still there, just under my skin. This time, I'll arrive clean. Clean enough, maybe, to keep at least some of the worst of it from sticking to me again.

When I emerge from the bathroom a short time later, my skin singing and red, Noor and Mia are in the kitchenette, scraping and rinsing and stacking the breakfast plates. Still talking as though they're the only ones in the apartment. Gal is a shadow through the balcony-door curtain. There is the faintest smell of weed smoke. All is calm. I feel a sudden peace. And sudden hunger. I grab an apple and a small container of yogurt and sit at the table, watching Mia and Noor enjoy each other's company.

"So, what is the plan?" Gal asks when he comes in a few minutes later, closing the balcony door.

"Aside from being at the hospital for visiting hours," I say, "I don't have a plan, not really."

Gal grabs an apple and bites into it, waiting for me to say more.

"I was going to wait and see. I don't know what to expect."

"Will they allow you to see him?"

"I'm family, so —"

"But not blood family."

The wind leaves me. That's true. How, in all the time I've spent thinking about and agonizing over this, has that not occurred to me? Different last names. Nothing to prove that Jesse has been a part of my life from breath number one. No photos, appropriately linked ID, records of any kind, nothing the hospital would take as proof. Shit.

"Well, we're here now," Mia says, stepping out of the kitchenette and wiping her hands on a dishtowel. "Let's just go. There's no crime in trying."

"This is true," Gal says.

Noor says something about having to work later and doing a dark load downstairs in the laundry room and us staying as long as we want, then disappears. She emerges carrying a cracked beige laundry basket filled past the brim with tumbled clothing. Grabs her keys and walks out. Mia stretches high and rolls her shoulders and walks down the hall to the bathroom. The dull hiss of the shower bleeds through the door.

I dig the burner phone from my pocket to check the time. A splash of green. A text from Aunt Viv, time-stamped early.

— Good luck today. I hope you find some answers or
   closure or whatever
— thx. still good on ur end?

I wait a long moment for a response, but there's nothing. I put the phone down to find Gal looking at me. His scars and his expression are impossible to ignore. Or to remain silent around. The ultimate truth serum.

"I feel like I need to say something to Jesse, but I don't know what."

"You will."

"There's no playbook for this. I'm —"

"You speak well. You are intelligent and kind. You love him, yes?"

The flood of affirmation stuns me so much that all I can do is nod. These are not compliments. Gal is not a complimentary person. His words are always measured out as precisely as marijuana from a government pot shop. But I guess he's seen something in me. Jesse would probably like him. *Will* like him. I can picture them sharing a joint in the park and trading bits of army wisdom. *Hurry up and wait. Embrace the suck. Watch your six. Gotta live the dream, troop.* They wouldn't trade war stories, though. They're not like that.

"I have heard you speaking with him. In the forest."

"You're kidding."

"I wondered who would receive such careful words. But now I know your story."

"How much did you hear?"

"Enough. I may be deaf in one ear, but my other hears a lot."

Have you ever been around a person but kind of tuned them out to background noise? Gal is like that. He's a constant presence, but for some reason I never thought of him as an active one. Even after Pat's attack. Gal was just there to help. More than convenient, to be sure, but I still haven't allowed myself to think of him as having a part in this weird play I'm staging.

"Thank you again for helping me the other day. When Pat ambushed me."

"He is a small boy with small ideas. It was necessary."

"Maybe, but all I did was tell you not to tell anyone. I should've thanked you. And trusted you."

A dismissive wave. "It was nothing."

"Tell me what?"

Mia's voice, sudden enough to make both Gal and me jump a little. She has padded to the kitchen, soundless in bare feet. Her hair is a wet, spiky mess. A small canvas bag, which I hadn't noticed either on the drive or on our way into Noor's apartment, rests under her arm. A change of clothing. Of course. She's in fresh shorts and a new tank top, making me feel grubby by comparison. Me focused on the destination. Mia planning the journey.

I hesitate, but Mia's looking at me patiently, like I could admit I torture kittens and she'd still hear me out before passing judgment. So I tell her about Pat and his attack, feeling the tiniest bit embarrassed that I have that kind of story to tell at all. Another one to add to a pile that's already too tall for someone my age. She glances down at the bandages on my wrist, now a couple of adhesive strips covering the lesions that haven't fully healed. I must scratch them in my sleep. Her eyes narrow when I tell the part where Pat unzips his fly and pisses on me, where Gal arrives almost in time. Mia looks ready to run back to Hamilton to find Pat and put him down for me. Pin him. Grind him into his very own patch of the greasiest poison ivy.

"Why didn't you tell me?"

It should be obvious. Shame and pride and the last piece of embarrassing teenage guyhood I'd want anyone to know about. Bad enough that Gal had to rescue me. But I don't say those things. I shrug.

Then Mia does another unexpected thing. She steps close and puts one arm around me, the other holding her bag. It is the perfect pressure, soft but strong and warm. No one else gets these kind of hugs, I'm sure. My embarrassment melts into her and is gone by the time she releases me and nods at Gal.

"Thanks for being there," she says to him.

Like claiming me in her own way. The good kind of possession.

Gal's face twitches into a scarred lightning smile before returning to neutral. He moves to the front hall and pockets his wallet and keys. Just as he bends to put on his shoes, Noor returns, nearly knocking the door into him. They perform an awkward dance in the tiny hallway, trying to manoeuvre around each other and uttering low words of apology in Arabic, back and forth. They both laugh, honest and unselfconscious. There is a moment of eye contact. Slight smiles are exchanged. A spark of something.

I stare. I've never thought about his age. He's Gal. Too wise and world weary to be bothered by the sudden pinch of attraction. Old. Scarred. Half-deaf and broken. I've only seen him based on his appearance and the history of violence he carries. I open my mouth to say something, maybe a too-late apology, but Mia nudges me before I can. Through her pleased, I'll-take-credit-for-this-introduction look, her eyes tell me to keep quiet, to let the moment play out. Not about me. Right.

The moment ends, transitioning back to our previously scheduled momentum. Mia and I move toward the door, to our shoes, and toward the big out-there questions that still need to be answered. Noor steps aside as we ready ourselves to go.

"Good luck today," she says.

"Thanks."

That's all I get out. I was hoping to thank her for letting us stay. Not a prepared speech, but for sure more than a single mumbled word. You do that when people offer something of themselves to make your life easier. I've been raised to make sure people know when they're appreciated, and I can hear Mom's and Jesse's voices in my mind, telling me to say my thanks out loud. They're both so big on generosity and gratitude. But once again I stumble on *thanks*. My new breaking word.

I can see a weight in Noor's eyes, a shadowed knowledge, and I wonder how much Mia has told her. Noor nods at me, smiles, and reaches out, pulling me into a wrestler embrace. Hard enough to squeeze some air from me. No pain, though. Just that core strength she and Mia share. She breaks off and holds me at arm's length. Looks me up and down. Finds my eyes. The shadow is gone now.

"Yeah, you'll do," she says. "You'll do just fine."

NO ACCESS

The long-term-care duty nurse sits back in her chair
and folds her arms. She is all business. Short blond hair
in a pixie cut. Pens secure in their sleeve pockets. A
clip-on watch dangling from her shirt pocket, next to
an ID card. LTC 102234 / S CRUMMEY, it says underneath a grainy photo of the nurse when her hair was
longer and darker. I wonder what the *S* stands for. She's
dressed in purple scrubs that wash out her already pale
skin, making the dark smudges under her eyes look like
bruises. Teal running shoes fringed in neon yellow. No
jewellery.

She says, "There's nothing I can do."

"But —"

"Your student ID tells me you're Wendell Sims, but
you don't have anything showing a relationship to the
patient. Besides, he's on restricted access because of who
he is and what he did."

"I'm worried about him."

"Maybe so, but we have to think about his rights, too. You could be anyone. We've had a lot of gawkers. Not so many recently, but still."

Gal steps forward. "What if I told you I was his brother, and this young man is my nephew?"

In the harsh lighting of the hospital ward, Gal's accent and appearance seem more pronounced. The nurse tilts her head and sighs. Skeptical doesn't begin to describe it.

"And you have proof?"

"Only my word."

"Do I need to call security?"

I look down the hall, wondering which room Jesse could be in. But the doors all look the same to me. I see one with a small desk beside it, a bald security guy dressed in black seated behind. That has to be Jesse's room. I want to run over and burst into the room, but the guard looks strong and fit. Not a chubby rent-a-cop, but someone who knows his job. I'd be on the ground and in cuffs in a heartbeat. But I'm so close. Too close to give up now.

I turn back to the nurse. "Jesse is my stepdad. I came all the way from Hamilton to see him."

"Look, kid."

"His middle name is Dominic."

"I'm sorry."

Her apology sounds so final. More than her previous threat to call security. Those were testing words. Not ending words, like these. So I list off every piece of information I can about Jesse. Date of birth. Our street address. His eye colour. And so on. As I speak, the nurse checks her computer records against some of what I'm saying. Confirmed. But when I describe Jesse's scars, the horrific ones he brought home from combat, I see her weakening. Too much inside knowledge to ignore.

"I know those scars," she says.

"You do?"

A nod. "Very well. Too well. He's been here a while. But we have protocols."

She doesn't reach for the phone, though. She is softening. Looking for the final reason not to send me away. I take a deep breath. "I was in the school library."

"But that's where he …" She can't finish her own sentence. She gives me a long, searching look. Another person rendered speechless. The breath stolen from so many conversations.

"Yes."

"Oh my god." Her eyes fill. She brings her fingers up to push the brimming tears away. "I'm so sorry."

I just nod. Me, too.

"It hasn't been that long," she says, "but I guess we've all tried to move on, you know?"

"I do."

I've reached her. I don't say anything, but part of me wants to ask about her connection to the shooting. I also don't want to. You worry how you could cut into a person by asking a question.

Another nurse appears from somewhere down the ward and steps into the duty station. The two nurses could be twins, but the new one's hair is a dark pixie, and her scrubs are aquamarine. She notices our nurse wiping her eyes. "Sarah? You good?"

So. *S* is for Sarah. She looks up and tries to smile. "Fine, Teresa, thanks."

The other nurse hesitates, as though she's not quite sure if she believes her, then nods. She walks past, too fast for me to catch any of the information on her ID badge, and sits behind a nearby computer. Lost in her data entry within seconds.

Sarah tries again. "It's not about moving on, I don't think. You'd know better than anyone that's not really possible. It's more like …"

She pauses and wrestles with something. In that pause I can hear everything around me, from the hush of the ductwork to the faint rustling of Gal's and Mia's clothes as they breathe. And this moment of clarity arrives, and the sounds from that day come back. Not the screams and the moaning, or the weeping of shattered parents and loved ones, but the regular sounds. Beeps from machines. The *skkriik!* of the mesh dividers between the trauma bays. The clicks and clunks of medical supplies on tables. The tearing of sterile packages. Urgent but calm voices. The voices of people whose job is to stitch the broken back together when the unthinkable happens.

"You were here," I say. "Afterwards."

Sarah nods. "All day and all night. We all stayed."

They stayed. And were stained, too. And came back to this terrible, hopeful place, day after day.

"I didn't know that."

"God, there were so many kids. No one could leave. But it was too much. I asked for a transfer from the ER afterwards. And ended up here."

"On this ward, of all places," Mia says.

"With Jesse," I say.

"We're supposed to think of him as just another patient."

"But he's not."

"Not even a little."

Sarah fingers her ID badge, half obscuring her photo and other information. She looks at me and smiles, her eyes squinching up, trapping the overhead lights. She tilts her head down the hallway, lifting her chin toward the security guy, who's finished his coffee. He's popped the dark brown lid from the maroon paper cup and is looking into the bottom like he can refill it if only he thinks about it hard enough.

"It's too bad, really," Sarah says.

"I'm sorry?" I ask.

"That I can't help you. That I certainly can't tell you he always leaves about five minutes after finishing his coffee," Sarah says. "Magazine in hand. Post-colic thing, I imagine."

"Post what?" Mia asks.

"Colic," Sarah repeats patiently. "Of the colon."

"He has to take a crap," I say. Mia chuckles. Jesse would call it something else. *Gotta go to the shitter, Dills. The Thunder Jug. Drop the kids off at the pool. If I'm not back in ten minutes, wait longer. Ha ha.*

Sure enough, a short while later, the guard is fidgeting in his seat. He gets up from the chair and hitches his utility belt higher, his flashlight and handcuffs and pepper spray clicking. He picks up his magazine and folds it in half, tucking it under his arm. Yawns. Starts walking.

He passes by and nods at us, just another family seeing just another patient. One of a thousand faceless people hoping to get better.

Sarah looks at the watch on her scrubs and declares she has to go check something. She rises and stands next to her colleague, pointing out something on the computer screen. Her back to us.

Permission, kind of.

"Dills, go," Mia whispers, gently pushing me toward Jesse's room. "We'll wait."

GOODBYE

There are two beds in the room. Only one of them is occupied. Jesse's army pension paying for semi-private, but the hospital unwilling to fill the other bed. Even with another paying customer. Forcing that person to recover next to a mass murderer. Someone with loved ones who'd visit. Where would they stand? Where will *I* stand?

I close the door behind me and move deeper into the room, forcing myself to walk rather than run. The horizontal blinds on the window are partially closed. The divider between the beds is drawn partway, obscuring Jesse's bed from the hall, the curtain's gaudy peach and dusty blue further dimming the light into a depressing blush. The smell is depressing, too. A stale mix of floor wax, disinfecting agents, hand sanitizer, urine, and something dank underneath it all. There is a rhythmic sound of air moving in and out. Ventilator. My anticipation fades, the smells and sights and sounds unexpectedly bringing me lower.

I step past the divider.

You're here. Finally.

"I'm here, Jesse."

My voice is barely a whisper. Not to be stealthy, or because of that strange reverence you adopt when you encounter sleeping people in hospitals. My throat has constricted itself. There is truth to what people say when you're about to witness the horrific:

> Prepare for the change.
> Nothing can prepare you.
> You might not know the person in front of
> you.

This is not Jesse. Jesse is a stocky guy, of a height you'd forget but strapped in muscles you'd remember. He takes a hard life seriously. He kept his form after leaving the military. He stayed ready. I'm supposed to be looking at hands that can skin a bush rabbit without a knife. Baseball forearms. A body as thick and cut as a fighting dog's. Not an ounce of fat anywhere. Mom will joke with him about it, pinching her own waist and trying to get a grip on his. "You can have some of mine," she'll say. He'll grab her close and kiss her neck, making her squirm but also giving her more chances to try to grab his skin. "You know I love every inch and pound of you," he'll say before she slaps him and tells him never to be so specific about a girl's weight. Mom never refers to herself or other women as girls, only women. But she lets herself think of herself as one around him.

This is someone else. Under the thin sheet I can see that there's nothing left. A skeleton wrapped in paper-thin skin, faintly yellowing. A couple of taped-down IV tubes look like they have barely enough vein and flesh to be secured to.

And this face isn't Jesse's. It isn't anyone's. It's a mess of cavities and pits and scars where his smiles and frowns and laughter used to live. Holdout wounds that have refused to heal. No mouth. No nose. Eyes sutured closed. A breathing tube sewn into his throat, space-age whites and blues against the jaundice of his face. A couple of small bandages are stuck at the top and bottom of what's left. All this damage by his own hand as the police closed in. He kept one round for himself. Maybe the monster everyone thinks he is.

Stay. Please.

His voice is pleading, strained, like he's worried that my heart will propel me out of here.

I stay. I stand for a long time, listening to the air get pushed into him and drawn out again. Watching the machines and their polite LED lights. Tracking where all the cords and tubes go. Trying to decipher the mystery numbers and bars and lines on all those screens. Do they predict how long he'll hold on? Ten minutes? Thirty? A week?

All this time I've been holding on to nothing. Like a disappearing breath in the cold. I've been cultivating his voice in my head and his memories in my brain and the idea of what he still might be. But this is not someone who intends to wake up. There's nothing left to support a life. Nothing to recover. No justice. Not even a trial, a formal pageant in advance of a preordained verdict. No chance at redemption, even for the only person who refuses to hate him. Restoration. Reconciliation.

"You never meant to come home, did you?"

My voice sounds like I've swallowed a handful of sand. Why did I say that? As though Jesse could walk out. From the moment I saw his ruined face and wasted body, I knew my plan had to change. There can be only one destination for all of this. It was supposed to be simple. But all my simplest hopes are gone.

No regrets, kiddo. That's what he should be saying to me right now. He hates dwelling on things. He taught me about survival but he never told war stories. He didn't have to. I read online about where his unit was deployed, one of the most notorious cities in Iraq and the toughest valley in Afghanistan. They humped their gear and their hate all over hell. They spilled blood, had theirs spilled. He had to survive somehow.

I now see so clearly that when Jesse took me into the woods, it was more about movement than about being in the outdoors. "Keep moving. You can't kill what you can't hit," he told me. Hunting another way to keep form. To stay alive. On that one hunting trip, he taught me how to use a knife to dress a small deer. There was so much blood, but his expression remained calm. "Don't focus on the mess," he said. "Focus on the job. There will always be blood."

"So what happened, then?" I say. "If you had it all figured out, how could you —"

I stop. Of course I do. *Kill all those innocent people* are the words that usually come next. Unlike those who weren't there, I can't say them so easily. The faces arrive too quickly when I try. A best friend named Ethan who sat next to me in every class we shared. Teachers. Kids whose names I only know from the news. I feel bad about that, even though they were in other classes, other grades.

"Why did you come to my classroom first?"

This is the first time I've ever said those words out loud. My next question should be *Did you want to hurt me?* but I won't ask it.

I'm sorry. I don't know what happened.

I know what the first part is. It's a non-apology, where you say sorry but don't say why. Vague. Dismissive. And the next part? "Playing the memory card," Mom calls it. *What happened? Do you mean before, Jesse? After? During? To you as a person? To the dead? To those who survived and have to live with Windsor every day? Probably forever?*

"That's it? That's all I get?"

Nothing.

"Why did you ask me to come?"

Still nothing.

And so I get mad.

No, Jesse, I think. *Not after months of defending you. Reminding everyone of the way you were. Holding on to the old you, who loved me and helped me learn about things and always had an answer. Not after driving all this way because you asked me to, only to find that you aren't you anymore. That nothing more will happen because you've given up.*

I feel my hands grip the base of the bed, hard enough to be painful. I want to hit something.

"You don't need me."

My voice is no longer constricted, but low and hard. You do that to deliver the truth, even when it's the toughest kind. Jesse taught me that. "Yelling and screaming and carrying on are tools of the weak," he said. "Make *them* listen to *you*." It has to be that way because of what has to happen next. What I have to do. What he needs to hear.

"I'm done, Jesse. Don't talk to me anymore."

I reach into my pocket. I have to dig deep. I take out my great-grandpa Gene's watch, the braided lanyard making reassuring pressure points against my fingers. I unravel the braid, the strands unweaving into a kinked spray of olive-green paracord, until the watch is released. The watch goes back into my pocket. Its cracked crystal face is cool through the thin fabric. I clench the loose strands of paracord in my fist before tossing them onto the bed beside Jesse's withered leg.

My heart wants me to turn away and move back into the hallway. But I can't. For a long moment I don't understand why. Then something inside twinges about that sad little nest of paracord. It sits wrong, incomplete, on the bed and inside me. I pick it up and find I can walk out. But I don't take it with me. I drop it into the garbage on my way out. It hisses into the small white bag lining the bin and then I'm back in the hallway. I don't look back.

ARRANGED

Teresa, the other nurse, is in the hall when I emerge from Jesse's room. She glances at the clock on the wall and says something to me, but I don't hear her. I feel like I'm in a cocoon, my thoughts providing noise cancellation for everything else. I can feel myself looking dumbly at her. She smiles and points at my wrist. The bandage covering the last spots of PI rash has flapped loose. She motions me to follow her down the hall and takes me to a supply cart around a corner. She grabs some gauze and tape and an irrigation syringe and sits me on a gurney. Physically. Two hands on my shoulders. But I don't want to sit. I want to get back to Mia and Gal and get away from here.

The sound comes back as she removes my dressing. She's saying something about infection. "It'll just take a sec, hon."

"No, they're waiting for me."

Teresa looks at her watch. Frowns. I don't like that frown. Why the urgency? I get up, pushing her restraining hand away.

"Please sit. I don't want —"

"I have to go."

When I round the corner, there is a constellation of flashes, spotting my vision. Cameras? A bunch of voices swell and there is movement beyond the orange spots burned into my retina. I'm surrounded. Reporters and photographers. Normal-looking people holding cameras and phones and shouting questions at me. Shouting my own name at me. How did they get that? No one knows I'm here. More flashes. One constant bright light. That must be a video camera. I try to look beyond the gaggle for Mia and Gal, but I can't find them.

I feel a firm hand holding my bicep and trying to guide me. I'm annoyed — what's with everyone trying to move me where they think I should be going? — but the flash of purple in my peripheral vision feels familiar. Purple scrubs. Sarah. She leans in and speaks loudly in my ear. Says Teresa's name and drops an F-bomb and tells me she didn't know the media had been called. She moves toward a glassed-in room across the hall and slides open the door. All the blinds are drawn. Gal and Mia are inside.

One of the photographers tries to get an arm in and snap some blind photos, but Gal grabs the arm and slams it upward. The camera doesn't break, but there's a squeal of pain from outside. The arm and camera pull back.

Sarah slides the door closed and leans against it. "Shit."

Mia rushes over and gives me a great big hug. Doesn't speak, just holds on like there's no one else in the room. Gal and Sarah don't say anything either. I can hear the clamour outside. The reporters are actually yelling questions through the sliding glass door.

"They won't come in," Sarah says. "Privacy laws. It's illegal to open a closed hospital door without permission."

"What's going on?" I ask. "Why are those —"

"The other nurse called them while you were with Jesse," Mia says.

"I'm so sorry," Sarah says. "Teresa must've figured she could make a few bucks."

"I don't understand."

"You're the Windsor Shooter's son," Sarah says, "and you came here. That doesn't happen every day."

"Stepson," I say.

"Still …"

Sarah doesn't finish the thought, but of course she doesn't have to. My presence is unusual. I might've been avoiding it all summer, but for everyone else it's an exciting development in a near-dead story. Everyone gave up on Jesse a long time ago.

"That doesn't make what she did all right," Mia says.

"Of course it doesn't. I'm sorry," Sarah says again.

"You don't need to apologize," I tell her. "Thanks for helping me."

"Did it help? Your visit, I mean?"

"I don't know yet. It wasn't what I expected."

She nods. "That's not unusual on this floor."

"And thanks for this, too. Helping all of us."

"It's the least I can do. I feel terrible. We take privacy so seriously." She sighs. "Or we're supposed to, anyway."

"Will you get in trouble for this?" I ask.

"Probably not. Well, maybe. But I'll be fine. What do I pay union dues for if not for situations like this, right?" She laughs for a split second before cutting herself off. Shakes her head as though she can't believe that came out of her in this moment. Adrenalin. I get it.

"How do we get out?" Gal asks.

Sarah moves past us and to the back of the room. Waves her ID badge in front of a small, nondescript box on the wall. The back wall, another sliding door, opens with a hiss. "Go this way. There's an elevator down the hall that can take you to the parking garage."

"What about the reporters?" Mia asks.

"This area is staff only. It's how patients from the different floors get moved around for tests, surgery, that kind of thing. No one will hassle you."

Gal moves into the hallway. I almost pause to thank Sarah again and to wish her well, but Mia takes my hand and leads me out before I can. More leading when I'm not sure I want to be led. But I let her. The door slides closed behind us.

The ride down to the parking garage feels slow, like an hour passes before the doors open into the exhaust-smelling gloom. I worry about reporters staking out the car, but no one's around when we get there. Gal gets out his keys and clicks open the doors as soon as the car comes into view. The horn beeps and the yellow hazards flash in the low fluorescent lighting. The car next to ours is still warm, clicking and muttering as its engine cools down.

Inside Gal's car we sit and stare out the front windshield. No speaking. No need to. We can hear our breathing. You forget about real silence until you find it again. Everywhere else is noise and motion.

TOLD

It's so bright outside. Emerging from the parking garage to the main parking lot feels like I'm seeing sunlight for the first time. Gal pulls a warped pair of sunglasses from behind the sunshade and puts them on, and Mia draws a grubby hat down low. It's creased and folded, and I wonder how long it's been in Gal's footwell. There's nothing for me. All I can do is hold my hand up to shield my eyes.

We leave the hospital grounds without incident. All seems normal. No TV-satellite trucks fringe every foot of the perimeter, no police cruisers block the entrances and exits, no family cars are parked at panicked, crazy angles. Not like last time, when Mom was finally allowed to drive me home. I look back at the building, brilliant white against the sky, and realize for the first time that Jesse would've already been there as I was leaving. He tried to kill himself precisely forty-nine minutes after the first shots were fired. *Fo-wer-niner mikes after the first rounds went downrange*, he'd say, exaggerating the words. *Fo-wer* for *four. Niner* for *nine. Mikes* for *minutes.* To sound clearer on a military radio. It was hours before things were settled and documented and straightened out enough to let the survivors leave, so he was definitely there. Rushed in on a gurney like all the others. Alive and worth saving. His own piece of the commotion he created. I wonder sometimes how he could've messed up his own death. He should have known better, right?

"We will need to find a mechanic," Gal says.

"I just want to go," I say.

"The spare will not make it all the way back to Hamilton."

Mia pulls out her phone. Opens Google Maps for a nearby mechanic. They argue about near or far, small mechanic or franchised tire specialist. Gal only trusts the independents. Mia says that speed is important and also that the franchise will probably have the tire in stock. Gal reluctantly concedes the point. Mia turns and gives me an impish thumbs-up. Smug victory. I try to smile back. I probably look like a gargoyle. They decide on a place out in the suburbs.

As we drive, I pull out my burner phone to text Aunt Viv.

— all done

— And?

— it was weird

— I bet

— everything ok at home?

There is a brief pause. It feels like forever before her text arrives.

— Dills, your mom was beside herself last night so I
    told her. I know I said I wouldn't but I had to
— told her what?
— Everything

I begin and delete a dozen replies. Between the hospital media ambush and now worrying about Mom, what's happened seems too big for texting. I should call Aunt Viv. But I'd have Gal and Mia listening on my end, and I'm not sure I'm ready to talk about it. I should definitely call Mom. The acid heat of guilt rises in my gut and I don't know what to do with it.

— ?????

Aunt Viv is impatient as I type and delete and type and delete. Probably wondering if I'm writing a novel. She deserves more. Mom deserves a hell of a lot more. And yet I'm not there.

— we'll be home in a few hours

As soon as I hit Send I power off the phone. I hope she's not too pissed about my lack of response. I hope she's staying close to Mom.

I slide the phone into my pocket and look out my side, watching the traffic get lighter as the city thins into its outskirts. Gal and Mia are chatting in Arabic now, punctuated by brief laughs and groans. Reliving the hospital in a language I can't understand. I don't mind, though. I let the now familiar but unknowable sounds wash over me and lean my head against the window. The safety glass is warm from the sun. I close my eyes and try to make sense of what's happened as the highlight reel of the trip and my summer and everything rushes past my eyelids.

LOVELY

I don't know I'm sleeping until potholes in the tire place's parking lot knock my head against the window and wake me up.

> LIGHTNING TIRE & LUBE
> while u wait!!

A compromise. An independent tire specialist. I almost smile.

"Hey, Dills," Mia says.

"Hey."

"You sacked out pretty hard."

"I guess I needed it."

The lot is empty. There's a small sign between the service bays that tells us to park there and honk the horn, so we do. The garage door trundles up on its guides and a small, wiry guy walks to the driver's-side door, wiping his hands on a rag. His skin is so brown, it's almost black. Stained red hat. Navy-blue coveralls that look bright next to his skin. Stitched to the chest is a white Lightning Tire & Lube patch fringed in red.

"Leave the keys in the ignition. Oil change is twenty minutes or so. You can wait in the waiting room."

"No oil change," Gal says. "We need a new tire. We are running on the spare."

"No problem, sir. That'll be a bit longer, maybe thirty minutes." He kneels and checks out the spare on the back left and scans the rest. "You'll want to change both right and left in the back, though, if not all four."

They go back and forth about brands and styles and prices. Gal settling on a mid-range pair of all-seasons for the rear that sound so expensive to me. I again have the empty urge to offer repayment, but this time say nothing. Gal holds out a hand, which the guy takes, looking pleased at the formality of a handshake to seal the deal.

He says, "I'll put the new ones on the front, rotate the others to the back. Okay?"

"You can do all of this in thirty minutes?"

He flashes a smile. "Twice, if I had to."

"All right."

We all step out of the car and the guy slides in, moves the seat forward a few inches, puts the car into gear, and zips into the bay. Like it's all one motion. No hesitation. No brake lights until the car stops in its spot above the mount.

The waiting room is a small rectangular space. The front window of the store is to our back as we enter. A TV blares high in the corner, angled toward the chairs lining two of the walls. A table under the window warms in the dusty sun, bearing the weight of a space-age espresso machine, an untidy spread of old magazines, and a wobbly rack of pamphlets and promotional material. A customer service counter divides the space between us and the service area. The door behind the counter is propped open for air movement, letting in the sounds of air tools and metal working metal. Just past the smell of oil and hydraulics and metal is the burnt smell of old coffee.

A young woman, maybe university age, sits behind the counter, clicking around on the computer there. She doesn't look up as we enter. A single other customer, a tanned man in a camouflage T-shirt, sits in a far chair. A matching ball cap pushes down on his impossibly blond hair, which sticks out like a scarecrow fringe. Though he's sitting, I can tell he's a big guy. He looks folded into the chair like clothing into too-small luggage. His eyes are glued to the TV. Some twenty-four-hour news channel, a clash of traffic cams and anchors and news tickers and weather icons. Every element screaming, *Look at me!* It hurts my eyes, so I sit in one of the free chairs and look at the framed tire posters hung wherever there's a few square feet of wall space. Mia sits next to me, Gal in the next chair down.

I think about Jesse. It's the pause that lets it happen. The waiting. Gal closes his eyes, patient as a park bench. Mia has her phone out and is scrolling through email or something. So normal. I feel normal, too, and that makes me uncomfortable. I've taken in the wasting body of my stepdad, a guy I've defended and puzzled over for months, but I don't feel anything. I've said goodbye, but it doesn't seem like a farewell. No telling how much longer he'll live, so my visit and my words are probably meaningless. Like a handful of water poured into a Cootes Paradise creek in the hopes of freshening Lake Ontario, absorbed long before reaching the marsh, much less the lake beyond. I'll never know.

I pull out my phone and power it on to send a text to Aunt Viv about the delay, but decide not to. What's thirty minutes when she doesn't know our specifics anyhow? The phone's screen brightens and urges me to swipe in. I wait for Aunt Viv's delayed texts to arrive, but there's nothing. Maybe she understands why I didn't respond. But if she told Mom everything, there's no reason not to have given Mom this number. I should see a cascade of worry in the register, red letters and numbers for every missed call. I should see it now and I should've seen it when I texted before. The little voicemail icon bold and red with a number that signals Mom's level of concern.

But, no. No numbers, no cascade.

What should I do with that? Put the phone away? Stick to the plan? Realize that there's nothing to be gained from a phone call where all you can do is inevitably break the connection? There's a certain logic to that. A certain attractiveness, too, in holding on to some measure of control. I tell myself to power down again, but my fingers don't listen. They're working on my heart's instructions. *Call your mom. Now.* Driven by an image of a mother so heartbroken and betrayed she can't text or call her only child. I watch my fingers do the touchscreen dance across the familiar numbers and the phone is up and there's a ringing sound and a pickup click interrupting the second ring.

I wait for the voice. The hello. Nothing.

"Mom?"

Is there a hissing on the line, or is it my mind filling in the lack of response from her?

"It's Dills."

Still nothing.

"Say something, Mom. Please."

"Are you safe?"

"Yeah. I'm with Gal and Mia and we blew a tire yesterday and we're getting it changed somewhere out in the —"

"Stop."

"Mom?"

"That's enough."

"I saw him. I saw Jesse."

There's a deep, brief moan on the other end of the line.

"He looked so different. He —"

"Please stop. I can't. Not now. I'm glad you're safe. But, Dills, I just can't."

And the click on the other end of the line is so final and dreadful that it must have filled the room. Gal and the other guy haven't moved. I lower the phone and look at Mia. She's watching me but not saying anything. I hear myself saying that I called my mom as if Mia didn't already hear everything on my side. That she hung up.

"I don't know what to do with that," I say.

"It's a lot to process."

"I need to get out of here. Walk, maybe."

We rise from our seats, pocket our phones, and step toward the door.

"Do not go too far, please," Gal says as we pass, not moving, eyes still shut tight.

Mia and I reply in unison that we won't. We glance at each other and walk out, the cheerful bells above the door signalling our arrival back into the world. Like we've been delivered by reindeer and sleigh. I swear they didn't ring when we came in.

Mia sets her phone's timer to ten minutes, a signal to turn around. I love that. It's the kind of detail only she could bring into the situation. I hear myself ribbing her about it. As another diversion from the strangeness of the day, I suppose. She's a good sport about it and gives back as well as she gets. Better, in fact. We're actually laughing when her alarm sounds.

"Thanks," I say. "I needed this."

"Me, too. I'm glad to be here, but it's quite a ride."

We turn and walk for a few steps. I breathe deep and shake my head. "I'm worried about Mom. She sounded so shattered by this. What if —"

Mia stops me with a kiss. She literally steps in front of me and halts my forward momentum with her hands on my shoulders. Gentle but with that bear strength behind them. She rises on her toes and plants her lips on mine, firm and warm and dry. My body is suddenly drawing in all the inertia from every car that passes, the sun, the turning of the planet. I want to wrap her up in me and carry the kiss to where kisses like that always suggest you go. But she breaks away and drops down to her heels, her eyes sparking. She moves a single finger to her lips like she wants to gauge the heat there. I haven't even moved my arms from their dumb place at my side.

"You're lovely," she says.

"Oh. Uh, thanks."

"You should've seen your face when you talked about your mom. Sweetest thing I've ever seen."

"Sometimes I think she won't make it through all of this."

Mia shakes her head, looking at me with a kind of wonder. "You survived the shooting — I can't imagine what you've had to carry — but you're more worried about her. Call me cheesy and Hallmark, but with you on her team I think she'll do fine."

"I have to tell her about Jesse. She won't be ready."

"You're a good son, Dills. Wow."

"Aside from running away and not telling her."

"Sure. And the LoJack and breaking the conditions of your sentencing."

"Right. And those."

We grin, shaking our heads at the impossibility of everything, and resume walking. On the way out, we watched the landscape change, from the tire place nestled among low strip malls, industrial buildings, gas stations, and fast-food joints, to the faceless rows of identical houses that surround us now. New pavement. Tiny trees and brand-new sod, the edges browning. Big SUVs in every driveway.

Mia and I walk back to the tire place, talking quietly, just loud enough to hear each other over Saturday traffic, a pair of teenagers no one looks twice at.

RECOGNITION

When we get back, the car has been backed out of the bay and is idling in the lot. Inside, Gal is leaning against the counter, signing the work order. The mechanic stands behind the young woman at the desk with keys in hand, ready to hand them over. Without taking her eyes from her computer screen, she slides the credit card terminal over to Gal, who pays by chip and secret number.

The mechanic drops the keys into Gal's hands. "You serve?"

Gal turns his good ear toward the guy. "I am sorry?"

"The pattern of your scars. Sprayed. Like from a blast."

"Oh. Yes. A long time ago."

"The Sandbox?"

"I am sorry?"

"Iraq? Afghanistan?"

"No. Israel."

The guy nods. "Panjwaii for me. Bunch of us came back with scars like that."

Gal nods, looking unsure what to say.

I do, though. You pick that up when you spend enough time with a vet in public. "Thanks for your service."

Jesse didn't talk about it except when the Corolla's veteran plates got noticed. Strangers pumping his hand or slapping him on the shoulder and repeating those words. He'd ask for the bill at a restaurant or arrive at the counter of the coffee shop only to find that the order had been paid for. Little handwritten notes, always anonymous. "THANK YOU FOR YOUR SERVICE." "It's embarrassing as hell, Dills. But awesome too, you know? It means something." Mom would get the same thing when she was out and about, always gently making sure that Jesse's name got mentioned. Turn the conversation back to what he gave. Lots of people shaking their heads and telling her that she served as much as anyone. Mom embarrassed by that, too, of course.

The man's eyebrows go up and he smiles. "You're welcome. Thanks for saying that."

Jesse always said "you're welcome" and "thank you," too. "Good manners are currency you can spend, kiddo," he'd tell me.

I feel Mia's hand on my shoulder. I follow her eyes to the TV on the wall. It's still muted. Bizarre watching such a familiar scene unfold like a silent film. Amid the tickers and scrolling text, the live-action frame is showing the scene in the hospital. Shaky, handheld footage. I watch myself come around the corner with the nurse who called the media. Sarah bustles me into the observation room, the camera bumping and shaking as the door slides shut. The scene cuts back to the moment I come around the corner, slowing down and zooming in, pausing on my grainy, video-stilled face. "WENDELL SIMS, SON OF WINDSOR SHOOTER." Cut back to the studio, where an anchor is speaking to the camera, serious. I imagine phrases like *moments ago* and *exclusive* and *saw it here first*. My last school photo hovers over her shoulder. Younger, chubbier, but still me.

"Shit," I say.

"Yep," Mia replies.

"I wonder who gave them that pic?"

I look over at the other customer, who's watching the TV, his face slack and passive. Something clicks. He sits upright and looks over at us. Back at the TV. At us. TV. He hikes his camouflage cap up on his forehead. In a nanosecond he has his phone out and he's typing. Then he's calling someone and watching us intently. I can almost hear the phone connecting on the other end, the news station's receptionist answering, asking how she can direct his call.

Gal's watching all of it, too. He shakes his head and says we should go. As we get into the car, the guy appears in the shop's window, now speaking into his phone. So this is what conspicuous feels like. People know you. They stare at you like they have something invested in what you do. Who you are. As we drive away, I get the tiniest glimpse of what it has taken for Mom to keep me safe and anonymous. And I feel shame that I might've made all those efforts and worries mean nothing.

SIEGE

The trip back to Hamilton feels quicker than the trip out. Gal pushes the car up past the limit, but there's something more to it. Like time has compressed. An hour in, we pull into a service centre to fuel up and take care of some basic human needs. We're almost surprised by the need to stop. The events of the morning pushing aside the urge to pee, the pang of hunger. We get our bagels and drinks to go, Gal sipping his coffee as he pulls back onto the highway, moaning about bad coffee and how sofas aren't meant for sleeping. Mia and I pass a large hot chocolate back and forth, each sip cooler than the last. I take a single bite of my bagel before spitting it out and wrapping the whole mess back in its bag.

The rest of the drive is uninterrupted. No one says much. Too much worrying about what might come next. In my case, I think about the reporters and video and my new notoriety. Mom's too, probably. And I try to imagine how I might apologize for the unforgivable.

And then we're home, driving up the main neighbourhood road and turning onto my street. Gal stops as soon as my house comes into view. Four or five shiny white vans, emblazoned with call letters and bright graphics, are parked around the house. Two of them have satellite dishes transmitting to the sky. I see a familiar blue car parked by the side door. Walters. Knowing that we only use the side door to go in and out of our house. First to arrive, I'm sure. An edge on the competition.

"That was fast," Mia says.

"Once they had my name …"

I don't finish. No need to. Simple web searches and public records and you'd land on Sims in minutes.

There's no car in the driveway. Aunt Viv's Prius still in the shop. Mom's car gone for who knows how long. Our house looks under siege.

"What should we do next?" Gal asks.

"Drop me off at the front door," I say. "Then go home."

Mia turns. "No, Dills, we should —"

"Guys, thanks so much for doing all this for me. But I have a feeling it's going to be super ugly when I walk in that door."

"We can help."

I shake my head. "I need to do this on my own."

"Are you sure?"

"No. Not of anything anymore. But at least it's just me facing the music."

"For now," Gal says.

Mia clicks her tongue behind her teeth. "Hey, come on."

"He did not drive himself, yes?"

I ask, "Gal? Mia? Trust me, okay?"

They look at each other and nod, and Mia turns to look me right in the eye. I feel pinned down in the back seat by it. Her dark eyes boring into me. Unsettling and reassuring all at once. The strength of it. Bear. Tiger. Pick your apex animal.

"Call me as soon as you can."

"I will."

I pull out the burner and text Aunt Viv.

— we're here r u home?

Her reply arrives almost before I'm finished typing.

— Yes
— unlock the front door i'm coming in
— Do you see the reporters?
— they're all watching the side should give me an
  extra second or two
— Hopefully!
— lol right

I slide the phone into my pocket. "Okay. I'm ready."

Gal puts the car in gear and accelerates the final distance, cutting a turn at the last second to stop at the curb closest to the front door, and I'm pulling the handle and stepping onto the sidewalk. Slamming the door. Slapping my hand on the roof to signal I'm clear. Watching Gal pull away. For a second, I can't see the circus, but Walters looks around the corner of the house, recognizes me, and holds her phone out in front, shouting a question of some kind. I realize I haven't moved from my spot. I dash up the stairs to the door. Walters's questions are pebbles launched at my back as I reach for the door handle. The rest of the reporters are behind her.

"Wendell, why did you go?"

"Wendell, how does it feel to —"

"What next?"

"Did you talk to him?"

Aunt Viv has swung open the door and stands aside as I rush in. She closes it against the cacophony of voices, which fade to dull chatter through the heavy steel. I stumble into the living room and put my hands on my knees. Maybe ten steps in total and my heart is pounding, my breath as thin as if I've sprinted a mile or a klick or something far and uphill. The hardwood floor blurs.

"Dills. You're home. Thank God."

Mom's voice. Mom's firm hands on my arms, my shoulders, lifting me upright, moving to my face, my neck, my chest, my arms again, and back to my hands. Checking for damage. My eyes clear and she's right in front of me, looking me up and down and at all points of my face, as though there's no way to focus on one. Needing to take in all of me.

"Mom, I'm so —"

One of those hands gently covers my mouth. She's shaking her head. That look is called "Don't Say a Thing Right Now, Young Man." I smell soap and skin and something rusty. Solder and flux, ground in. Committed hands. One keeping me from speaking, the other now rising up to embrace me, hard enough to steal some of the breath I've only just regained. Both are shaking. She's shaking. My eyes fill. How close I've brought her to coming apart. Like I said, she feels everything.

"The phone," she says, releasing me and stepping away. "The one Viv gave you."

"What about it?"

She holds out a hand. The other wipes away a single tear on her cheek.

Aunt Viv takes a step toward us. "Vick, he should have the chance to —"

Mom turns toward her and silences her with a look that you'd say was expressionless if you didn't see her eyes. I dig the burner out of my pocket and lay it in her hand. It's still warm. She gives it a long, accusing look and turns away, her filthy workshop shirt — one of Jesse's old Class A uniform ones, a faint green that can look white from a distance — flapping behind her as she disappears through the door that leads downstairs.

DIG

A short while later I walk up the stairs and into the living room. The noise outside has gone down. Reporters back to their places, back into siege mode. Gramma Jan has come down from her room and is sitting in the easy chair. She is pale and thin. And pissed. She's watching the front door like she could shoot fire through it. Aunt Viv has seated herself on the couch and looks up as I enter. I shake my head. Mom won't come out. She won't speak to me. She locked the door to her workshop and fired up her grinder, making conversation impossible.

"She'll be all right," Aunt Viv says. "We just have to —"

"Give her time, yeah, I know," I snap at her.

"Easy, Dills."

"Why is everything about time? Seems like there's either too much or not enough of it."

"Maybe life's biggest damn secret," Gramma Jan

says. "That and love. Regardless, you never get it back. Time, I mean. Maybe love, too."

"That's pretty dramatic, Mom," Aunt Viv says.

Gramma Jan glares at her and points. "Sit in my chair for a few days, Vivian, then we'll talk about what's dramatic."

"Okay. Sorry. It just felt extreme is all."

Gramma Jan grunts and goes back to her burning study of the door. As soon as she's sure Gramma Jan can no longer see her, Aunt Viv rolls her eyes. She doesn't seem to care that I'm in the room. That I can see her. I get this glimpse of the teenager still inside. Apologies as a selfish kind of peacemaking. I sit at the other end of the couch and settle in for a wait. Wondering how and when the waiting could end.

"I imagine you don't want to talk about it," Aunt Viv says.

"About what?"

"The trip."

I'm annoyed at the non-question. The kind of thing you say because you should, not because you want to. Half-hearted. Leading. Hard to turn around without an unnatural amount of force. *Actually, I'd love to talk about it, Aunt Viv! Why don't you put your feet up and let me tell you* all *the details!* Meh.

"I want to talk to Mom first," I say.

"That makes sense."

"It was … eventful. I can say that."

Gramma Jan snorts and stands up. Too quickly. She has to grab the back of the chair to steady herself. Her clothing — the family uniform of jeans and frayed

T-shirt — hangs on her. An unsteady scarecrow. Her face is flushed and her eyes have narrowed. An unsteady and livid scarecrow.

"That's it," she says. "This ends now."

Aunt Viv stands, too. "Mom?"

"Reporters chasing you all over like you're some wounded specimen. Following you home. Goddamn vultures."

"What're you going to do?"

"I'm going out there. Beat them off with a broom if I have to."

"I'd watch that press conference," I say. Reaching for an inappropriate levity.

Aunt Viv gives me a look. *Don't encourage her*, it says. She moves next to Gramma Jan as she reaches for the door handle and puts a hand on her mother's hand. "Stop."

"They can't treat my family this way."

"They're following the story, Mom. They'll go away if we ignore them."

"When?"

"I don't know. Not long. Surely this isn't worth more than a news cycle."

I don't think she's right, but I don't say anything. Of all of us, Aunt Viv is by far the most media savvy, so surely she knows they'll feed on this for at least a few days. The stepson of the Windsor Shooter making a pilgrimage to see his wasting father in a distant hospital? Caught on tape outside the room? Tracked home to where he and his mother have made a new, anonymous life? Rich material. It's feast or famine in the news industry, and this is at least a holiday meal. They'll gorge themselves to bursting and let the calories sustain them a while.

"I want them off my property."

"They'll go back to their spots on the road and sidewalk if no one goes out. Public property."

"It's still harassment. I should —"

"They're not breaking any laws. And it won't help, going out there, looking like —"

"Looking like what, Vivian?"

No response. Aunt Viv's intentional dangler left in the air for Gramma Jan to grab on her own. Looking like an elderly, sick, crazy woman. While Mom and I cower inside. Gramma Jan's outburst would be a delicious addition to the meal. The perfect side dish that gets praised as much as the main.

Gramma Jan frees her hand from Aunt Viv's loose grasp and opens the door a crack. Immediately, reporters fire questions through the gap, a vertical slash of diminished light. Grey clouds instead of blue sky out there. I can see Walters's bright red jacket and her blond hair. A few seconds pass, feeling like an eternity.

Gramma Jan closes the door and stands still, head down, one hand on the silver handle and the other against the doorjamb. When she turns back into the living room, she looks paler. Thinner. Defeated. She grabbed hold of what Aunt Viv didn't say. Maybe it was the sight of the reporters. Maybe the noise. Whatever it was, the realization soaked her through. That the media would insist on learning more about her. They'd scoop and dig and do what they do. And they'd find her cancer as surely as the tests the doctors did a few weeks ago. She'd become part of the story. Part of the reality she was trying to banish. Part of that sickly pot-luck that was being assembled about my family. More calories.

NO APOLOGY

It's evening now. Late. Dark outside. I'm in the kitchen, staring into the cupboards, hungry but not seeing or craving a thing. Aunt Viv leans against the counter. Mom's still in her workshop, and Gramma Jan went to bed a while ago. In the end, I told them the story. It was bursting out of me anyway. Gramma Jan tried to stay awake, but lost more colour with every passing minute. Her body pulling its limited supply of blood back to its core to combat the pain and fatigue. She stopped me as I talked about Noor's apartment, then said goodnight and eased her way upstairs. I watched Aunt Viv deflate as she watched her mother leave. She wondered out loud when they'd have to move Gramma Jan to the main floor. When the stairs would become too much. I didn't say anything. It would need to happen soon. *Way too goddamn soon*, Gramma Jan would say.

"So you and Mia …?"

"I suppose."

"*I suppose*?"

"It's good. I like her."

Aunt Viv smiles. "As your older and wiser and scary aunt, my official position is that you're too young and that no one, of course, is good enough for you."

"And unofficially?"

"I met her. She's nice. I'm happy for you."

I exhale. "I'm glad, Aunt Viv."

"Just don't rush it, okay?"

"I won't."

"Good."

There's a knock at the side door. Aunt Viv gives me a weary look and tells me to stay put and out of sight. She doesn't have to. The last thing I want is to give some eager reporter a chance to stick his camera in the door to get a picture of me like they did at the hospital. I hear the whoosh of the door opening followed by a few seconds of silence. The murmur of low voices. More silence. Then the heavy clunk of the sticky door. Aunt Viv steps back into the living room.

"He's in here," she says over her shoulder.

Sean walks in, looking like hell. Untucked shirt. Hair sticking up. Unshaven. He's removed his shoes, which Gramma Jan calls "a common-sense sign of respect," but his brown socks look worn. And they're sloppy, as if he's too tired even to pull them up after removing his shoes. This all at a glance.

I stand up out of reflex. He waves me down again and kneels on the floor next to me. He tugs on the LoJack's nylon strap, checking for extra give. For compromise. He pulls out a little black device from his pocket that looks like a beeper, holds it next to the ankle monitor, and pushes a button. Three green LEDs light up in sequence and the device in his hand emits three quiet and cheerful chimes. Satisfied, he stands and drops onto the couch next to me, tossing the device onto the coffee table.

"Okay, then," he says by way of greeting. But he's looking at Aunt Viv. Sad eyes. She's still leaning against the doorframe separating the living room from the hallway, arms folded.

"Hi, Sean," I say.

I don't say any more, aware of the delicate balance of fact and fiction that we've built around this weekend. Something is obviously making him worry about the integrity of the LoJack, but I can't guess what. Aunt Viv has been clear — there should be no anomalies in my movements to find. No digital trail.

And yet.

"So here's a little story, yeah?" he says. "There's this youth probation officer who procrastinates a lot, and sometimes has to use his Saturday mornings to get caught up on paperwork. Imagine him heading to a local café to take advantage of its excellent sausage biscuits, strong espresso, and free Wi-Fi, and imagine him ordering and sitting down. Imagine a TV on the wall, which he watches while he waits for his breakfast. And guess what he sees?"

Ah. I know where this is going.

Aunt Viv is obviously processing the same thing, studiously willing herself not to look at me. Like I'm willing myself not to look at her. But she does speak first. Maybe thinking that she can control the narrative. "What does he see?"

Sean laughs, quick and harsh. "Get this, Vivian, you'll never believe it. He sees one of his clients on the news, caught on film at the hospital in Windsor. But the youth worker thinks *That's impossible!* He'd have gotten an alarm if the client had left town. Some of his clients wear ankle monitors, yeah? So he checks his monitoring app, and guess what?"

Aunt Viv does not respond to this one.

Sean throws up his hands. "The app tells him that there's no problem, that his client hasn't gone anywhere except for a few short walking jaunts around the neighbourhood!" His voice has gone up a few levels. His eyes move between Aunt Viv and me, as narrow as toothpicks. "In two places at once! What do you make of that, guys?"

"Quite a story," Aunt Viv says.

"Oh, it is," Sean says. He snorts. "It really is."

He sits back against the couch cushions, folds his arms, and falls silent. We hear footsteps on the stairs from the basement, and Mom steps into the hall. She waits while Aunt Viv, who's still blocking the doorway, stands aside to let her in. Her eyes rest on Sean. I can see deeper shadows under her eyes. More exhaustion and weight to bear.

"Sean? What's going on?"

He gives a quicker, less sarcastic version of the story. Same result for us. Silence. But Mom hasn't been brought in, so she's confused. "I don't understand. Is there some malfunction?"

Sean points at the diagnostic device on the table. "I checked, and all's well with the equipment."

"So how can this happen?"

"That's the mystery of it, isn't it, Vivian?"

He's glaring at her again. Mom follows the look.

"Why would she have anything to do with —"

She goes quiet, too. Everyone waits. Breaths are held. Mom looks her sister in the eye, pinning her down with a scrutiny I know can melt glass. Aunt Viv tries but can't hold it. I get that feeling. You have to look away to protect your delicate insides. Mom exhales through her nostrils, an extended, low hiss of constricted air.

"You didn't," she says to Aunt Viv.

"Vick, there's no need to —"

But there's nowhere to go from there without admitting everything, so Aunt Viv stops herself.

Sean is watching all of this intently. Very, very interested. And looking more and more pissed off by the millisecond. "You screwed me, Vivian."

"Don't be so dramatic."

"I should report this."

"You do what you need to do."

"But you know that I can't —"

"As I said —"

"Because what do I show the court, yeah? The digital record? Spotless. But then they say they've seen the news. *Oh, right, that*, I say. *Well, I've been hacked*. They say, *Course you have, so let's order an inquiry*. I say, *Great. Easy*. Until they discover that I've been dating the hacker."

"I'm not a hacker."

"I can't believe you did this to us, Vivian," Mom says.

Aunt Viv winces but doesn't respond. She glances over at me. *Remember the plan*, the look says.

Mom tries to get a response out of her again and again, but still Vivian doesn't say anything. Sticking to her resolution that you can't be incriminated by something that never gets said. She folds her arms again and simply looks at the floor through the onslaught. Sean occasionally pitches in or answers a question, but I can see he's wrung out. Resigned. All he sees is a bleak, unemployed future. If not worse. He hasn't done anything other than his job, but he still got led on and used, and he'll live out the consequences.

Meanwhile the person who started it all fades away in a distant hospital bed. Jesse will never face a trial. He'll never answer for what he's done. I can't get my head around that. He was all about accountability. I remember one time when I broke a spoke on my bike trying to tighten it. I heard somewhere that you have to keep them tight, not realizing that cheap kids' bikes aren't made that way. The spoke bent and popped out and I tried to ignore it, but a bike needs every spoke to work or it limps along on a warped rim that you can't hide from anyone. "Stop," Jesse said when I tried to worm my way out of it. "Don't make it worse by lying. One, take responsibility. Two, fix what you've broken. It's that simple. Clear as mud?" But there are some mistakes that can never be fixed. Sometimes what's stolen can never be recovered.

This can't get that far. I won't let it.

I slap the coffee table with my hand and stand. The effect is instantaneous. The living room goes quiet and all eyes find their way to me. Aunt Viv sees what I'm about to do and she moves from the door, shaking her head. But I give her a look of my own, hoping it's strong enough, and she stops.

"I'm sorry," I say. "This is all my fault."

"Wait," Mom says. "Let's —"

"No, Mom. I have to own my shit."

Own your shit. Jesse's language. ("But tell your mom I said *stuff*, right?") Mom's eyes widen and shimmer. She starts to say something more but I hold up a hand.

"Visiting Jesse was my idea. I thought he wanted me to go. I had to go, too, I guess. It wasn't what I expected, but —" Then it's my eyes that are filling. The disappointment of it. The reality. I wipe my palm across my eyes and look at Mom. "It is what it is, right?"

It is what it is. More of Jesse's voice, channelled through me. Time to let go.

She nods and gives me a small, sad smile. "It is what it is."

I take a deep breath and turn toward Sean. "I went to Windsor last night."

"No kidding," he says, rolling his eyes.

"If Aunt Viv restores the system to show the trip, can you charge me properly?"

"Is she admitting that she hacked me?"

Aunt Viv glares at him but says nothing. But I don't think it matters. I can see some strength return to Sean's bearing. He's seeing a way out of this.

I say, "I'm admitting I left town. Can you charge me?"

"I don't charge anyone, remember? I'll merely report that you broke your sentencing conditions. The consequence will be up to the court, although for you I suspect it'll be just an extension, rather than escalation. You'll have to tell the judge where you went."

"And why," Mom says to me.

"I know. I'll take whatever comes."

"You must've had help," Sean says.

I look at the floor, not wanting to say anything to get Gal and Mia in trouble, but I nod. It's pretty obvious I couldn't have gone on my own. Sean waits for me to offer more, but I won't. This is on me.

I don't know how long we all stay suspended like that, between what's said and unsaid, but finally Sean sighs and sits back on the couch.

"Ah, screw it," he says. "Don't tell me. Frankly, I don't need the extra paperwork."

"Thank you."

"Don't thank me, Wendell. There are no guarantees here." A pause. "They must be some amazing friends."

"The best."

"All right," Sean says. "This stays with me and I leave them out of it. As long as the other thing is taken care of, yeah?"

"Aunt Viv? Will you do it?"

There's so much resistance in her. She scowls and spends a long time looking at the floor, her eyes darting left and right. Weighing and figuring. Finally, without looking up at anyone, she nods. Sean's relief takes him over so completely, he looks like he could cry. Seeing that perfect lack of a digital trail. Saved.

He gets up and mumbles a good night, tells me he'll see me in the morning, and walks out. I lock the door behind him, peeking through the blinds. I watch for a short while, but there's only one news truck still there. Dark. No movement. Gathering dew on the windshield. Like they've gone to sleep. But I'm sure they haven't gone away or forgotten.

When I return to the living room, only Aunt Viv remains, sitting in the easy chair with her laptop. Already immersed, her brow scrunched up in concentration. She doesn't look up but tells me that Mom has gone back to her workshop, that she's pretty upset. Proud that her kid is taking responsibility but also worried what his actions and admissions will bring down on him. I go downstairs and stand outside her door.

"Mom?"

No answer. No sounds. No light cutting under the door to tell me she's present and busy and hopefully okay.

"I'm sorry."

Still nothing. I turn and go into my room and lie down on the bed. It's not that late, but I don't want to come out again. Something in me needs to lie in the darkness without doing anything. Apart from wondering about the impossibility of doing the right thing.

ON YOUR TERMS

Before work on Monday morning, I pause on our side step before heading over to the park. I'm surprised to see that the street is empty of news people. They were there all day yesterday. I guess our story isn't important enough for constant coverage. Media owners with tight budgets, refusing overtime.

I step away from the house and head west toward the park. A now-familiar rhythm. Aside from wondering when the media circus will return, it feels like any other day in this messed-up summer. Cooler, though. The sun isn't as high. Later sunrise. For the first time, I'm wearing a long-sleeve T-shirt under my safety vest. There's a depth to the coolness. Maybe fall isn't so far away.

I didn't see Mom at breakfast. Only Aunt Viv and Gramma Jan were up, getting ready for a last-minute appointment at the hospital. Something to do with adjusting the cocktail of drugs the doctors have Gramma Jan on. She was as pale as yesterday, and there were new tremors in her hands as she tried to eat her breakfast. She had a hard time with it. Her toast shook on its way to her mouth. Aunt Viv had to peel her hard-boiled egg for her.

Behind me, there's the quick beep of a car horn. I turn to see a small silver car pull up beside the house. Must be an Uber for the trip to the hospital. Aunt Viv emerges from the house and leans into the car's window to say something to the driver. He turns on his yellow hazards. She sees me and waves before heading back inside.

I walk quickly, trying to get a little heat in my bones. The park is quiet. The sudden coolness keeping the less diehard walkers and runners away.

Sean meets me at the field house with a stack of paperwork to read. He must've been up late to get it ready so quickly. Gal is starting his day, too, but lets Sean and me use his office. There's almost no smell of weed today, as though Gal has aired the place out for us.

"I will walk now," he says, getting up from the tiny desk. "Take your time."

"Thank you," Sean says.

His words are professional but clipped as short as a brush cut. Like he's still processing his unwilling role in my production. Like he doesn't want to say too much, too soon. Like he's deciding how pissed off to be at anyone who might've been involved. After Gal steps out, Sean rushes through the formalities about my admission of guilt and what happens next, and I have to sign a few forms.

"Your mum has a few things to sign, too," he says. "I'll head over to your place next."

"She wasn't up when I left."

"Is that unusual?"

"Very. She's an early riser."

"Well, this isn't like every other day, I suppose."

Sean's voice rises lightly at the end of his statement. Almost a question but not quite. I don't respond. What would I say? I haven't seen an "every other day" for a long time. All my days seem prone to shift in unexpected directions.

He gets up and slides the paperwork back into its folder as he walks to the door. He pauses, silhouetted against the brightness of the morning.

"Vivian came through, by the way. Your trip to Windsor is clearly indicated. The chronological vectors and my lack of immediate response are anomalous enough for an investigation —"

"Chronological vectors? And what investigation?"

He shakes his head, almost comic in its suddenness, and gives a small, sad smile. "Right. Sorry. I had your aunt in my mind as I said it. She'd know."

"She would."

"Your ankle monitor tracks speed, time, and distance, yeah? So it's clear you drove out of the city, which normally would've triggered a breach alert. That I didn't immediately register the breach or try to locate you is enough to get me in trouble, and enough for a records audit."

"Does that happen?"

"Hasn't yet," he says. "But it could. My work phone is tracked, of course, so if anyone notices my little GPS dot sitting at home while you're zipping to Windsor and back …"

"Right. Bad news. Got it."

Without another word Sean turns away and disappears through the door. His lack of farewell hangs in the cool, damp air like an accusation. I sigh, put on my helmet, and follow. Sean is already at his car, opening his door. Gal is out here, too, working on a service door down the side of the building. Tightening the hinges with a screwdriver. Out of earshot. Far enough to be polite.

"Do I need to worry about him?" Gal asks as I approach. He doesn't look up from his task.

"I don't think so. My admission seems to be enough."

"Good."

"Can I use your phone? I'd like to call Mia."

"It is early, my friend."

"She'll be up. She's an early riser."

"No, I was thinking of her parents. They might not know about —"

"And my call will only make them curious. Got it."

"Good," he says again.

And that's it. I wait for something more, but he is reimmersed in the task. The hinges needing all his attention. Like I wasn't there.

So.

Spike in hand, I walk out into the field. The dew on the grass is thick and cold and in seconds soaking into my toes. I head into the woods across the way, thinking I can stay on the paths until the sun gets high enough to burn off the moisture.

Time passes slowly. I find only the occasional piece of trash. Lots of time to think. And to fall into that old habit of waiting for Jesse's voice. Which doesn't come. It feels strange doing the job without knowing whether or not his voice could arrive at any moment. Yet what could he say now? I don't know how to feel about that.

FAR FROM PERFECT

Mom finds me before lunch. I'm working the treeline on the far side of the aviary. Eastern exposure. Full sun. The grass here is dry. I'm avoiding the shadows.

She's dressed in jeans and a long open sweater, her hair in a simple ponytail. Which is surprising — she prefers to pile her hair on top of her head in loose bunches, cool off her neck and out of her work. She looks tired but at peace. Her eyes still carry the dark shadows underneath but also a calmness I haven't seen in a while. And she's going grey. More than occasional streaks of white and silver line her light-brown hair. I don't think I've noticed that before. A green plastic shopping bag hangs from her left hand, bumping against her leg as she walks. She smiles and waves.

"Lunch?" she says, holding up the bag.

"Is everything all right?"

"You're a hard one to find. Good thing I ran into the park manager."

"Gal. He's my supervisor."

"Right. Funny I've never met him before. What did you call him?"

I say the name again.

"Oh, okay. He introduced himself to me by his last name. Amar, I think it was."

"I've only known him as Gal. Sean called him Gary on the first day."

Her head tilts and she purses her lips. Nods. "Right. Gal. So that's who Viv was talking about. The one who drove you to see Jesse. Now that fits in a little better."

"Mia came, too."

"I know."

"So are you all right? What's up?"

"Your head looks good. The stitches, I mean. There's barely a scar."

"Mom …"

"Let's find a spot to sit down, okay?"

I point at a couple of benches on the south side of the aviary and ask if those will do. The sun is shining on the outside cages. Birds are visible in only one of them. A handful of tiny green and yellow parakeets, squawking loud enough you'd think there were dozens. Mom smiles at the sight and the noise and says that it's perfect. We walk over together. I watch her closely. Part of me is happy that she looks so at ease, but the rest of me doesn't fully trust it. You can be afraid of a sudden peace that appears in a loved one too soon.

We sit on opposite ends of the bench, leaving a space between us for the meal. Mom opens the bag and lays out the food. Bread. Sandwich meat. Cheese. Mustard.

Apples. Yogurt cups. A couple of those miniature bags of chips you give out at Halloween. She wordlessly assembles a sandwich and hands it over to me. Bologna and cheddar and mustard. A new combination to me. I take a bite and chew, Mom watching me as I eat. Expectant.

"It's good," I say with my mouth still full. "Really good."

She looks pleased. "That was my favourite sandwich when I was a kid. I'm glad you like it."

I always thought PBJ was her favourite. The things you can't know, I suppose. I finish chewing and swallow. "What's going on?"

"I had a craving. Bologna sandwiches and chips and a picnic. Lucky for us the store had everything." She reaches into the bag and pulls out the receipt, crumples it up, and worries the small wad of paper between her fingers.

"No, I mean —"

"I know what you mean, Dills. In a minute. First things first."

She flicks the wadded-up receipt back into the bag and pulls the far side of her sweater across her body. From a small pocket sewn to the front she withdraws a brass-coloured object engraved with an unfamiliar style of writing. And something else I haven't seen in her hands since before the shooting. A small joint the size of a .22-calibre short round, held tight in a binder clip. A pinner. She and Jesse used that word whenever they smoked up together. Their ritual. They'd grin at each other, and whoever had the joint would hold it up before sparking up and would say "Pinner time, lover!" like it was a horny, sacred toast.

"Really? Now?"

"Yes, really," she says. "Yes, now."

I watch Mom place the joint between her lips and open the brass lighter and flick the wheel. She touches the flame to the tip of the joint and breathes in so deeply she might hold the entire summer in her lungs. She exhales and smiles, closing her eyes. A single tear escapes, but she lets it course down her cheek. A good tear. She doesn't stop smiling as it dashes under her chin and soaks into her collar. She inhales again. Exhales. I wait.

"This must look strange," she says.

"Wow, yes."

"Mr. Amar — Gal — hooked me up."

"Wait, what? He did?"

"I could smell it on him. So after I introduced myself, I just asked."

"And he gave it to you?"

She inhales again, holds it, then blows the yellowish smoke at the sky. "Yep. Rolled it right there in front of me. Clipped it. Gave me his old army Zippo, said I could return it later."

I glance at the lighter again. The engraved script is Hebrew, of course. There is also a crest, like you'd see on a military shoulder flash. And nicks and scratches and dents. The tarnish of the brass a long history.

"This is so weird," I say.

"I'm drowning in weird, Dills. This feels normal."

What do I say to that? It's so accurate. Maybe I understand far too much.

The pinner is already almost burned down. She tokes a final time, this one even longer and deeper. Her eyes narrow but shining. As she exhales she talks about how she and her friends used to run all over the park. The secret places they found. I think about Mia's spot in the hedge and wonder if Mom might've used the same space. She talks about how they used to make fun of the lawn-bowling-club members, their white clothes and hats and formal ways. About how old they seemed to her and her friends.

And she laughs about the poison ivy, how mad Gramma Jan used to get whenever a new rash appeared. I look at my own wrist, realizing that the bandage fell off at some point, but don't say anything. I let her talk. She hasn't said this much since the shooting. There's a fragile need in her I'm afraid to frighten away. I can pinpoint the hour when it began, of course, but it feels undefinable, too, like it's possible that entire histories could get forgotten.

"You saw him," she says. "You saw Jesse."

I nod.

"I never went to the hospital after the shooting. Sometimes I wanted to. Mostly I didn't. The media was camped out, of course. But I was so angry."

"Everyone was. Is."

"But not you."

"I am now. He's given up. He's not even willing to try to come home, to face me, to make one thing right."

"You shouldn't carry this."

"I don't know how I can't."

"Me being angry at him has nothing to do with why. I'm as mad at myself for not seeing …" She sighs and looks at the distant trees for a few long seconds. "Of course, there were all the little things. Little signs. Like breadcrumbs to what happened. But —"

"He always seemed okay to me. Normal."

"Maybe he was to you. For you."

"Everyone hates him."

She snorts. "These days people don't know what to hate. Or how."

"They all talk about him like —"

"No. Something inside him cracked. Something beyond his strength. That's it. People need to think there was more, but he was just broken. That's it."

"I didn't know you felt that way. I thought —"

"I'm sorry, Dills."

I hold out my hand and she places the lighter into it. I flick it open. Closed. Open. Closed. The sound of it echoes sharp around us. "I'm sorry, too, Mom. For all of this."

"'Sorry is as sorry does,' as Gramma Jan likes to say."

One of the most confusing things I've ever heard. Yet it makes a kind of sense, too. *Sorry* needs to get said, but it can't really fix anything, can't bring anyone back. Mom reaches out and fingers the edge of my safety vest above my shoulder, worrying a spot where the nylon is beginning to fray. A mom thing. Looking for something to repair.

"Tell me about the trip," she says. "Tell me every-thing."

So I do. Every detail. When I get to the part where I first saw him, I have trouble getting it out. My mind and soul pushing those details so far down I can barely grab them. Scars. The pieces of a person lost to gunfire. How a damaged person can be there and not there. The details hurt when they claw themselves out, and I fight myself as I'm sharing them. Even with my mom, who needs to know. We both lose it a couple of times. But you know what? Some amazing things get said. But those are just for me and her. I hope that's all right.

"So now we just wait," she says. "For the end."

"Yeah."

I get up and help her pack away the garbage. She tells me she's going to sit for a while and enjoy the sun and the quiet and the sweet little high she's riding. I put on my helmet and take hold of the spike, but as I'm about to walk away, the sounds of hard laughter and bikes being bashed over rough pathways clatter through the trees beyond the aviary. Three boys burst out of the trailhead and skid to a stop in a cloud of their own dust a few dozen feet away.

As the air clears, I recognize them. It's Pat and a couple of friends who move around the school in a rough, awkward pack. Nameless drones. When Pat sees me and my mom, his eyes widen. He turns to his friends and tells them to head over to the basketball court, that he'll catch up. They snicker and give him a hard time about it, but roll away, laughing, when he threatens them in a voice too low for me to hear. When they're safely away, Pat pedals over, dismounts, and leans his bike against its kickstand. The canteen sling is a diagonal, insulting slash across his chest. My hand clenches tighter around the spike. Only he can ruin a moment so perfectly.

"Hey," he says. And that's it.

"I recognize you," Mom says. "You're Patrick."

"Yes, ma'am. From Wendell's school."

Well, if that word doesn't threaten to knock me out cold. *Ma'am*. That he used it. That he knows it at all. "One, always be polite to your elders, no matter what. Two, always introduce yourself and say *sir* and *ma'am*. Clear as mud?" Jesse's voice — the one I hear in my memories — arrives untouched from the past, so pure I almost respond out loud. But, no. Not in front of Pat. Not again. No more material for him.

"What do you want?" I ask, hard.

Ordinarily Mom would snap at me to try again, to remember my manners. But she doesn't. She understands what fed my stupid, misguided need to go after him with the knife. My actions not justified, of course, but there's no need to paint things gold when they're already stained red.

"Hey, uh, I saw the news. I had no idea."

"So?"

"What happened to you … with your dad … it …" He stops. Looks down at his feet. Kicks the grass. "Well, it sucks."

On a scale you can't imagine, Pat. But there's no way I'm talking to you about it. You look like you want to say more but I'll stand here, spike in hand, if you don't mind. Waiting for you to rip something open again.

He looks almost ready to say something else, but instead he shakes his head, quick, like he's flinging away an unpleasant bit of business. He unslings the canteen and holds it out, the pouch dangling in the chasm between us. I reach out and take it back. There is the faintest smell of bleach. Like he washed and disinfected it. Must be my imagination.

It's not enough. Not even close. But Mom isn't feeling any of that. She's looking at him with a sad smile and nodding. An appreciative, half smile you allow to burn through your grief. Momentary. Maybe because of the weed. Maybe something else. Pat looks up and sees her face and puffs out a breath. Embarrassed but relieved. Then he turns his attention back to the ground, kicking some poor bunch of grass free from its roots.

"So, yeah," he says. "Okay."

And with that he turns back to his bike, mounts it, and rides away across the grass. No goodbye. Mom and I share a look. Learning to accept what's been offered. Whenever we can.

YOUR STORY

On my way home that evening, when I head back to the field house to store my stuff, I see a familiar blue car parked on the street nearby. Walters comes out of the building, cellphone in hand. Escorted by Gal, who shakes his head and turns back into the gloom. Looks like he's not co-operating. Good. She leans against the wall and raises the phone, closes her eyes, and talks to it. Recording details. I change direction slightly, hoping she won't open her eyes and see me. I can keep my garbage-collecting gear at home for one night. I'll explain it to Gal in the morning. He'll understand.

Wishful thinking. Not a millisecond after I make my decision, Walters opens her eyes and zeroes in on my safety vest. Smiles. Steps away from the building and walks, fast, toward me.

I stop and wait for her. In that same millisecond, what her presence means has become clear. Talking to

Gal means she found out the specifics of my sentencing. And if she was able to find out about that, well, everything has been laid bare.

"So now you know," I say when she draws close enough.

A momentary look of surprise. She nods. "I do."

"Are the other reporters camped out at our place?"

"Probably. Or at least some of them."

"What do you want?"

"I want to tell your story."

"You and everyone else."

"Not everyone wants to tell this part."

"Isn't that what every reporter says?"

"I was in court, remember? No one else is trying to go this deep, to look beyond your trip and the shooting. I think you have a lot more to say. As a survivor, sure. But about moving here, too. About your stepdad, if you want. And obviously with your mom's permission."

Stepdad. It's not a passcode or anything, but no one else has had the sensitivity to use the proper term. And because the shooting happened in a school, to kids, there's been a lack of survivor perspective. I get that. Kids are vulnerable. They need space to heal. But part of me thinks it would be good if other people could understand more about what happened. From those who were there. In our own words. Reconstructions and interviews with first responders and hospital staff only go so far. How can we get better unless we prevent the tragedy of children knowing how black and surprisingly small the muzzles of assault rifles are? Of children seeing friends butchered in front of them. The sights, the sounds, the smells. The voids that are left when friends and teachers are snatched away.

"I guess that makes sense," I say.

"I'm glad."

"Mom grew up here."

"I know."

"You went to school together."

"Yeah."

"She brought me back here after the shooting. Home, for her. Not for me. It's hard to think about, much less talk about."

"I get that. I'm sorry."

"A lot of people say they're sorry."

"Please don't misunderstand. Obviously, I hate that you or anyone went through what you went through. But I'm more sorry that we can be so awful to survivors. The media, I mean. I think we can do better."

Uh huh. My head tilts, skeptical.

But she beats me there. She winces, as though she's only then heard herself. "God, I sound like such a cliché. Anyhow, take this."

Walters reaches into her satchel — which is identical to one Mom carries, only hers is a deep maroon, while Walters's is a coyote brown — and pulls out a stack of business cards held together by a stained rubber band. I like that. Functional. Plain. She slides a card out and holds it out to me. Blue newspaper logo. Her name and contact info in raised black ink. White cardstock.

"Call any time. Day, night, whenever."

"Okay."

"And don't worry. We have fickle appetites. Things will quiet down quickly after everyone files their stories about your most recent adventures."

"Which you'll do, too."

"True. I have bills to pay, after all. But there's no deadline for the bigger story. Take your time. When you're ready."

"If I'm ready."

"Right. And make sure you tell your mom."

"I will."

She says a quiet goodbye and walks to her car. Drives off. I stuff the card into my pocket and go home, ducking my head and saying nothing to the full-auto questions from the reporters. There are fewer of them now, but those who remain make up for it with increased repetition and intensity.

GOODBYE, PART II

Mom's in the kitchen chopping vegetables. The smells of heat and chopped things fill the air. She smiles when I walk in and puts a finger to her lips. Gramma Jan's dozing in the living room easy chair, head back and mouth open, a hardcover open on her lap. Mom comes over and gives me a hug.

"Smells good," I say, my voice low.

"Thanks. I'm hungry today." She winks.

"I can tell."

There is a faint skunkiness wafting from her hair and clothes. She releases me and goes back to the cutting board and her ingredients laid out on the counter. Carrots. Celery. Onion. Zucchini. Brown rice measured out in a cup. All for the pot of gently boiling water on the stove. I can't remember the last time she made homemade soup. Homemade anything, really.

"Did Cathy find you? She stopped by right after I got back from our lunch."

"Cathy?"

"Walters. Sorry."

I nod.

"What do you think of her?" she asks, lifting the cutting board above the hot water and scraping in the chopped veggies. She wipes her hands on a dishtowel. "Did she tell you what she wants to write?"

"Yes."

Mom pours the rice into the pot. "Me, too."

"Part of me wants to trust her."

"I don't. I'm not sure what good it would do. Talking to her made me want to pack us up again and find somewhere else to start over."

"I don't want to run away again."

"Me neither, Dills. But —"

Mom's cellphone rings. The chimey bells and vibration are nauseatingly sudden and loud in the stillness of the house. She reaches over as quickly as she can, but the damage has been done.

Gramma Jan stirs, her eyes fluttering open. "Answer the damn thing, Victoria." Her voice like river stone dumped from a truck.

"Sorry. I thought I had the ringer off." Mom taps the green button. "Hello?"

She listens, frowns, and looks at me. She places a hand over the microphone. "Reduce the heat when the soup boils, okay?"

"Sure."

"Thanks," she says over her shoulder as she heads into the family room. I try to hear what she's saying, but she's keeping her voice down.

Gramma Jan groans as she gets up from the chair behind me. She's paler now, almost transparent. Beads of sweat appear on her lip, despite the coolness of the house. Only huge, deep pain can do that. She shuffles into the kitchen, leaning on a new cane. High tech. Like you could build an airplane out of it.

She sees me looking. "Stupid thing. Made the mistake of falling in front of the doctor."

"Can I get you anything? Your meds?"

"Hell, no. They got me on the strong stuff now. Bottles and bottles of it. Makes it hard to think. And go to the bathroom. God, painkillers bung you up something good."

"Gross. TMI, Gramma."

"TMI?"

"Too much information."

She snorts, but it brings a fresh flash of pain. Her features twist and she has to exhale long and slow to manage it. She sits down on one of the kitchen chairs, rests the cane across her thighs.

"Gramma —?"

"NEI, you mean. Not enough information. If telling you about my inability to take a shit keeps you from making the same mistakes I did, so be it."

"Mistakes?"

"Mistakes, regrets. They pile up."

We hear the beeping of the keypad on the side door and a clunk as the door is closed hard on the frame. Enough to rattle the other doors in the house, old things on old hinges. Aunt Viv comes in, shaking her head, her mouth set. She drops a loud, long, acidic F-bomb. When she sees Gramma Jan and me standing there, she hooks a thumb over her shoulder toward the reporters outside. "Leeches," she says. "Every damn one of them."

"Language, Vivian. In this house —"

Aunt Viv rolls her eyes. "Yeah, yeah, purity of word and thought and all that. Wonder where I get it from."

"Don't be sarcastic with me, young lady."

Aunt Viv moves beside Gramma Jan and leans over for a side hug. "How are you feeling?"

"Oh, I'm super, dear." Her voice is exaggerated, that of an old woman in a classic movie. She holds up the cane. "I'm bionic, don't you know!"

I'm watching this in real time and yet I can't believe it. Half apologies and hugs and witty repartee. Makes me feel like I'm witnessing the interactions of some alien family in a parallel universe.

Aunt Viv lifts her chin in greeting to me. I give her a low wave. No words right now. All this bizarrely comforting strangeness is leaving me without much to say. She holds up and shakes her keys, declaring that her car is fixed and humming along, which you'd expect given how much coin she just dropped on the dealership. Her phone beeps and she glances at the screen. Frowns.

"Bad news?" Gramma Jan asks.

"No," Aunt Viv says, distracted. "I was expecting that by now he'd …" She stops.

"He?" Gramma Jan asks.

Aunt Viv shakes her head, embarrassed to have revealed as much as she did.

"She's talking about Sean," I say to Gramma Jan.

"You're too good for him, Vivian."

Aunt Viv squirms. Visibly.

I ask, "He hasn't come around?"

"I wasn't expecting a full pardon or anything, but still."

"He was pretty pissed."

"Still is, apparently," Aunt Viv says, looking perplexed. An unfamiliar emotion for her. Usually it's all confidence and brashness. As though she fully expected that Sean's emotions should be as hackable as the tech she deals with. But apparently his anger is offline. And all his own.

Mom comes back into the kitchen, looking like someone has punched her somewhere tender. The three of us watch her put the phone down and move to the stove. She stirs the soup without looking at it. She isn't seeing us either, even as she starts talking.

"That was the lawyer. Jesse's and my lawyer, I mean. From Windsor."

She pauses. Gramma Jan, Aunt Viv, and I exchange looks but wait for her to continue.

"You know that the lawyer has power of attorney. But the hospital also has her as Jesse's first emergency contact. Not me. God, what a fight that was. Me, trying to build space between what happened and our family, and the hospital administrator needing to fill in his forms —"

"What did she say?" I hear myself asking.

"I was worried that someone might access the records. I didn't want our names to —"

"Victoria Sims," Gramma Jan says, her voice as firm as I've ever heard it. "Tell us."

Mom takes a deep breath. Exhales. "Jesse's dying."

"And?" says Aunt Viv.

"He's dying, Viv."

"He's been dying for months."

Mom's mouth opens and closes. Aunt Viv's words true but as blunt as ever.

"He never woke up," I say. "We've kind of known this was coming, right?"

"I guess that's true," Mom says, her hand coming up to rub her right temple. Hard. "But the lawyer said that his organs have begun failing. That it's just a matter of time."

"I don't know what that means," I say.

"No one does, kiddo. It's just what they say."

Aunt Viv and Gramma Jan offer advice, weigh in on next steps, on what it could mean. I can hear the attempt at comfort in there, the need to help shore up what might crumble. Well meant, all of it. But it basically centres on getting ready to move on from this. To let him die while we carry on here. Embark on the next phase of our involuntarily shifted life. Like the ground has become permanently uneven but we can work and learn to get our balance back. They're eclipsing Jesse, though. And not seeing a mother, either. Not seeing a wife.

There are lots of words but Mom isn't hearing any of them. She's moved herself into that hazy place you go when you understand that grief is on the way but you can't quite see its shape.

It feels like a long time before Mom does anything, but finally she moves. She turns off the stove and slides the soup to the cool space between the elements. She picks up her cellphone. Unlocks it. Dials. Gramma Jan and Aunt Viv seem to notice that Mom is moving independently of their ideas, and they fall silent as she makes the call.

"Hello? Are you still open? … Good … I know it's late notice, but do you have anything available for tonight? … Windsor … A large sedan would be fine … Yes, I need a pickup."

She rattles off our address, thanks the faceless person on the other end of the line, and disconnects the call. Looks around the room.

"I need to pack," she says. "He'll be here in fifteen minutes."

"I want to come with you," I say.

She shakes her head and points down at my ankle monitor. "You literally can't, Dills."

"This doesn't feel finished."

"It's not. Not yet."

Mom lays a hand on my shoulder as she passes me. She tells me that I'm first on her list of people to call when there's anything to update. Then she's gone upstairs to her room to pack.

Gramma Jan and Aunt Viv resume their conversation, quieter now, as though they're afraid Mom will hear them through the ceiling. They talk for a few minutes. Aunt Viv's phone chimes a few times with new texts but she ignores it. They fall silent. *All talked out, thank God*, Jesse would say. He hates small talk.

Gramma Jan stands, slow and fragile and shaking, leaning on her space-age cane. "I'm taking my old bones to bed, kids."

"But Vicky's still —"

"Tell me in the morning, Vivian. I'm done in."

Aunt Viv nods, moves to Gramma Jan's side, and takes her arm, which sparks a round of weak but flinty swearing. She doesn't refuse the help, though.

Mom comes back into the kitchen as they make it to the hallway door, a canvas bag slung over her shoulder. She has jotted a few notes down on a piece of paper that she pushes into Aunt Viv's hand. She faces her mother and sister and tells them to take care of me. To watch out for me. She goes quiet. So do they.

A series of short knocks on the door fills the space. Everyone looks at it. Mom shifts, adjusting the strap of her bag. More silence. And another series of knocks, louder this time. Mom calls out that she's on her way and she'll just be a minute.

"You should get going," Aunt Viv says. "Call whenever you need to."

"I will."

Gramma Jan sighs. Loud. "I don't know what to say to you, Victoria. I'm so tired."

"Me too, Mom."

"Just come home when you can. This is home now."

Mom breathes deep and folds Gramma Jan into a tentative hug. Like holding a butterfly. But Gramma Jan drops her cane and grabs her daughter hard. Fierce. Long. Whispers something into Mom's ear I can't make out. Mom nods. Aunt Viv comes in and joins them. Full eyes everywhere. I feel like I'm witnessing history.

Mom wipes a tear away and smiles at her mother. Eyes narrowed. Tells Gramma Jan not to die while she's away. Says she might need her around for what happens next. Gramma Jan laughs, quick and harsh, like it's all she can manage, and says something in her failing voice about hell freezing over and wild horses and unfinished business. Aunt Viv picks the cane up from the hardwood floor and helps Gramma Jan into the bedroom down the hall.

I walk Mom out. The reporters are gone for the night. No cameras flash. No questions are machine-gunned at us. The driver, a tall, lanky guy with bad skin, wearing an ill-fitting shirt and rental-company tie, offers to carry her bag. She refuses. Of course she does. But she does link her arm in mine and hold tight, like my weight can keep us grounded.

At the car, she tosses the bag into the back seat and faces me. She gives me a hug and I return it because that's what you do. But I wait for her to let go first. She's holding so tight and long and has her face buried in my neck. I realize she hasn't held on to me like this since the hospital released me to her after Windsor. So much of the blood covering me ended up on her that she had to throw out her clothes, too.

She tells me how sorry she is for all of this. How proud she is of me. Which is awkward because she's been amazing, but now doesn't seem like the time to argue. And finally, she tells me she'll say goodbye to Jesse for me. Because she knows, somehow, that I didn't get to.

Part III
Everywhere

POTENTIAL

Mom's been in Windsor for more than a week. Jesse is holding on longer than anyone predicted. I don't know how to feel about that. "Death is a part of life," he said to me once. "No sense in dwelling on it. We all end up in the same place. Pushing up daisies. The great dirt nap, ha ha." But even as he spoke, I could tell that his eyes didn't believe the words. And now the lie is clearer. Death is more than a part of our lives. It's a twisted blood relative who refuses to leave. Maybe ever.

The cordless handset rests beside me on the side step. Still warm from my nightly phone call with Mom. She calls after supper to fill me in on the day's happenings. Tonight we didn't have much to talk about. The medical staff is monitoring Jesse. The reporters saw Mom arrive and made her part of the story for a day or two. Her lawyer threatened legal action, so the hospital got better at keeping the reporters away from the ward. But they've been waiting outside the building less and less often anyhow — Mom hasn't commented and Jesse hasn't died, so there's nothing to feed their fading appetites. Tonight, without the scrutiny, Mom sounded more at ease, a little more like herself.

Mia sits next to me. She arrived while I was on the phone. She hands me a glass of lemonade with mint, a gift from her mother. Everyone knows about me and Windsor now. There are gifts. Letters. Emails. Floral bouquets. Boxes of candy. Anonymous casseroles appearing on our doorstep. Mia's mom keeps a small thermos in the fridge filled with the lemonade for Mia to bring over every night. Her dad in the dark about it. A mom's tiny, sympathetic rebellion.

Mia one-arms me closer so she can kiss my cheek. Her lips are warm. "How's your mom?"

"Tired."

"I bet."

"Waiting for Jesse to …" I stop. I still can't say it. "Uh, waiting is hard enough, but this thing with Gramma Jan is stressing her out."

There was an episode this afternoon. Over the past few days, Gramma Jan's pain has been getting worse and worse. She refuses to take anything stronger than Tylenol, and the pain affects her balance and her ability to make good decisions. When I got home from the park there was an ambulance parked beside the house. Lights off, the paramedics moving around in no great hurry. Just another call to an elderly person's home for just another fall. Gramma Jan was inside the vehicle, strapped to the gurney and pissed about it. There wasn't time for many details, but Aunt Viv said there'd been a bad fall and a blackout and a long period where Gramma Jan didn't remember who she was.

Their departure has left another hole in the house. I sat by myself for a long time before messaging Mia on my iPod and asking her to come over.

"Any news from Vivian?"

"No."

"She's tough, your grandma."

"She is."

We sit in silence. I sip the lemonade and feel the tartness and sweetness competing on my taste buds. The high of the mint at the back of my mouth. Delicious and foreign and slightly subversive.

"And Jesse?"

I shrug. "The same."

"How? Aren't all his —"

"He's going, but no one can say when."

"That sucks."

"Mom sounds like she wants this settled. Me too, kind of. And not."

"Yeah."

Settled. Weird to say the word, much less think about its meaning. Feels like fantasy. Way out there. Glimpsed only in my imagination. That thing other people get to have while not realizing they have it at all.

"What's this?" Mia moves the cordless phone and picks up the envelope pinned underneath. The phone a paperweight to keep the letter from blowing away. She runs a finger over the printed crest and return address of the youth-court division. Looks at me. "May I?"

I nod. "Sean dropped it off today in the park."

She slides the carefully folded paper from the torn envelope. Reads it. It's only a couple of paragraphs.

"So you have a date for the hearing," she says.

"A week before school starts."

"Are you worried?"

"Not really. Sean says he's already spoken to the judge. He thinks she'll add more hours of service rather than escalate."

"Good. I'm not ready for prison romance."

"Ha ha."

Mia folds the letter and gently, precisely, slides the paper into the envelope. I watch her hands as she returns the letter to its spot on the cement. You couldn't call her hands delicate or graceful, but they're perfectly steady. Surgical. She sees me looking, laughs, and does a pantomime of a hand-model presenting a piece of jewellery, a bracelet maybe. I can almost see diamonds there, ablaze in the setting sun. She leans in, her arms sliding around my middle, and rests her head against my shoulder. We watch the sun fall toward the horizon. I have her warmth on one side and the failing summer evening's coolness on the other. I shiver.

Mia asks, "Should we go inside?"

"Not yet."

"Let me get you a blanket or something. You're a popsicle."

"Okay."

She gets up, opens the door, and disappears into the house. A cicada in a nearby tree starts trilling. The sound goes on for a minute or so before weakening in a long, steady decline. And silence again. Odd to hear one this late in the day. Or at this temperature. Usually they do their best to deafen me from the trees only on the hottest afternoons. Mia returns with the fleece throw blanket from the family room sofa and wraps us both up in it.

I start talking. Again. I've been doing that more and more since Mom left. I tell myself I'm not going to, but Mia sits or walks with me and out everything comes. Maybe tonight it's the blanket's sudden warmth that does it, loosening me up like injured tissue. I don't know. But my memories come out in a jumbled mess. Details I've never told anyone. About questions I'll never get the answers to. About Windsor and Ethan and the blood and the sounds I still hear when I close my eyes or try to fall asleep. About best friends who die afraid and alone and so horribly that you don't want to make any more friends because they can be taken so easily. About Gramma Jan, how there are a thousand kinds of cancer we have to worry about. About school and fear and life and how nothing is certain until it is.

I feel like there should be millions of tears, but my voice never breaks, not once. Because of Mia. At some point I realize she hasn't said a word but has reached out and taken my hand, has pulled it onto her lap, and is now holding it with both of her own. Her wrestling hands, so unbelievably warm and calloused and strong. I think about how a friend can hold another friend together. About how good that is. How necessary.

Beside me on the step, the cordless phone begins to ring, echoing along the sidewalk and down the street. NO CALLER ID is splashed bold across the amber screen. It feels like a long time before I pick it up, but it's probably not. Maybe a second or two. But so many thoughts fill that instant. About what happens next. What might get said. It could be nothing at all, everyday talk that won't change a thing. It could deliver the unexpected, where miracles happen or where everything threatens to fall apart. Or it could be the call I'm expecting, that simple and final piece of information that tells me it's time to move on. That it's all right to heal. Maybe even to forgive.

So.

I lift the handset and push the Talk button. I clear my throat to make sure I have a voice for this part. I want to be heard.

"Hello?"

At the other end of the line, there's a voice I know and love and trust. Low. Calm. Telling me there's news.

ACKNOWLEDGEMENTS

First, to everyone who has been touched by gun violence, to the survivors, victims, and their heartbroken loved ones, I am grateful for the courage and grace you've shown in sharing your stories. Thank you for trusting us with your memories and pain and rage, and for somehow still daring to hope.

Thank you again to Rachel Spence, Scott Fraser, and the rest of the team at Dundurn for bringing me into the family. Special thanks to Jenny, Susan, Sophie, and Babs for their laser-applied specialties. It's a pleasure to work with such a dedicated and professional crew, and my work couldn't be in better hands.

A million thanks to Rachel Eliza Griffiths, who graciously allowed me to borrow a few lines of her sublime and devastating poem "26" for my epigraph and title. Also thanks to writers extraordinaire Karen Bass, Amanda Leduc, Roz Nay, and Anne Valente, who read this novel and said some really nice things. Buy and read their books, everyone: you will be challenged and changed for the better. And, of course, much love to all my writer friends, who inspire and push me to write better.

And what a privilege and honour it is to live and write in a country where literature is honoured and valued! I'm thankful for everyone who loves and supports the arts, but Valhalla exists for those who support public funding. Thanks to the Canada Council for the Arts and the Ontario Arts Council, whose granting programs have given me and so many other scribes the financial space to create.

Thank you, Cootes Paradise, Churchill Park, and Westdale.

To those who serve, have served, and will serve their country: thank you. We send, you go, and too often it costs everything. We see you. What you've done matters. We need to do more for you.

Finally, to my people. To God, who makes it all possible. To the saints at HPL and SJE. To my family, immediate and in-law and extended, for all your support; I am spoiled for love. To my girls, Nora and Alida, for making me care even more about what's to come, and for giving me a reason to keep telling my stories. You are safe and loved, and I know you'll strive for a world where every child can feel the same. To Rosalee, my amazing wife, first reader, and the mother of our girls, you are so much in everything I do and every word I write I can't even begin to define how much you mean to me. Fifteen years, my Left. Imagine that. Here's to a whole bunch more.